✓ **NORTHUMBERLAND COUNT**

You should return this book on
below unless an extension of

Application for rene

Fines
ov

IAN FLEMING PUBLICATIONS LIMITED

www.youngbond.com

Also available in the **YOUNG BOND** series

Written by Steve Cole:
Shoot to Kill

Written by Charlie Higson:
SilverFin
Blood Fever
Double or Die
Hurricane Gold
By Royal Command
Danger Society: Young Bond Dossier

www.youngbond.com
www.ianfleming.com

Also available by Steve Cole:
The Z. Rex Trilogy
Tripwire

YOUNG BOND

HEADS YOU DIE

STEVE COLE

RED FOX

RED FOX

UK | USA | Canada | Ireland | Australia
India | New Zealand | South Africa

Red Fox is part of the Penguin Random House group of companies
whose addresses can be found at global.penguinrandomhouse.com

www.penguin.co.uk
www.puffin.co.uk
www.ladybird.co.uk

Penguin
Random House
UK

First published 2016

001

Text copyright © Ian Fleming Publications Limited, 2016
Cover artwork copyright © blacksheep-uk.com, 2016
Wave, boy and coin images copyright © Shutterstock, 2016

The Ian Fleming logo is a trade mark owned by the Ian Fleming Estate,
used under licence by Ian Fleming Publications Limited.

Young Bond is a trademark of Danjaq, LLC, used under licence
by Ian Fleming Publications Ltd. All rights reserved.

The moral right of the author has been asserted

Set in Bembo Schoolbook 13pt/17pt by Falcon Oast Graphic
Printed in Great Britain by Clays Ltd, St Ives plc

A CIP catalogue record for this book is available from the British Library

ISBN: 978–0–782–95241–1

All correspondence to:
Red Fox
Penguin Random House Children's
61–63 Uxbridge Road, London W5 5SA

MIX
Paper from
responsible sources
FSC
www.fsc.org   FSC® C018179

Penguin Random House is committed
to a sustainable future for our business,
our readers and our planet. This book
is made from Forest Stewardship
Council® certified paper

For Tobey

The only thing necessary for the triumph of evil is for good men to do nothing. Cowardice will suffice for its triumph. Courage will suffice for its overthrow.

Edmund Burke, 1770 (attrib.)

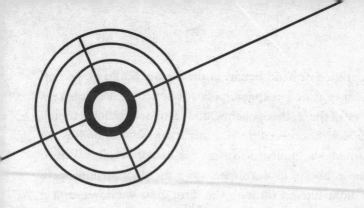

Prologue
Secrets to the Grave

If you're found in here, you're dead.

Sarila Karatan hurried along the dark corridors of the lab building, searching for the right door. The boss of Scolopendra Industries must have stepped up security since her briefing: the private estate stood in a quiet Cuban backwater, but boasted more guards than a military base. Dodging the armed patrols – and the venomous wildlife imported from outside Cuba – had proved a challenge.

A contact had tried to warn her off this assignment. '*You don't cross Scolopendra – he doesn't fool around,*' he'd said. '*The man's a maniac: big plans and big-hitting friends.*' She'd taken the warning lightly; assumed he'd wanted the job for himself.

Now, though . . .

Ahead, the corridor ended in a heavy steel door that reflected her trim, dark silhouette back at her. The emblem of Scolopendra Industries – a sharp red claw in a black circle

– was printed at head height in the centre. Sarila slipped off her military-issue backpack, pulled a bunch of skeleton keys from one of the leather pouches, and set about finding a match for the lock. Success came in under sixty seconds, and as the key turned, she pulled down on the heavy handle. With a hiss, the rubber seal disengaged and the door swung open. Dawn light filtered through the dirty grey windows, and a chemical stink filled the air.

Sarila stepped into the lab with her backpack, skin prickling as she took in the cloudy vials and bell jars that lined the shelves. It was horrible: in each container was a part of some unknown animal – little limbs with skin and fur peeled back to expose the flesh beneath.

Get on with the job, she thought. *Find the safe, take what's inside, get the hell away*.

She headed for a heavy-duty steel cabinet. It stood in front of a glass partition that ran the length of the room, a kind of inspection window that separated the lab from a darkened area beyond. If her information was correct . . .

Yes. The safe, a dark-green cube, was mounted inside the cabinet. Sarila crouched and began to turn the dial. Her insider had supplied the three-digit combination, but what if it had been changed?

She only released the breath she'd been holding when the safe door swung open. Inside was a strongbox marked with the Scolopendra name and insignia. With sweating hands, Sarila pulled it out and slipped it into the backpack's main compartment.

Then she froze. She'd heard something . . .

A guard, outside?

No. It sounded closer. Like someone dragging along a heavy sack.

With a chill, Sarila realized that it was coming from the other side of the glass partition; and it was getting closer.

'*¿Hola?*'

The voice was faint. Young and female. Pained.

What the hell . . . ? Behind the cabinet, Sarila raised her head and peered into the gloom. If she was seen here now, she—

A bloody hand swung up and slammed hard against the glass.

Sarila recoiled, cried out. For a few moments she stared at the thick crimson smear as the palm pressed against the partition.

'*¡Necesitamos ayuda!*' The call for help from behind the glass was hoarse, desperate.

But Sarila had already fled the lab, charging back down the corridor. *You've got what you came for*, she told herself, clutching the backpack tightly. *Now get out. What are you – a child, to be so distracted?*

She almost collided with a guard coming the other way.

The man raised an automatic weapon, a Bergmann-Schmeisser MP18. But Sarila was faster and heaved the backpack into his face; the weight of the strongbox inside sent him crashing into the wall. She grabbed his head and twisted round hard. Through her fingers she felt the crunch as his cervical vertebrae snapped. The man dropped, a dead weight, to the floor.

'No' – Sarila hefted the backpack over her shoulders and picked up the MP18 – 'I'm not a child.'

Professional instincts pushed fear aside, and she headed for the window she'd forced open earlier. The pink sun hung sleepily over the high wooded hills. Everything seemed quiet. All she had to do now was make her way to the nearby marina before—

The alarms went off.

Sarila swore, and ran like hell through the scrubland beyond the lab complex. The blare of klaxons rose up behind her, and almost immediately she saw two guards approaching. Without slowing, she opened fire, aiming for the legs. The men howled and screamed as they were cut down. Sarila ran on past them. 'They'll live,' she muttered.

Her lungs were bursting as she ploughed through the tree cover – and found Scolopendra's private marina at the base of a wooded hillside. She scanned the boats moored there – a motor yacht, runabouts in several sizes, a smart sixty-foot motor sailer – but her eyes settled on a sleek, custom-built cruiser made of tough mahogany. The open cabin at the forward end of the cockpit would give her shelter. Most importantly, it looked fast.

You'll do.

Dry-mouthed, sweat-soaked and panting, Sarila flew down the wooded slope to the marina. She leaped aboard the cruiser, dropped the MP18 and hit the starter. The engine barked but then fell silent.

'Come on!' She pressed the starter again, and this time a throaty note roared confidently through the boards beneath her, almost drowning the voices calling in Spanish from the hillside.

The guards had caught up with her.

Sarila took off the backpack and pulled out a stick grenade, a German Model 24. She unscrewed the cap at the base, yanked on the pull-cord to prime it, and then tossed the grenade into the cockpit of the massive motor sailer beside her. At the same time she pulled down on the throttle lever and the cruiser roared out into the private harbour. *Come on!* Sudden heat seared her back as an explosion gutted the calm of morning. Shrapnel peppered the water and the cruiser's roof. Sarila turned the wheel, making for the short channel through the cliffs that led to open water.

Glancing back through the shimmer of heat and roiling smoke, she glimpsed guards swarming down the hillside, caught the rattle of gunfire. She prayed she was out of range; prayed that she would pull off this job like all the others.

The blood-smeared hand against the glass slammed hard in her memory.

Fanned by the breeze, the flames from the motor sailer took hold in the runabout beside it; suddenly a tankful of diesel ignited, and the blast left guards scattered on the ground. Machine-gun fire started up once more but it was sparse and faltering, the bravado of a beaten enemy.

A sharp bend in the inlet obscured Sarila's view of the mayhem she'd left behind, and she breathed a shaky sigh of relief . . . until she saw another boat ahead of her; a runabout marked with the Scolopendra circle and claw.

Sarila tensed – then realized that it was travelling *away* from her, leaving the estate behind, just as she was. A young girl was at the helm; she had dark braided hair and was maybe fifteen or sixteen. *What the hell . . . ?*

Head down so she couldn't be identified, Sarila overtook

the girl in the boat and powered onward. 'Keep your mysteries, Scolopendra,' she muttered. 'I'm out.'

The cruiser made open sea in just minutes. Sarila was glad to find plenty of fuel in the tank; she would strike out east through the chains of tiny islands and make for mainland Cuba. In maybe five hours she would reach the swamps and forests of the Zapata peninsula and meet her employer, as arranged.

The hours passed uneasily, accompanied by the fierce growl of the cruiser's eight-cylinder engine, until finally the mainland came into sight. On the low cliffs stood a stubby ancient tower like a friendly thumb raised in greeting.

But the throb of the cruiser's engine had masked the approach of a seaplane. Sarila looked up through the window as it circled overhead, and swore. There was that damned sign again, the red claw in the black circle: INDUSTRIAS SCOLOPENDRA. She hadn't planned on pursuit by air coming so quickly.

Like a massive predatory bird, the air yacht came lower, nearer, twin propellers blurring, landing sleds suspended on either side of the long coral-coloured body. A man leaned out of the co-pilot's seat; he was holding a machine gun. '*¡Apaga el motor!*'

'Kill the engine?' Sarila's answer was to turn the wheel hard to port, clinging on as the cruiser tilted sickeningly. Bullets raked the vessel, shattering the cabin windows. Sarila ducked and threw her arms over her face as glass flew around her. As the thump and chatter of bullets came to a stop, she scooped up the MP18.

'*¡Apaga el motor!*' the man screamed again as the air yacht touched lightly down on the ocean not fifty feet away, its

6

belly ploughing through the water while the skids held it on the surface. '¡Apaga el motor!'

'I'll kill you!' Sarila rose up and returned fire. Bullet holes winked open in the side of the air yacht like little black eyes as it lifted back into the air, engines roaring, climbing out of range. She hadn't hit the co-pilot. The plane would simply circle round for another go. How many rounds were left in the mag?

The cruiser was now only a couple of miles from shore. Perhaps if she dumped her backpack and its treasure overboard, Scolopendra's men would stop chasing and leave her be. They weren't to know that she had the means to recover it again. All she had to do was—

Another burst of gunfire tore through the cockpit. Sarila shrieked and dropped the gun as her left arm spat blood. She lost her balance and fell to the deck.

Shot. She could feel the blood pulsing from the wounds, the spreading wetness, sticking sleeve to skin. The boat rocked sickeningly as Sarila fumbled with the wheel, worked the throttle, tried to push on. Her left arm wouldn't move. Water was pooling around her ankles – the cruiser must have been holed by the gunfire: it was taking in ocean as fast as she was losing blood. She gripped the MP18 – and stared at her hand as she waved it threateningly up at the sky . . . but she couldn't focus. Her fingers became those of the crimson smear on the glass in the lab . . .

Sarila must have closed her eyes because when they opened again, she was rib deep in dark seawater, slumped over the wheel, her good hand still gripping her backpack. The seaplane was circling above like a vulture.

She was so close to land! The coast was barely a mile away. *God willing*, she thought, *I might get out yet*. She'd run things close before and always made it.

Sarila was praying for the usual miracle even as the waters closed over her head.

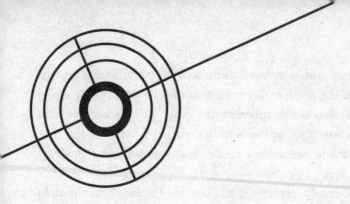

1

To Catch a Thief

James Bond pursued his target through the narrow, crowded streets, fighting to keep him in sight.

To catch the pickpocket would be a challenge, James knew. The thief was fast on his feet, picking a path through the endless little alleyways of Old Havana. And with sunset scorching the Caribbean skies, tourists and locals alike had been drawn out in their hundreds, enticed by the promise of adventure that hung on the sultry evening air. While James fought his way through the hordes, the thief was increasing his lead.

Yes, to catch him would be a challenge.

James smiled, stepped into the road to escape the kerbside scrimmage, and put on a sprint.

A honking Dodge pick-up truck thundered towards him, so wide it all but filled the road. James angled his body sideways as it powered past. The flared front fender almost took his legs off, but he refused to slacken his pace; finally he was reducing the distance between him and his quarry! He could see the stolen wallet still clutched in the pickpocket's fist and vowed again that he *would* retrieve it.

There was something inside that was far more precious than money . . .

'Stop, thief!' James yelled, but his English brought only sharp looks from the Spanish-speaking locals.

The pickpocket darted left into a side street. Without hesitation, James followed, barging between a grizzled post-card seller and a huddle of young women, muttering apologies. He reached the alley's mouth as the pickpocket neared its exit; it led to a major road, where noisy traffic roared past in glimpses.

James quickened his pace, hurled himself past the strolling couples and souvenir hawkers. His dark-blue cotton shirt clung to his back with sweat, his white linen shorts were smeared with dirt, and his brown loafers, not yet worn in, were blistering his heels. But a steely confidence held James as he turned the corner and saw the thief waiting at the side of the road, just fifty feet ahead, poised for a break in the traffic.

The pickpocket saw James coming and darted recklessly forward. Braking automobiles screamed out across the asphalt. A motorcycle in the nearside lane swerved and crashed into the side of a Cadillac roadster, which in turn collided with a red-and-white Alfa Romeo 8C Tourer. James followed boldly in the pickpocket's wake. Horns sounded, shouts went up. The Cadillac was shunted forward as a truck rear-ended it; its V-shaped grille almost clipped James. The thief was halfway across, heading for a swathe of parkland on the other side, when he all but bounced off the silver Lanchester 18 that screeched to a halt just in front of him. The pickpocket stopped dead for a moment, then scrambled desperately round the back of the automobile.

'I don't think so . . .' James threw himself forward and grasped the boy around the legs in a rugby tackle that would've gladdened the hearts of his masters back at Eton. Both he and the thief landed hard in the dusty gutter at the side of the road.

The boy twisted round, scrawny and indignant, and unleashed a torrent of angry Spanish in James's face. There was more shouting from the stalled drivers, aimed at them both; the Cadillac's driver, old, tanned and pouchy, got out of his car. James snatched back the stolen wallet, stood up and waved it at the angry audience, hoping they'd understand the purpose of his pell-mell pursuit.

But they didn't watch him for long. The pickpocket, accepting defeat empty-handed, was off again and the driver of the Cadillac dashed after him, shouting; James knew threats when he heard them, whatever the language. Still, he no longer cared what befell the boy. The mission had been accomplished.

Turning his back on the melee, James checked the wallet. He was surprised to find a small fortune inside – almost five hundred dollars. But the real treasure was there, tucked behind the bills: an old, battered sepia photograph. It showed James's late father, Andrew Bond, posing outside the family home in Switzerland with another man, the owner of the wallet: Gerald Hardiman.

James smiled fondly at the picture. His parents had died in a climbing accident when he was just eleven, and he still missed them badly. This photograph, snapped one sunny winter's day in the 1920s, was a memento of happier childhood times. Hardiman had just been putting it back into his wallet when the pickpocket struck.

Without a backward glance, James quickly headed through the little stretch of parkland, making for the place where he'd left his friends – the Malecón, a wide, sweeping promenade that bordered the ocean.

'Now,' he murmured, 'the rest cure can continue.'

Rest cure? Who was he trying to fool! That chase had left his body more invigorated than twenty days of rest could achieve, while his success was a boost to the spirits. Plus James liked to repay a debt, and knew he owed Hardiman a good deal for his kindness. Upon hearing that James and his friend, Hugo, were stranded in California after recent misadventures, the old boy had stepped straight in to help.

As James reached the busy esplanade and started scanning the crowds, he remembered his delight when Aunt Charmian had called from her archaeological dig in southern Mexico (she was always on a dig somewhere) to share the news.

'I've talked to Gerald Hardiman,' she'd said, the familiar voice so warm and rich even over the crackling line. 'He insists you must both stay at his place in Cuba until I can join you all – which with any luck will be within a week . . .'

The warm air was heavy with the aromas of the sea and food and flowers, and as he walked, James grew introspective. He had only fond memories of Hardiman – a regular Bond houseguest in both London and Switzerland throughout

James's early childhood – but the tortuous journey to Havana was something he'd sooner forget.

Adam Elmhirst, the British agent who had cleared up after the field trip from hell in Los Angeles, had arranged for James and Hugo to make the journey as quickly as possible: they had travelled by air in a DC2 to Dallas, stopping off to refuel at Tucson. From Dallas they had got a ride with an American Airlines mail plane that stopped six times along the way to Atlanta, before flying Eastern Air Transport down to Miami. Hardiman had met them there, dead on their feet, for the last leg – a Pan Am flight into Cuba that had landed safely earlier that day.

Still, we're here now, James thought. He gazed over the seawall, drank in the lazy grandeur of his first Cuban sunset, and smiled. *Nothing to do but relax in good company and enjoy all that Havana has to offer . . .*

'Blood and sand, James, there you are! We didn't know what had befallen you . . .'

James turned and found a beetle-browed young dwarf hurrying along the top of the seawall. He smiled. Shared travel and adventure had left him and Hugo as close to friends as James could ever allow. 'Sorry to dash off.' He held up the wallet. 'All in a good cause.'

'You caught up with the little sewer rat, then! Not that I doubted you would.' Hugo shook his head admiringly. 'That should snap Mr Hardiman out of his funk.'

'Funk?'

'Well . . . don't you think he seems a bit distracted?'

James bit his lip. He knew what Hugo meant. Hardiman's face was as crumpled as always, but the kindly eyes looked haunted. On the flight to Cuba he had come out with all the usual exclamations about how James had grown, pressing him for updates on school and sporting achievements – but had hardly seemed to listen to the answers.

'I expect he's just tired after flying out to meet us so early.' James pushed a curl of hair off his forehead, looked around. 'Where is he, anyway?'

'Can't be far behind. I climbed the wall for a height advantage – the better to spy you, of course – so the crowds didn't slow me down.'

James scrambled up to join Hugo. He took in the trails of tourists, the street sellers pushing postcards and parasols, the lottery agents weighed down with numbered tickets as big as licence plates, the souvenir hawkers and the musicians in traditional dress serenading passing lovers.

'Hey, look.' Hugo's attention had been taken by the headline on a nearby stall selling the *Diario de la Marina*. He translated it for James's benefit: '*Mystery woman's body washed up on coast. Shot, then drowned . . .*'

'Puts our long, rough journey into perspective, doesn't it?' James said, his interest caught. 'Wonder what it was about?'

'You've got a chunky wallet there,' Hugo noted. 'Why not buy a copy? I'll translate for you.'

'You'll have to ask the wallet's owner.' James grinned as he finally spotted a tall, stooped man in a crumpled linen suit and Panama hat emerge from the crowd. 'Here he comes!'

'James! Thank heavens!' Gerald Hardiman waved in greeting and quickened his step. 'Are you all right, lad? Did you get the little—?'

'Got the lot.' James jumped down and handed him the wallet. 'It's all there.'

'Oh, bravo. Well done, James.' Hardiman opened the wallet, saw the money inside, and kissed it with a grin. 'Thanks to you we will eat tonight!' His Scots tones seemed too deep for so slight a frame. 'This calls for a celebration, eh? For the conquering hero! We'll go somewhere really top drawer . . .' He trailed off, his face clouding as he noticed the newspaper stand. 'Oh, dear Lord . . .'

'We just saw that.' Hugo glanced at James. 'Good and lurid to sell the evening edition.'

'I suppose,' Hardiman said distantly. He fumbled in his pocket for a coin to buy a copy.

As he did so, James noticed a handsome automobile slow to a crawl on the far side of the wide street – a Hispano-Suiza Coupé de Ville, its livery black and scarlet. A young man with dark skin sat in the driver's seat, which was open to the elements. His passengers would travel in the private compartment behind, hidden in stylish seclusion.

The driver was staring at Hardiman, and James saw that a thick scar ran vertically from nose to chin across the lips, like a long stitch pulled too tight.

James nodded at the fancy car. 'Is that someone you know, sir?'

Hardiman turned, and the coin dropped from his fingers and bounced on the pavement.

At once, the Hispano-Suiza pulled away again. Hugo stooped to rescue the coin, offered it back to Hardiman. '*Find a penny, pick it up, all day long you'll have good luck.*'

Hardiman said nothing as he stared after the disappearing automobile.

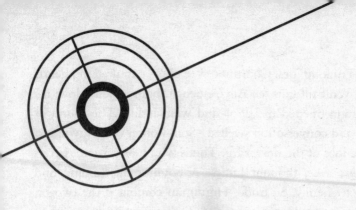

2
Alley Fight

It didn't escape James's notice that Hardiman was heading straight for the nearest crowded street in Old Havana; he was gripping the newspaper tight, like a baton. Crowds spilled over the pavements, slowing traffic to an angry crawl. Hugo let James and Hardiman push their way through, following quickly in their wake.

'I thought we'd eat here.' Hardiman gestured to a shabby but lively-looking restaurant named Just Jawin'. 'I often do when I'm in town.'

'Do you come to Havana a lot?' James wondered. Hardiman had taken him and Hugo to drop off their luggage at the musty apartment he rented in Calle Villegas, in the old town. The once grand building was now beginning to crumble; it rose from a restful flower-filled patio like an old gravestone from a well-tended plot. 'Your real home's on the other side of the island, isn't it?'

'In Trinidad, yes. Charming wee city – captured my heart, it did. Wait till you see Ancón beach, boys – you'll love it.' Hardiman opened the door and went inside. The sound of music and conversation swelled. 'Still, I often visit Havana to use the labs at the university. That's why I keep rooms here.'

Makes sense, thought James. A botanist by training and research chemist by trade, Hardiman combined the two by studying rare plant species and discovering what uses they might have in science and industry. 'Are you working on something at the lab now?'

'No, no,' Hardiman said quickly. 'I've got an appointment with somebody, is all.'

The head waiter approached them hesitantly. 'Señor, forgive me . . . The owner, he tells me, sorry, but no more meals on the tab until payment is—'

'Now, now.' Hardiman's smile grew forced and he looked around. 'I think perhaps you've mistaken me for someone else. See . . . ?' He pulled some dollar bills from his wallet and tucked them into the waiter's pocket. 'Seat us at a good table, eh?'

'Ah! Señor, forgive me, please.' All smiles now, the waiter bowed and led them to a table at the rear, overlooking a small courtyard where flowers hung in loose splashes of colour.

As the waiter moved away, Hugo eyed him sternly. 'That fellow needs spectacles. What a liberty!'

'Just a misunderstanding,' Hardiman said airily. 'Lots of tourists imitate my style, you know. Trendsetter that I am, eh?'

Across the room James saw an older, stern-faced man

approach the waiter; judging by the immaculate suit and expansive air, he was the owner. As the waiter pulled the dollar bills from his pocket, the man scowled across at Hardiman suspiciously.

'Right, then!' Hardiman placed his rolled-up newspaper on the floor beside him. 'Menu, menu, menu. Who's hungry?'

As it turned out, not Hardiman. James noted that he ate barely a mouthful of the dishes he ordered for the table: tomato, lettuce and avocado salad; a sweet plantain omelette; dark lentil soup; a thick yellow tamale casserole with rice and black beans; and *ropa vieja*, a shredded shank of slow-cooked beef with olives and capers. Hungry after their long journey, James and Hugo shared the dishes between them while Hardiman watched and flashed a smile now and then.

'Remember the time you came skiing with us in Chamonix?' James hoped good memories might conjure a little more of the old Hardiman. 'I must've been six . . . Bumped into you off-piste. Knocked you halfway down Mont Blanc . . .'

'Always one for a bit of rough and tumble, eh, James?' Hugo said, before turning to Hardiman. 'What happened?'

'Andrew – James's father – raced into the forest after me. Found me with my legs wrapped around a tree. Laughed so hard he could barely stand . . .' Hardiman's warm chuckle died in his throat as he glanced across the restaurant to the front window.

James followed his gaze – just in time to notice a dark figure shift away from the window and walk down the street. 'Is . . . everything all right, Dr Hardiman?'

'What's that? Oh, yes – fine. Everything's fine.' He rose abruptly, patted James and Hugo clumsily on the shoulder. 'Excuse me, boys. I'll just take care of the bill, eh?'

As Hardiman left, Hugo leaned towards James. 'Do you think that head waiter really *did* make a mistake? Perhaps Hardiman's been, er, financially embarrassed, and that was a debt collector he saw through the window?'

'He said it was a misunderstanding.' James watched Hardiman give the waiter a generous tip. 'Anyway, he has plenty of money now.'

As they made their way back to the apartment, James tried to banish his disquiet.

'I'm fit to drop.' Hugo yawned. 'It's a good job I haven't far to fall.'

James smiled. 'I hoped there'd be time for a game of cards before turning in.'

'Well, I'm worn out myself, boys,' Hardiman said. As they reached the doorstep, he groaned and slapped a hand to his forehead. 'Damn it, I meant to pick up some coffee. Well, the all-night store's only three blocks from here—'

'I can go,' James said quickly, happy to make Hardiman's life easier.

'Would you like company?' Hugo asked half-heartedly. 'Slow, lethargic, hindering company . . . ?'

'It's all right, Hugo,' James told him. 'After my earlier jaunt through the streets I think I can manage a couple more blocks alone.'

'You're a good lad, James.' Hardiman seemed grateful, and passed him a silver dollar. 'It's two hundred yards down to the main road, and just on your left.' He paused and glanced around. 'I know you can look after yourself, but . . . just be careful, eh?'

James nodded. 'I'll see you shortly.'

He set off along the quiet street. The humid night tasted of salt and smoke. Ornamental streetlamps lined the shadows with silver. A bored-looking woman whistled to James from a doorway, shouting promises of a good time in broken English, and he hurried past. High overhead the houses leaned towards each other as if whispering secrets.

James had barely gone two blocks when a girl's shouts attracted his attention: '¡Suéltame! No voy contigo . . . !'

They were coming from a side street up ahead. James didn't understand the words, but the fear and anger were evident. *Another pickpocket?* He hesitated for a moment. *It's not your business . . .* Then the crash and rattle of an overturned dustbin compelled him to check and be sure.

Silhouetted in an automobile's headlights, James saw struggling figures at the junction up ahead – a man and a girl. '¡Está intentado secuestrarme!'

Taking a deep breath, James ran forward out of the shadows. 'Hey!'

The man froze as the girl turned to James in shocked surprise. She was tall and painfully thin, with dark skin and long black hair thrown over her face; there was something feral about the features in the oval face. The man was young and lithe, his frame swamped by an expensive suit. As James got closer, he noticed the livid scar that made the man's mouth a gruesome, puckered cross.

With a chill, he realized it was the same man who'd been

staring at Hardiman from the Hispano-Suiza Coupé de Ville – which was parked just behind.

'English?' The girl reached out to James with her free arm. '¡*Ayuadame*! Help—!'

'¡*Silencio*!' The man yanked her backwards, forcing her towards the car.

'*No hagas esto . . .*' The girl twisted in her captor's grip. '*Por favor*, Ramón.'

'Ramón?' James echoed. So the girl knew her attacker.

Ramón sneered at him. 'This not your business, little boy.' Through his scarred lips he bared white teeth that were as broken as his English. 'Go home now.'

For a moment James wondered if he'd blundered in on some lovers' tiff. Should he leave them to it? And yet the girl was turning such large, imploring eyes on him, damn it, he couldn't just turn and go!

Just then a large figure lurched out of an alleyway behind the car. Hope quickened James's heart. *Perhaps I've got backup . . .*

But Ramón was smiling: this was *his* backup – a big bald block of muscle in a raincoat. One enormous palm was open, the other clenched inside a leather glove. The threat in the hulking giant's eyes was unmistakable.

Ramón smiled at James's reaction. 'This is *El Puño*. The Fist . . . Stay and you will know why.'

James felt a flicker of self-doubt. Two against one, over a girl he'd never met before? He hadn't meant to rival St George for chivalry, but if he walked away now . . .

El Puño lunged forward with surprising speed; with his bare hand he grabbed James by the shirtfront. James gasped as the pain spiked adrenalin through his limbs, and brought his knee up hard into his attacker's groin.

But El Puño didn't double over as James had hoped. He merely grunted and tapped James on the side of the head with his gloved hand.

It was like being struck by concrete.

Senses reeling, James fell back against the wall. That was the fist, all right – this ugly giant well deserved his nickname! The girl shouted as she renewed her struggle with Ramón.

The cry galvanized James. Using the wall as a springboard, he launched himself at El Puño in a desperate shoulder-charge, cannoning into the broad chest. The huge man staggered backwards and rocked against the car, off balance. James bent down, grabbed his ankles, and then heaved back with all his strength. But the massive man would not be moved; he simply kicked James away like a dog.

James cried out as if the blow had hurt more than it had, and rolled backwards. He saw Ramón forcing the girl into the back of the Hispano-Suiza.

As El Puño strode forward, James scooped up some dirt and hurled it into the pudgy face. Blinded for a moment, the man spat and recoiled.

Ramón started forward to join the fray – but the girl's slender arm snaked out through the window and crooked tight around his throat. Ramón made a thick retching noise and his scarred face twisted.

James scrambled up and punched him in the stomach. The man doubled over so hard he broke the girl's grip, allowing James to twist him round and propel him into El Puño.

By now, the girl had reached through the window and

unlocked the door. Like a shadow, she slipped out and raced away down the same alleyway that had hidden El Puño. James pelted after her.

'You gonna bleed for this, boy!' he heard Ramón shout. 'I will open your face!'

James did not look back.

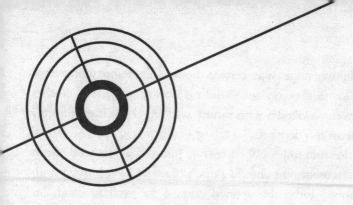

3

Separations

Heart hammering as he raced away, James knew that he would *never* get used to the thrill of danger. That was its allure. So much of life was routine and boring, but danger had no rules. It happened anywhere, could take so many forms.

'And it looks me up wherever I go,' he muttered to himself.

The alley emptied into a main road that was crowded with tourists and partygoers; it throbbed with the passionate music of a *guaguancó*, led by the chiming rumba rhythm of the claves. James could see no sign of the girl, and swore under his breath. Now he'd never know what in hell he'd been caught up in! Unless Ramón and El Puño found him, of course – in which case he imagined they'd let him know . . .

James ran on, angling his body sideways to dart between clumps of people, turning at random, lungs already burning.

Only when he was certain he wasn't being followed – either on foot or by car – did he stop running. His clothes were sweat-soaked but his mouth was dry. The city felt hotter by at least ten degrees.

As the adrenalin ebbed away, James felt his head throb with a nauseating pulse; El Puño's blow had left him with an egg-shaped lump. He leaned against the wall to catch his breath, tried to process what he'd just lived through. No doubt Ramón had been watching Hardiman down on the Malecón . . . and he could well have been the man James had spotted through the restaurant window. So it seemed an unlikely coincidence that Ramón had chosen to park so close to Hardiman's apartment on Calle Villegas.

What about the girl – where did she fit in?

I need to speak to Dr Hardiman, James decided.

He tried to get his bearings. It wasn't so hard since the stone cupola of the National Capitol Building towered over the neighbourhood, a useful landmark. Warily he began to retrace his steps through Old Havana, sticking to the busiest streets. Between wrought-iron grilles and slatted shutters, the walls were plastered with hand-painted signs and posters advertising local events. The shops had no doors; everything from bars and cigar stores to beauty parlours opened straight onto the narrow pavements.

As he walked, James chanced upon a late-night grocer's. He bought the promised coffee, along with a glass bottle of milk, warm and close to turning. He'd drunk nearly half of it by the time he got back to Calle Villegas. There was no sign of the Hispano-Suiza, or Ramón and El Puño, or the girl.

James knocked on the door. Hardiman quickly came to

open it, Hugo peering out from behind him, both looking worried.

'James! Where've you been?' Hardiman almost dragged him inside and closed the door. 'You're in a mess, lad.'

'Not another pickpocket?' Hugo pointed up at the bump on James's head. 'What happened?'

'Two men happened. Hard.' James followed Hardiman up the stairs to the small sitting room, which was cluttered with mismatched furniture. A breeze teased the curtains through the open window, and James was grateful for it. Hardiman fetched a clean wet cloth and some iodine for the bump, and James explained briefly what had happened.

'I'm sorry.' Hardiman dabbed at James's head. 'I should never have let you go out alone at night. It's my fault.'

Perhaps, thought James. 'The man's name was Ramón, sir. He was the one you saw watching you from the red-and-black automobile when we were down on the Malecón.'

Hardiman flinched. James saw more than just concern now on the familiar face; he saw guilt. 'Sweet Lord, I never imagined they'd attack a child.'

James felt his stomach clench. 'You *do* know him, then.'

'Who is he?' Hugo's eyes were china-doll wide.

'Ramón Mosqueda, and his fellow thug El Puño – the Fist – are employees of a man I've worked for in the past.' Hardiman turned away, troubled. 'He says he wants me – *needs* me – to work for him again on a . . . special project. I want no part of it, but he needs my expertise.'

'He can't force you to work for him, can he?' James frowned. 'Whoever he is.'

'Audacto Solares isn't a man you say no to. He's a great

27

biologist . . . amongst other things.' Hardiman paused. 'These days he likes to call himself *Scolopendra*. It's from the Latin term for a species of giant centipede he discovered, *Scolopendra deltadromeus*.'

'Well, creepy-crawly or not,' said Hugo, 'why would his men start out by following you and end up trying to kidnap a girl?'

Hardiman rose stiffly and crossed to the window. The rattle of trams and the growl of motorcars quarrelled in the dark. 'You're sure she got away?'

'She ran like hell. I couldn't spot her. But I suppose . . .' James shrugged. 'Who do you think she is?'

'I don't know.' Hardiman slammed the window shut. 'She could be anyone.'

'But—'

'Please, James, leave it, eh?' He smiled suddenly, a ghost of the old Hardiman showing in the crumpled face. 'If your aunt were here, she'd tell you to get some rest and see how that lump feels in the morning, would she not?'

James shrugged. 'I suppose.'

'Then get some rest and see how that lump feels in the morning.' Hardiman put a hand on James's shoulder. 'I don't think you're concussed, but I know a doctor at the university. We'll get you checked out.'

'The university?' Hugo raised his eyebrows. 'Wouldn't a hospital be—?'

'The university will be easier,' Hardiman insisted. 'Bed, now, boys. I know your journey here was quite an ordeal. Sleep's the best thing for you.' He gestured to the spare room.

Awkwardly, James and Hugo rose and said goodnight to their host. But, unable to sleep after the evening's violent turn, the boys played poker by candlelight until almost one a.m.

Afterwards James lay awake, the sheets kicked away, listening to Hugo shift uncomfortably in his bed. The night was stifling despite the open windows. A Westinghouse table-fan blew warm air around the room and an oil lamp sputtered, shaking shadows across the stuccoed walls.

'Penny for them,' Hugo murmured. 'Your thoughts, I mean. Not your cards.'

'I was just working out how many times I beat you tonight,' James lied.

'Thirteen!' Hugo sighed. 'Still, unlucky in cards, lucky in love, they say.' He paused. 'The ignorant fools.'

'You're lucky we were only playing for matchsticks.'

'You're lucky you won them all, or I'd have set fire to your bed.'

James smiled. A minute drifted by; he listened to the whir of the fan, snatches of Spanish in the street, a man singing languidly over the rhythm of a *habanera*.

'D'you think old Hardiman does know who that girl was?' Hugo murmured.

'Yes. And I think he's in trouble. Question is, what kind of trouble? He said he was in Havana to meet somebody. Could it be the girl?'

'Well, from the sound of things, he's in no hurry to meet up with his old boss again – Scolo-whatsit . . .'

'Scolopendra.' James nodded. 'Perhaps that's why those hired apes have been keeping tabs on him. So Scolopendra knows where to find him—'

The telephone in the living room rang, silencing their whispers.

'Late for a social call,' James murmured.

'Perhaps it's an *anti*social call . . .'

'That's what worries me.' James got up, went over to the fan and switched it off. The sudden silence seemed louder than the hum of the blades. He heard the click and scrape as Hardiman picked up the telephone.

'Hello?' A pause. 'Scolopendra – how did you get this number?'

It's him. With a thrill of foreboding, James padded over to the door and opened it a crack, hoping to hear more.

'. . . No, I've had no contact with her.' Hardiman sounded uncomfortable. 'I'm sorry, but I don't know where she is, truly.'

The girl I ran into? James thought.

'No, I didn't know your laboratory had been ransacked – how *could* I have? I was in Miami, picking up friends of the family. Did you lose anything . . . ?' James could hear fear edging into Hardiman's voice. 'I can see why you're upset, but . . . I've already told you, I have no wish to return to that particular project, no matter how much you're investing . . .'

Hugo popped up beside James. 'I consider eavesdropping morally wrong.'

James frowned. 'If Hardiman's in trouble, I'd like to—'

'Shush, James, I can't hear.'

'If I knew where she was, I would tell you,' Hardiman went on. 'But I don't. I've had no contact with her.' Another, longer pause. 'I *won* that money, if you must know . . .

30

Er, on the roulette table. Is it any of your business where I was . . . ?'

'Quite an interrogation,' Hugo hissed.

And Hardiman sounds nervous, James noted. *I'm not sure he's being straight with his answers.*

'Scolopendra, please excuse me. It's late and I have company staying here for the next few days. I wish you success with your business here in Havana. Goodbye.'

The phone was slammed down into its cradle. There was a pause, then the floorboards in the living room creaked as Hardiman began to pace to and fro.

'What's it all about?' Hugo murmured. 'This mysterious girl Scolopendra's looking for . . . that money he says he won . . . not wanting to take you to a proper hospital . . .' He sighed. 'I thought I'd feel safer once we reached Cuba. But after your adventures today, and now this, I'm actually looking forward to ten tedious days on a liner back to England.'

'Only five days till we set sail,' James reminded him, 'then all this is behind us.' But he had the feeling that whatever Hardiman was mixed up in, there would be no quick get-out for the old boy.

James went back to bed, troubled. He felt under his pillow for his treasured air pistol, Queensmarsh, keepsake of a recent skirmish. Once a crude mongrel cobbled together from different parts, it had been repaired and restored and was now extremely accurate. He resolved not to leave the apartment again without it.

Hugo yawned and switched the fan back on. This time he put it on its highest setting; the blades buzzed around enthusiastically, although the breeze remained feeble. 'Perhaps things will seem clearer in the morning,' he said.

'They will, I'm sure,' James agreed, enjoying the movement of air against his skin. Queensmarsh felt snug and smooth in his hand. A girl called Boudicca had carved the name into the stock, after the place in which he'd won the weapon; he thought of Boody now and wondered if he'd ever see her again.

But no – it didn't do to look back. The past, with all its pain, stalked the shadows like a hunter, never far behind. James chose not to confront it; to keep his gaze fixed ahead. What else were life's struggles for, if not tomorrow?

The fan hummed on like a swarm of drowsy bees. James closed his eyes and fell asleep, willing the new day onward.

The roar of an engine in the street outside rose over the noise of the fan. James woke to find a pale blue sky waiting at the windows. He was thirsty, and got up to fetch water from the kitchen.

As soon as he reached the living room he knew something was wrong. A chair had been overturned, and there were papers and letters scattered over the floor and furniture. A dent in the wall leaked plaster dust.

'Dr Hardiman?' James called uneasily. 'Are you there?' The door to the main bedroom stood wide open. The sheets had been stripped from the bed, luggage opened and clothes strewn around. Heart sinking, James hurried downstairs into the hall. The front door stood open. The glass panel beside it had been removed – allowing someone to reach in and undo the catch.

Feeling sick, James rushed out into the deserted street. 'Dr Hardiman!'

The echo of his cry died into indifferent silence. James and Hugo were alone now.

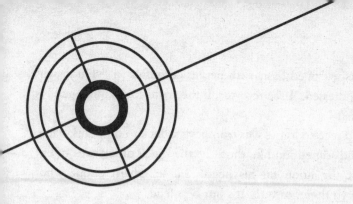

4

At Knifepoint

James stormed back into the bedroom, shaking Hugo awake. 'Dr Hardiman's gone. The apartment was broken into last night.'

Hugo blinked blearily. 'What the hell . . . ?'

'Everything's a mess.' James quickly threw on some clothes. 'Whoever took him was looking for something.' He swore. 'That damned fan! I never heard a thing.'

Rubbing his eyes, Hugo got out of bed. 'You're sure Hardiman's not just gone out for a walk or . . . ?' He paused, took in the chaos in the living room. 'All right. No need to dignify that with a response.'

'We must go to the police. It's the only thing we can do.' James searched through the papers in the living room for an old guidebook he'd noticed the night before. 'Will your Spanish be up to it?'

'Lived in Madrid for a year. My Spanish tutor had

a bookshelf piled high with penny dreadfuls . . .' Hugo was getting dressed. 'I seem to recall the word for "kidnapped" is *secuestrado*.'

For a second James was transported back to that dark alley. '*She* said something like that . . . the girl Ramón was after.' He felt the lump on his head. 'I'll tell them about what happened there, as well. It's our best lead.'

'We don't know that your friends from the alley had anything to do with this.'

'But we know they work for Scolopendra. And you heard Hardiman last night – Scolopendra wanted him for some job or other, and wasn't about to take no for an answer.'

'I hope you're wrong,' Hugo said, buttoning his shirt. 'Right then, James. Ready when you are.'

With the help of the map, they headed south through Old Havana's narrow, teetering buildings and projecting porches. The design was deliberate, as it meant that the direct sun could penetrate for only a few hours each day. Even so, after only a few blocks James found his skin prickling in the heat. He kept tapping Queensmarsh, tucked discreetly into his waistband, expecting trouble at any time.

The police station was an ugly, one-storey cement building on the south side of the Calzada de Guanabacoa. In his rusty Spanish, Hugo outlined the emergency to the officer in charge, and was told that someone would take their statements as soon as possible.

At first James was grateful for the cool shelter of the reception. But after waiting for almost two hours, it started to feel more like the cells than the front desk.

Eventually they were summoned for interview by an officer

about as large and stony as the building he worked in. Hugo tried to explain what had happened. James didn't understand what the officer was saying in return, but his expression was clear enough: dismissive; bored; no time for tourists.

Hugo turned to James. 'He says they have no records on file of the men you've described.'

James cursed. 'Did you tell him we think this Scolopendra character's involved?'

When he heard the name, the officer's already sour face curdled further. He spoke again.

'Scolopendra is a very important man here,' Hugo translated. 'His conduct is beyond reproach.' The policeman went on talking, and Hugo sighed. 'Seems we're to wait at home, stay out of trouble, and if we don't hear anything from Dr Hardiman, we can come back tomorrow. *Late* tomorrow.'

James was incredulous. 'The police won't help us?'

'I've tried to act like we're helpless minors, but . . .' Hugo looked apologetic as the man went on talking. 'He seems to think Hardiman had it coming. A lot of people in Havana have made complaints about him, he's run up some serious gambling debts.'

'Gambling debts?'

'He owes money to more than one restaurant, and he's done a bunk on more than one angry landlord. Officer Unhelpful here puts the vandalism down to someone trying to scare Hardiman into paying back money he owes. No shortage of possible culprits.'

'And that's it?' James stared at the policeman. 'Hugo, tell him he can't just ignore this . . .'

Hugo started to speak, but the officer's chair scraped loudly against the concrete and he heaved himself up, leaning heavily on the table. His gaze flicked slowly between the two boys.

James didn't need an interpreter for that one. He turned to Hugo in disgust. 'Interview's over.'

They retraced their steps back through the city, the fierce heat doing nothing to lift James's mood. Hardiman, with his crumpled charm and friendly optimism, was a totem of happier childhood times with his parents. Over the years they'd swapped postcards, spoken long-distance on the telephone at Aunt Charmian's; he'd seemed more like an uncle than a family friend. To think of him now as an ordinary person with real weaknesses . . . It was an unwelcome shock. James was cross with himself for feeling it so deeply.

'Could we call Agent Elmhirst, do you suppose?' Hugo pondered.

'While he's cruising back to England?' James grimaced. 'He flew to New York but from there it must be at least five days by ocean liner. I've got the number of his London office, but what can they do, four and a half thousand miles away?'

'They could have words with the British ambassador here.'

'Does Cuba even *have* a British ambassador?' James felt weary. 'Before we do anything else, let's go back to the apartment. Check it again for any clues. Maybe ask the neighbours – someone might have seen something.'

'Do you mind if we grab a swift breakfast too?' Hugo met James's slightly reproachful look. 'Starving ourselves won't help. Besides, it's bad for one's health to face foreign bureaucracy on an empty stomach.'

When they got back to the apartment, James reached in through the gap in the frame and opened the front door. As he did so, he heard a muffled thump from upstairs.

Hugo's eyes widened. 'Hardiman's come back?'

'Or somebody else,' James said, starting up the stairs. 'Hello? Dr Hardiman—?'

As he stepped into the living room, he glimpsed movement to his right, and turned.

A frying pan was swinging towards his face.

Instincts kicked in. James brought up both arms in an X to deflect the blow as much as possible. Pain lanced through his forearms as he heard the clang of metal on bone; he cried out, knocked the pan from his attacker's grip, swiped viciously with the back of his hand at—

A girl?

His knuckles struck her lower jaw. She gasped and fell backwards onto the tiles, her black braids falling over her eyes.

'What the . . . ?' Hugo had followed James up the stairs. 'Is that the girl you saw last night?'

'No.' Rubbing his arms, James stared down at her, dumbfounded. She looked little older than he was, and had honey-coloured skin and handsome features. Her navy dress looked worn but of good quality. 'I don't know who she is, but she tried to brain me.'

Hugo was wide-eyed. 'God, James, you haven't killed her . . . ?'

At that, the girl's eyes opened, fierce and dark. James felt her legs scissor around his ankles and twist. He lost his balance and fell against an old coffee table, which splintered under his weight. Suddenly she was on top of him, arm pressed to his throat.

'Hey!' Hugo ran forward to push her off. But then another girl – much taller and scrawnier than her friend – came running out of the kitchen. She was holding a knife, and shouted in Spanish as she jabbed it at Hugo. Hugo broke off his counter-attack and raised his hands. And for a moment James stopped struggling too. He recognized the voice, caught a glimpse of her face.

'That's her,' he gasped. 'The girl I saved last night.'

'Does she know that?' Hugo was still transfixed by the blade pointing at his face. 'She doesn't seem very grateful.'

But as the wild-looking knife-girl gazed down at James, her aggression gave way to confusion. She gestured with the blade and said something in Spanish.

'*Sí. Es él.*' Hugo nodded enthusiastically. '*El muchacho en el calléjon.*'

The girl with the braids looked down at James, then spoke in accented English. 'You are the boy who saved Maritsa last night?'

'If your friend here is Maritsa, yes,' he said carefully. 'My name's Bond. James Bond.'

Her face darkened. 'And so, James Bond, when she ran, Ramón got to you, yes? Paid you money to help them catch Señor Hardiman?'

'Of course not. We're staying—'

'Tell me where he is!' She gripped James's shirtfront, hissing

40

into his face. 'What did they do to him?'

'We don't know! If you'd only calm down—'

'Not until I know where he is!'

James bucked his body with sudden force, threw her off him. She rolled over and got to her knees, but he was on his feet first. Maritsa raised her knife again – but James had already pulled Queensmarsh from his waistband and pointed it at her. She dropped the knife and took a step backward.

'Now, listen,' James said, 'Dr Hardiman is an old friend of my family. Hugo and I were going to stay with him for a few days. We want to know where he is a damn sight more than you do.'

The girl looked up at him. 'They are your clothes, then, in the smaller room?'

'Yes. So what do *you* care about Hardiman?'

'Gerald Hardiman is more than my friend. You could say . . . he is a lifeline.' The girl pulled a tightly folded piece of paper out of her pocket and slapped it down on the broken table. James picked it up and unfolded it: he saw the apartment address, written in Hardiman's own hand, and underneath:

Jagua –
Expect action early Wednesday. Be ready to leave quickly. Meet in Havana soonest. Safe passage for us both with luck.

'And you're Jagua?' James murmured.

The girl nodded. Her face was flawlessly smooth; the strong features might have been chiselled from stone, no trace of emotion beyond the rebellious attitude in the curl of her lip and the lifting of her eyebrow. Her eyes were as dark as her braided hair, and though her gaze was cool, James had no doubt that there was fire behind it. About her throat she wore a St Christopher on a golden thread, together with a small silver crucifix. Her tennis pumps – striped red canvas with rubber soles – seemed at odds with her formal dress, but James supposed running away was harder in smart shoes – and judging by the wear on the rubber, running was something this girl did a lot.

'Hold on.' Hugo looked between James and Jagua, baffled. 'I thought Maritsa was the one who was nearly kidnapped . . .'

'Ramón tried to take Maritsa when he saw her,' said Jagua, looking at her friend, who was frowning. 'He guessed she might know where I am. He is sly, like the crocodile.'

James passed the note to Hugo. 'When Scolopendra called last night, he asked Hardiman what he knew about a missing girl, remember?'

'Right.' Hugo scanned the scrap of paper and looked shyly at Jagua. 'So you really were supposed to meet old Hardiman?'

'Yes. I asked Maritsa to take a message to him, asking where would be safe . . .'

'But Ramón found her before she could pass it on.' James lowered his pistol. 'Just who exactly are you?'

The girl thrust out her chin. 'My full name is Jagua Belarmina Solares—'

'Hold on,' said Hugo. 'Isn't that the real surname of—?'

'Scolopendra.' James stared at Jagua. 'Audacto Solares. You're his daughter?'

'This is so. I have run away from home on the Isla de Pinos and so he sends men to bring me back. These men now have Hardiman.'

James raised an eyebrow. 'How do you know?'

'The trick with the front door – to take out the glass, reach in and turn the latch to enter quietly – is a favourite of Ramón's.' Jagua pointed to the dent in the wall; now that James looked more closely he could see four smaller dents within it. 'And I see this mark on many walls. On many faces also. It is made by a man who works with Ramón: El Puño.'

'El Puño . . . The Fist.' James put his hand to the lump on his head and looked at Maritsa; her dark eyes met his own, and she nodded. 'Well, will they have taken Hardiman back to this home you've run away from, wherever that is?'

'The Isla de Pinos – Isle of Pines – is Cuba's biggest neighbour,' Hugo offered helpfully, 'about thirty miles off the south coast.'

'I do not think he will be there,' said Jagua. 'Father has business here in Havana for the next two days, and he will want to question Hardiman . . .'

Left out of the conversation, Maritsa was looking towards the kitchen, holding her stomach. '*Tengo hambre.*'

'She's hungry,' Hugo translated.

'We have not had food for a long time. We eat while we talk, yes?' Jagua got up and headed into the kitchen, Maritsa at her heels. 'If we are to find Hardiman, we will need strength. Strength and luck.'

Hugo sighed. 'Sounds as if Hardiman hasn't had a whole heap of luck so far.'

'Maybe not.' James tucked Queensmarsh back into his waistband. 'But now he's got us on his side.'

'Ha! His troubles are at an end.' Hugo shook his head and followed the girls into the kitchen. 'Ours are just beginning.'

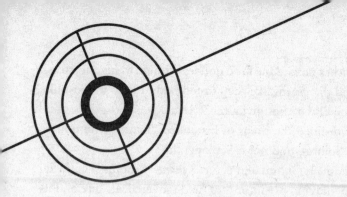

5

To Bring to Heel

They ate a hurried Cuban breakfast at the kitchen table: *tostada* – slices of Cuban bread, buttered and browned under the grill – dipped in *café con leche* – a strong espresso served with scalded milk. Despite his misgivings, James found the bitter drink and tostada went together well. Maritsa wolfed down her breakfast, stuffing her face with both dirty hands.

Hugo cleared his throat. 'Well, goodness. Here we are, eating together, and I haven't properly introduced myself. I'm Hugo Grande. Er, *mi nombre es Hugo Grande.*'

'*Grande?*' Maritsa swallowed and grinned suddenly, showing a chipped front tooth. '*Hugo es pequeño.*'

'Yes, I'm very small. Thank you for not stabbing me.' Hugo made to shake her buttery hand, then decided against it and turned shyly towards Jagua. 'Hello. You have an unusual name.'

'My father named me for a goddess known to his ancestors.' Jagua said the words like they tasted bad. 'I hate it – just like everything else he has given me.'

James drained the dregs of his coffee. 'Is that why you've stayed a Solares, and not a Scolopendra?'

'The name is for him alone. *Scolopendra* – the giant centipede – is a fast-moving predator that he discovered. Its bite and its poison are feared.' Jagua looked down at the table. 'It is a name he likes to live up to.'

'Likes . . .' Maritsa had turned to James, one side of her mouth turned up in a lopsided smile as she waved the last piece of tostada. 'You – likes this . . . ?'

'Yes, it's good. *Gracias*.' James took in just how painfully thin she was. 'I only wish Dr Hardiman were here to enjoy it too.' He turned to Jagua. 'When did he send you that note?'

'Five days ago.'

'Before he knew we were coming,' Hugo noted.

'One of the cleaners at Father's estate – she lives in Nueva Gerona but has family on the mainland – she was go-between, yes? Passed messages for me, if I paid her enough.' Jagua pushed aside her plate and dabbed at her mouth with a cloth – though when she noticed Maritsa watching, she dragged an arm across her lips instead. 'It was risky. Hardiman knew this. But I think something happened . . . something that made him think he could help us both at last.'

'At last?' Hugo queried.

'Hardiman lived with us on our estate for months. He is a man who sees much.' Her thin lips curved in a sad smile. 'Many times I wish he was my father, and I his daughter.'

'Jagua, I'm sorry if you're not happy at home,' James

began. 'But if you go back to your father, surely he will let Hardiman go . . .'

'No,' she snapped. 'I will not go back.'

'Surely—'

'*No*. You want to know why? I show you.' Trembling, Jagua stood up, reached behind her neck and unzipped the top of her dress. Then she tugged down on the left arm to expose a long mass of scarring – white welts sliced into the deep bronze skin.

James felt anger coil in his stomach. 'Your father beats you?'

'He says, only force can bring wild things to heel. This is what life with him is like.' Jagua struggled to do up her dress again, and Maritsa rose to help her with the zip. 'Hardiman, he would clean my wounds when Father had finished with me, and whisper: "Be brave, Jagua. Do not break. Deliverance will come." And I listen to him, and I do not break, even when Hardiman goes away. And before he goes, he tells me he will help me to run when he can.'

James couldn't help feeling a tiny twinge of jealousy at her closeness to Hardiman. He nodded to Maritsa. 'Does she run with you?'

'Always.' Jagua stroked her friend's tangled hair. 'I have known Maritsa all my life. My mother died when I was small, and Father spent much time away, so Maritsa's mother had to raise me also. It is a very poor place. Poverty is hard to escape.' A smile bloomed and died on her face as she looked at James. 'I don't suppose you would know . . .'

James shrugged curtly. 'You and your father seem to have escaped it.'

'Outrun it, maybe.'

Maritsa sat back down; divorced from the conversation in English, she began to eat leftover *tostada* from the other plates. Jagua watched her for a few moments, then gazed out of the window, remembering.

'Four years ago, when I was twelve, my father got very rich. Rich overnight, you say?' James and Hugo nodded. 'A plant he helped discover in Brazil – it is good for medicine . . . Anyway, he takes me away from Maritsa's family. We get a big home instead, like Americans. He invests in timber, takes over a big yard, makes things modern – new ways of working, with science and machines. Scolopendra Industries does well . . . but it changes him. And new "friends" change him more. We live in a private estate across the Gulf now, with swimming pools, gardens, his own private laboratory . . .' She suddenly looked back at James and Hugo. 'You are thinking, poor little rich girl, yes? In her prison of luxury. Well, my father schools me well, feeds me well. I am taught good manners, other languages – *Only in English when you talk to me, Jagua. Always in English, so we practise.* He chooses what I should be. Punishes when I say no.' Jagua's hand strayed to her scarred shoulder. 'And since he has met *her* . . . it is all so much worse.'

'*Her?*' James enquired.

'First she was his "business partner",' she said with a curl of the lip; 'now, his woman.'

James tried to hide his impatience. Jagua had suffered, no doubt, and he was sorry, but her unhappy home life was not high on his agenda; Hardiman was. 'I don't understand why Hardiman walked out on your father's work, but didn't leave Cuba.'

48

'He could not. Hardiman owes much money, to many people. Father pays off these debts in instalments. Pays the rent on his home in Trinidad.'

Hugo was puzzled. 'Seems very generous . . .'

'Just another form of control,' James guessed. 'In return, he expects Hardiman to jump when he cracks the whip.'

'Only something must have changed,' said Hugo, 'because when you wrestled his wallet back from the pickpocket, it was stuffed full of money.'

'And Hardiman knew well in advance what would happen at Father's yesterday,' Jagua agreed. 'An intruder – a woman – broke into the lab and took something – I do not know what, but it must have been important.'

'So Hardiman *was* lying on the telephone when he said he didn't know about Scolopendra's lab,' James realized. 'I wonder what this mystery woman stole . . .'

'While Father's men were busy trying to stop her, I took a boat and left. She took Father's fastest cruiser. She passed me, and I felt sure she would escape . . .' Jagua shook her head and shivered despite the heat. 'I followed her course to the mainland, though I could not keep up. I saw Father's men go after her by plane. I saw them shoot holes in the cruiser; saw it sink beneath the waves, less than a mile from shore . . .' She looked at James. 'And you wonder why I want to run away?'

'I'm sorry.' James remembered the newspaper headline in the *Diario de la Marina* the evening before. 'This intruder – she's the woman who washed up dead. No wonder Hardiman reacted the way he did when he heard.' He paused. 'Whatever she took from Scolopendra, she died for it. And now it's lying at the bottom of the sea.'

'All for nothing.' Jagua's eyes were hard and dark. 'I do not know who this woman was so I cannot grieve for her. But I grieve for the man my father used to be . . . and I fear the man he has become.'

'My fear's for Hardiman,' said James. 'If he lived and worked on the Scolopendra estate, he'd have good information on how to get inside the lab.'

Hugo nodded. 'You think he sold his knowledge to the brains behind the break-in – so he could pay off his debts and get away with Jagua?'

'Maybe.' James turned to Jagua. 'But surely the police must know it's your father's men who killed this woman? They'll investigate and—'

'The great Scolopendra has powerful friends,' she said, 'in the government, the embassies . . . The police will never move against him. And if they see me, they will hand me over to him, knowing they will be well rewarded.'

James didn't comment, but noted again how Jagua had put herself at the centre of the drama. 'Let's recap on what we know.' He put his fingers to his temples. 'Hardiman's been abducted. Scolopendra must suspect he's involved in the robbery at his lab as well as in his daughter's latest escape . . .'

'Half the city must be looking for Jagua by now,' Hugo added.

'And we can't turn to the authorities for help,' James concluded. 'Even my Aunt Charmian won't arrive for several days.'

Hugo sighed. 'Good pep talk, James.'

'But there's still the four of us.' James looked at Jagua and Maritsa. 'Right now, we're all Hardiman has.'

Jagua regarded him coolly. 'It is an alliance you propose?'

'Yes. If we pool our resources and work together, perhaps we can find Hardiman ourselves.' James held out his hand. 'How about it, Hugo?'

Hugo sighed again. 'Can't let you go it alone, can I? You bloody fool.' He reached up and put his hand on top of James's. 'I suppose I'm in.'

Jagua turned and spoke to Maritsa in Spanish. James waited tensely through the exchange. Finally she looked at the boys and pulled a silver dollar from her pocket. 'My father would no doubt decide on the toss of a coin.' She flipped the dollar – and Maritsa swiped it out of the air with a cheeky, lopsided smile.

'Jagua, *not* Father.' Maritsa pocketed the coin and placed her buttery palm against James's from underneath.

'We will stand together.' Jagua smiled and placed her long fingers on Hugo's knuckles. 'For the moment – yes?'

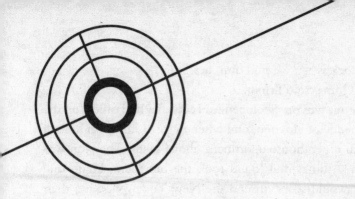

6
Fingertips

Within the hour, James and Jagua were waiting nervously for a motor bus on the leafy Avenida Carlos III; it felt a safer and less conspicuous way to travel than walking the streets. The stop stood in the shadow of an ancient tumbledown fort. Like so much in the city, it spoke to James of resilience; still upright despite everything the years had thrown at it.

You and me both, he thought.

'I am standing out more in these clothes than in my own,' announced Jagua beside him. She was wearing a white shirt of James's, along with a pair of Hugo's trousers as makeshift shorts. A Panama hat kept her braided hair tucked up out of sight.

'You look fine,' James assured her. 'Just like a boy.'

'A boy? Well, thank you.' Jagua's tongue was sweet but her eyes were acid. 'I think the hat suits Hardiman better. We give it back when we find him, yes?'

'Yes,' James said firmly.

The hunt was on. Scolopendra Industries had offices on the western edge of Havana, and when in town, the man himself stayed in a penthouse apartment above them. The plan was that while James and Jagua took the bus there, Hugo and Maritsa would scout around the New Town, working their way through lock-ups and equipment stores owned by the company. Every possible hiding place for Hardiman had to be eliminated.

For the thousandth time James imagined his old friend in some filthy hovel, menaced by Ramón and El Puño, and shuddered. 'You really think Hardiman's still here in Havana?'

'Father will want to speak to him in person. And Father is here.' Jagua paused. 'I suppose he may take Hardiman to one of the research stations . . .'

'The what?'

'Cuba has many cays – you know . . . tiny islands?' When James nodded, she went on. 'My father owns several – Cayo Esqueleto, Cayo Iguana, Cayo Soledad . . . more. And he has built wildlife places – you say "sanctuaries"? – on these islands. Only he and his teams may go there.'

James nodded glumly. 'Sounds like any one of those would make a good prison.'

'But so would the penthouse above his offices. It is close, and it is private.'

James thought for a moment. 'Perhaps . . . you could telephone your father . . . talk to him – try to find out—'

'You think he will tell me where Hardiman is?' Jagua

looked scornful. 'What if he says he will hurt Hardiman if I do not return? I do not dare talk to him . . .' A crafty look flitted across her face. 'At least, not until I have some way to make him listen. And perhaps this too may be found at the penthouse.'

'What do you mean?'

She looked up at James from beneath the brim of her hat. 'My father needs Hardiman for his special project. The project *she* helps him with.'

James nodded. 'This mysterious woman you've taken against?'

'She calls herself *La Velada*. You would say "The Veil". She flatters my father's ego; says only he can carry out this great task.' Jagua spat on the pavement in disgust. (*So much for finishing school!* James noted.) 'That the world will respect and fear him like no other if he completes it.'

'And the task is . . . ?'

'Who would tell *me*, the problem child, huh?' Jagua dropped her voice, glancing about furtively as she did so. 'Hardiman said only that this task will shock the world. He wants no part of it, but my father will not let him quit.'

James considered. 'You say La Velada is Scolopendra's business partner as well as his lover?'

'She inherits a big company, yes? It makes new drugs from things rare in nature. Such discoveries have always been Father's passion, and now he finds a lady who shares it.' Jagua's eyes had narrowed to slits. 'La Velada, she helps him to start a private business, to build and staff his own laboratories, to . . . exploit? Yes, exploit nature. Says how great his discoveries will make him. But she does not love him. She only uses him.'

James wondered if a daughter's jealousy was playing its part here. 'Uses him how?' he asked.

'Cuba has many special habitats – in Baracoa, Zapata, Pinar del Río . . . There are plants and creatures there known only to my father.' Jagua looked serious. 'I think she plans to cheat him of his discoveries. I have been collecting . . . what is it you say? Evidence.'

'Like a proper little spy.' James smiled his approval. 'Evidence of what?'

'I listen to her telephone calls in secret. When she thinks she is alone, La Velada talks often to people of my father, of this particular project and its progress.'

'Sounds as if *she* is the spy. Who's she talking to?'

Jagua shrugged. 'I cannot tell. Sometimes she gives instructions. Other times I think she takes them. She uses code, though: speaks sometimes in English, sometimes in Russian. I do not speak Russian well, but I wrote down all I could understand. Each time Father had business in Havana, I would hide my notes in my room at the penthouse. We are not there so often, so it is safer.'

James smiled. 'Very resourceful.'

'You patronize me, James Bond?' Jagua's eyes flashed. 'I have paid others to investigate La Velada also. If I can prove to my father that she is not who he thinks she is, that she tricks him, he may yet turn back from this "task" . . .'

'Meaning Hardiman's let off the hook because his services won't be needed.' James cleared his throat. 'I'm sorry, I didn't mean to be patronizing, Jagua. It's a good plan.' He looked up as a rusting Renault motor bus approached, engine rattling, headlights like eyes squinting myopically on either side of a narrow, extruded bonnet. 'Is this our transport?'

'About time.' Jagua jumped aboard as it slowed beside them. 'We go to my penthouse in style, yes?'

The bus was already jammed with locals. Some had dogs; one old man clutched a scrawny hen on his lap. After paying the driver, James and Jagua stood on the large open platform at the rear. They didn't talk. Drumming his fingers against Queensmarsh, James wondered how much he could trust this girl. Perhaps she was thinking the same about him . . . With every block, James felt his nerves twitch and his senses sharpen, a slow metamorphosis. A coming to life . . .

The bus chugged along through the bustling neighbourhoods. By the time they reached the town of Regla, at the bottom of Havana Bay, the crowds had dwindled and the urban landscape had given way to industrial sprawl.

Scolopendra's Havana offices were located near the harbour, where they left the motor bus. The brick building was hard to miss, James thought, taking it in from across the road. INDUSTRIAS SCOLOPENDRA screamed in crimson capitals from a hoarding, one word on either side of a sharp red claw within a black circle. Above the sign was a specially converted upper floor, with huge picture windows and a balcony offering incredible views over the bay.

The penthouse, James noted. Several of the mahogany shutters were closed. 'Are the windows shielded for shade, or privacy?'

'I do not know.' Jagua was glancing around, her hat low over her face. 'I *do* know that if I am seen here . . .'

'Hold still,' James hissed. 'The more you fidget, the more conspicuous you look.' He surveyed the rest of the building, which seemed in less good repair. There were deep ridges between the bricks where salt-damp mortar had crumbled, and wooden scaffolding stretched to the second storey; here some building repairs were underway – although there was no sign of any workmen.

'I want to take a look at the main entrance,' he said. 'Meet you in a moment.' He crossed the road and walked casually past the set of double doors that led into the lobby. The doors had been propped open, and James could see a smart receptionist typing behind the front desk. Further back stood two formidable-looking security guards in pale-blue uniforms, armpits dark with sweat. The man on the right was—

El Puño. James felt fear prickle through his body. *He's here*.

James continued calmly past the entrance, then forced himself to turn back for another look. This time he checked out El Puño's fellow gorilla, saw the small Beretta nestled discreetly in his jacket pocket. Swearing under his breath, he hurried back to Jagua.

She saw from his face that something was wrong. 'Well?'

'Two big guards in the lobby. One of them's armed. One of them's El Puño.'

'*El Puño?*' Jagua looked shaken. 'But he is employed for special assignments, not as a doorman.'

'Which could mean Hardiman's being held upstairs.' James felt a thrill of excitement. 'If I can get past El Puño and his friend—'

'You think you can get rid of them with your little popgun?' Jagua was shaking her head. 'El Puño alone would be impossible to beat . . .'

'Well, is there another way up?' James was growing exasperated. 'A fire escape at the back maybe?'

Jagua frowned. 'I don't remember.'

'Let's take a look.' James adjusted the brim of her hat to give maximum cover to her face and gestured to the building. 'Come on.'

Moving as nonchalantly as possible and trailing crowds when they could, the two of them explored the local area. The rear of the building could be reached from a narrow alley that cut between blocks. It was protected by a tall fence crowned with barbed wire; beyond that, the back door was heavily padlocked.

Jagua swore. 'This is hopeless.'

'Let me see the front again.' James wiped sweat from his forehead. 'Maybe there's another way.'

Leaving Jagua in the alley, he surveyed the walls above the scaffolding, the gaps and ridges in the old brickwork. It wouldn't be easy, but barefoot, he might just be able to find enough holds and crevices to climb from the scaffolding to the penthouse above the offices. And then . . .

James turned and hurried back to a grocery store he'd passed. A plan was forming in his mind.

When he returned to Jagua with the proposal and a small metal pail, she just stared. 'You think you can break into the penthouse in full sight, with only a sponge, a jar of honey and a newspaper?'

'Given the right incentive, I think that's all I need.'

'Apart from prayers for your soul and the luck of the devil.'

'Help from above *and* below, eh?' James smiled, slipping off his deck shoes and dropping them in the bucket. 'Nothing like hedging your bets.'

'I thought we said we would not stand out? This is crazy!'

'Let's call it bold. El Puño and friends are inside the building – they won't even see me . . .' James hooked his arm through the handle of the black bucket and hoisted it onto his shoulder. 'It's broad daylight. Anyone in the street will think I'm a window cleaner, or one of the builders – not a thief. I won't hold their interest for long.'

'If Hardiman *is* up there, what will you do? There could be more guards . . . my father—'

'I won't know till I'm up there, will I?'

'But window cleaners use ropes to hold them if they fall. You have nothing!'

'Besides your kind prayers for my soul and the luck of the devil.' James's nerves jangled, but he knew that chances had to be taken. 'What will you do – wait for me out here?'

'Like a good little girl?' There was a bitter edge to Jagua's voice. 'Listen. If by some miracle you do this, there is a pile of books on the floor in my room, yes? And a manuscript, written by a friend. In there is my evidence.' She touched the tiny crucifix at her neck and placed a hand on his chest. 'Now, go if you are going, but in the name of the Virgin Mary, be careful.'

'You too.' James hesitated, then handed her Queensmarsh. 'I don't want to drop my "pop gun" – and if you're found here it might help you bluff your way out.' She nodded, took it. Then he headed back to the scaffolding at the front of the building, and looked up at the sheer brickwork.

Well, he thought, *no sense in waiting around*.

Quickly James shinned up a scaffolding pole and heaved himself onto the platform. It was a simple matter to repeat the action and reach the second-storey scaffold.

Now for the real challenge . . .

Fingers and toes wedged in the gaps, muscles trembling with the effort, James slowly scaled the bricks between the windows. A breeze was getting up, and he was aware of the rattle and blare of trams and traffic; at any moment he expected to be spotted, and the alarm raised.

Carry on, he told himself. *Focus*.

His toes were soon bleeding as he scrabbled at the cracks in the wall for purchase, and his numb, raw fingers dug into the crumbling mortar. His route was dictated by the gaps in the brickwork, and frustratingly pushed him sideways as much as upward. When a dusty windowsill jutted out above him, James clung onto it gratefully. He glanced down, the massive drop twisting dizzily in his sight. His shoulder ached from carrying the bucket, and a muscle tremor was making his right arm shake.

Two weeks of taking it easy, he thought, *and you're out of condition!*

James carried on, dodged the window, hauled himself higher. The bucket felt as if it were full of lead, and the breeze began to gust dangerously. Pins and needles swarmed in James's hands and feet, and he was forced to slow down. He glanced down to check he'd not been spotted, and vertigo stirred again, dizzying his senses.

Suddenly he slipped, cried out as his bloodied toes scraped over brick. He barely clung on, fingers like gnarled, crimson-tipped claws as he regained his foothold.

Come on, he told himself, forehead pressed against the old brick. *The quick way down right now is not an option.*

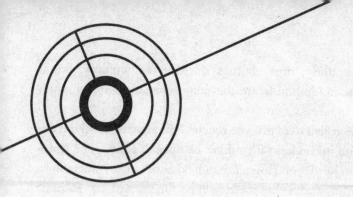

7

The Thief and the Lady Killer

The climb slowed to a nightmare crawl. Finally, sweating and panting with effort, James reached the underside of the penthouse balcony – just where its left side met the wall above him.

With the bleeding fingers of his left hand still jammed in the brickwork, his right grasped hold of a slender wrought-iron railing. He tensed, praying his aching arms would still support his weight. Then he pushed away from the wall and gripped another railing with his left hand. He clung there for a moment, muscles on fire, shoulder throbbing where the handle of the metal pail had cut in. Blood mixed with dirt was trailing slowly from fingertips to knuckles.

Summoning all his will, James dragged himself up and over the balcony rail, and with a surge of euphoria fell down onto the warm wooden floor. He collapsed face first, the

63

bucket rattling; dark shutters shielded the window, but if someone inside had heard the noise, opened them, saw him there . . .

James rolled over until he reached the shutter, blocking the base with his body so it couldn't be opened easily. The climb had been harder and longer than he'd anticipated, taken more out of him, and he lay there, willing the strength to return to his frame.

Encouraged that no one was trying to force the shutter open, he reached for the pail with shaking hands. Keeping low, he crawled across the balcony until he reached the door, which was locked but not shuttered. He couldn't make out much through the harsh reflections in the glass — just a sea of white marble and dark blurs of furniture rising like islands. He detected no noise from inside, and no movement.

Please be in there, Dr Hardiman . . .

It was time to see if his plan would actually work.

First James put his deck shoes back on and winced. Teeth gritted, he opened out the newspaper and blotted his bloody fingers. Then he poured the jar of sticky honey over the front page. Once he'd used the sponge to smear it thickly over the whole sheet, he stuck the newspaper to the glass panel at the bottom of the door.

Pushing pain into anger, James lifted the pail and struck it against the newspaper as hard as he could. The paper muffled the noise of the blow, and when at his second attempt the glass shattered, the honey stopped it from falling on the floor.

James carefully peeled the paper backwards, and the glass shards came away with it. The hole he'd made was just big enough for him to wriggle through. He nodded in satisfaction; it was his own take on Ramón's slightly more professional glass removal at Hardiman's apartment. 'Do unto others as they have done unto you,' he murmured, 'or to your friends.'

In moments, the marble floor was like ice against his chest and legs, and the cool of the apartment soothed his aching muscles. Carefully, James reached an arm through the hole in the glass and hooked his hand under the shutter to pull it closed. Then he got up and looked around.

The large open space felt more like a museum than a living room: the heads of different beasts – a bull, a lion, even an elephant – had been mounted on the walls, and huge stuffed specimens of bear, ape and alligator loomed in angry stances, as if ready to attack.

There was still no sign of anyone about. James explored. The glass eyes in the long-dead bestial faces seemed to follow his progress from door to door as he opened each a fraction and peered inside.

It didn't take long to establish that the apartment was empty.

James felt a crushing sense of futility. And yet, what was El Puño doing here if not guarding someone important? Perhaps Hardiman was somewhere else in the building. *And there's still Jagua's evidence*, he reminded himself, trying to stay positive. *You won't come out with nothing.*

He returned to what was clearly Jagua's room – a single bed, neatly made, a wardrobe half full of expensive clothes that looked barely worn, and shelves overflowing with dusty leather-bound reference books and encyclopaedias of the natural world. Her own selection, or her father's?

James spotted the pile of books by her bed and quickly found a typed manuscript entitled *A Field Guide to Birds of the West Indies*. There was no author name, but James was more interested in the thin folded sheets of paper pressed between two pages on the Cuban black hawk. He removed them, skimmed the handwritten Spanish, then stuffed them into his back pocket. He only hoped that Jagua was right; that these notes really did hold the power to set Hardiman free – wherever he was.

The flimsy pages didn't fully satisfy as spoils of war, so James decided to poke about the place for more. He left Jagua's room and crossed the corridor to Scolopendra's study. Jars containing fat, worm-like creatures with spiny legs and segmented bodies lined the walls. *Centipedes* . . . It looked like some grisly museum.

With a shiver of revulsion, James turned his attention to a large mahogany desk. A loose roll of graph paper lay on top of it. Opening it out, James was soon inspecting plans for a tugboat towing large amounts of timber across the ocean. On the back was a series of scrawled costings and estimates. A map of the West Indies had been rolled up behind it, with a route marked in red stretching eastward from an island south of Cuba, across the Caribbean Sea, past Haiti, and then out into the North Atlantic.

Frustrated, James rolled the papers up again. That Scolopendra brought work home with him was hardly a revelation, but a leather-bound diary lay on the desk blotter. James sucked blood from his stinging fingers and flicked carefully through the pages. Appointments had been noted in untidy capitals.

There was nothing marked down for yesterday, and nothing for today. But in the margins of tomorrow at five p.m., in a different, neater hand, had been written:

MACLEAN. GRAN CASINO

'Business or pleasure?' James mused. At least he knew where Scolopendra would be late tomorrow afternoon; that seemed more useful intelligence.

Although he searched diligently, James could find nothing else of interest in the office and decided to widen his search. In the master bedroom, oppressive with its black walls and stuffed wildcats glaring out from two of the corners, he found a diamond chain and earrings lying on Scolopendra's bedside table. Impulsively, James pocketed the jewellery, thinking Jagua and Maritsa might know somebody who could convert it into cash; they had little enough, and who knew how long it would have to last them? Besides, whoever heard of a break-in where nothing was stolen? He didn't want Scolopendra to suspect that the forced entry to this apartment had any other motive.

The gilt dial of the Duverdrey et Bloquel clock on the mantel told James he'd been in the penthouse for almost twenty minutes now. 'Time to leave,' he murmured.

He opened the heavy front door and stepped out onto a small tiled landing. Ahead of him was the concertinaed door to the private lift. Using that would alert the guards downstairs, so James turned to the fire door that led to the staircase.

Then he froze.

The sound of steel-tipped heels called from the steps behind the heavy door. Someone was coming.

James swore, ducked back inside the apartment and closed the front door. He hid behind the towering grizzly bear, its face frozen in mute accusation. James only hoped that the new arrival would spy the hole in the glass straight away and cross the room to investigate – allowing him to creep out unnoticed.

A key turned in the lock. James held his breath as the door opened, braced himself for fight or flight. But as he peeped out from behind a thick, furry arm, he saw that this was not Scolopendra.

It was a woman dressed all in black, wearing a veil, as if she'd just come from a funeral. It was hard to see her face, but her hair was as dark as her simple but elegant satin dress. The fabric was decorated with long silk tassels so that when she walked, the whole garment seemed alive with whispering movement.

James watched as the woman went straight to the Bakelite telephone on the table opposite. As she dialled with her back to him, James felt his heart thump harder. Would she notice the closed shutter, the hole in the glass . . . ?

He braced himself to run, peeped out from behind the grizzly. But he hesitated as the woman started to speak – not in Spanish, but in quiet, fluent English.

'La Velada. You can talk?'

So, thought James, here was Jagua's nemesis! And true to form, speaking in tongues on the telephone.

'I've identified the corpse myself. The thief was Sarila Karatan. Freelance arms dealer, operating out of the Middle

East and the Caribbean. We don't yet know who she was working for, but it's certain an insider gave her the necessary knowledge . . .' A pause. 'Yes, Hardiman has been acquired, and my investigation has begun. Launch may need to be brought forward . . . Yes, so long as the strongbox stays lost at the bottom of the ocean, no one can get at it . . .'

At least Hardiman's alive, thought James. *But just who are you talking to?*

La Velada tilted her head to one side, holding the receiver between shoulder and ear while she reached into her bag.

As she did so, James saw with a shock the ghost of his reflection in the glass of the display case on the wall opposite. *And if I can see it—*

The woman spun round to face James, a small nickel-plated Derringer held at chest height – and fired.

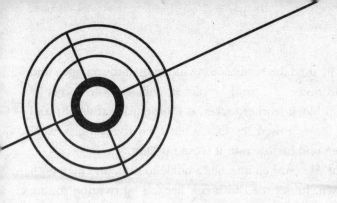

8

Plot and Counterplot

The shot shattered the calm in the penthouse. The stuffed grizzly rocked back on its plinth under the impact of the bullet – and James dived out of hiding.

He knew that if he stopped, even for a second, he was dead. He tucked in his head and launched himself into a forward roll as another shot was fired. The marble floor spat powder at his cheek. He turned, hurled the necklace he'd stolen at the woman's face; it struck her veil like a glittering snake and she stepped backwards, almost tripping over the telephone table. James scrambled up, bolted for the front door, swung it open and dived through as a third bullet sent splinters flying.

He charged across the landing to the heavy fire door, gripped the handle with throbbing fingers and threw it open. It struck the wall with a bang, which echoed as James thundered down the concrete steps. At each turn in the staircase he used the banister to swing himself round, speeding faster and faster . . . until he almost collided with someone wearing a black leather jacket, a motorcycle crash-hat and goggles. James raised his fists – but then the goggles were pulled free and he saw that it wasn't a man, it was—

'Jagua!' He crashed into her, unable to stop, and they both went down. James tried to break her fall by twisting round, pulling her on top of him, gasping as he hit the concrete.

She gripped his arms urgently. '*La Velada* – woman in veil, she is—?'

'Upstairs,' James gasped. 'She tried to shoot me. Almost killed me.'

'She has a gun?' Jagua helped James to his feet. 'The bitch will call El Puño. *That* is why he is here – her escort.'

'How did you get in' – James started after her as she hurried down the stairs to the first floor – 'dressed up like that—'

'Not now,' she hissed.

There was thunder from below as the door was smashed open. James glimpsed two large figures starting up the steps, and swore. El Puño and his friend were coming.

Jagua did not slow down. She reached a door marked '1' that led off the stairwell, and slipped through. 'You found my evidence, in the unfinished manuscript?'

'Yes.' James overtook her and pushed open a second door. It gave onto gutted brickwork with untidy tangles of wires dangling from the ceiling. Tarpaulins shrouded the glassless windows, darkening the space. Jagua ran up to the nearest and ripped it away, then climbed nimbly over the frame and out onto the wooden boards. James followed her into the glare of daylight and the throaty serenade of automobiles and motor buses. Jagua slid down one of the supporting metal poles to ground level; he followed her example, hands and feet stinging, legs almost giving way beneath him.

'This way.' Jagua had slipped her crash-hat back on; she pulled him after her as she raced towards the alley.

James heard shouts from inside the Scolopendra building. They were like a wind at his back as he pelted after Jagua into the shade of the alley.

He found her sitting astride a motorcycle, a handsome black Indian Four with a sidecar that was styled in sweeps of black and silver to a pointed prow, like a speedboat. At the back of the bike, a leather carry-case was fixed to a chrome luggage rack. James noticed a young bearded man in shorts and a vest lying slumped against the wall beside a small pile of parcels, apparently asleep. 'What happened?'

'I see him make a delivery nearby. I want jacket and hat for disguise. He says no. We bargain.' Jagua pulled Queensmarsh from her pocket and tossed it to James. 'I won.'

James caught his air pistol. As Jagua started the bike and twisted on the throttle, he searched in his pocket for the diamond earrings and pressed them into the young man's hand. 'Compensation.'

'James!'

He turned at Jagua's shout to find El Puño blocking the alleyway, his gloved fist raised.

Jagua's face was as fierce as the Indian's roar as she pushed it into gear and revved the engine. James leaped into the sidecar and held on tight as the rig jumped forward.

El Puño was still blocking the way.

As the Indian Four accelerated, James took out Queensmarsh, pulled the cocking lever up and forward, inserted a ball bearing in the barrel, and closed it. Jagua veered left, making for the narrow gap between El Puño and the wall. James aimed his pistol at the man's neck and fired, but the metal pellet merely bounced off the fist as it swept down in a killer blow. James ducked inside the sidecar as the windshield was smashed clear off, and his head almost went with it.

Then Jagua was swinging the Indian out into the road. James heard the bark of brakes behind them; a Buick had slewed to a halt in the middle of the road, its angry driver shouting at them. Jagua pulled away, cut in front of a truck and turned hard left into a row of shipyards and warehouses separated by glittering glimpses of the sea. James let out a breath he didn't know he'd been holding – just as Jagua made a sudden sharp right onto a tree-lined boulevard and almost threw him out of the sidecar.

'Boats, motorcycles . . .' James clung on tight. 'Is there anything you can't drive?'

'Seaplanes are not so easy.' Jagua shrugged. 'I like fast machines.'

Emphasis on the fast, James noted approvingly as they screeched round a bend.

Jagua jerked to a stop for traffic lights and lowered her head, sucking in deep breaths. 'That was close, no? If El Puño connects, you are dead.'

'Where did your father find him?'

'El Puño is muscle for hire. When his hand was blown off

in the Brazilian revolution, he had the stump crowned with a block of granite, fixed and pinned to the bone.'

James pulled a face. 'Explains his cheery disposition.' He tried to relax his cramped body. 'Nice trick with the dispatch rider, by the way.'

'I took some of his parcels, pretended they were for the sales department on the second floor. I was looking for Hardiman—'

'Your father's got him somewhere. Your friend with the veil said so, before she started shooting.' James remembered his narrow squeak. 'I can see why you're not in a hurry to call her "Mother".'

The lights changed to green and Jagua pulled away again. James ordered his thoughts as they made their way through the city, sticking to quieter roads wherever possible. He pointed out a petrol station, a one-storey building on a two-bit street, and suggested she top up the tank. 'Once this bike is reported stolen it'll be too risky to stop for fuel.'

'You are right.' Jagua drove onto the garage forecourt and killed the engine. The pump attendant emerged from his white stall, and James asked, '*¿Habla usted Inglés?*' When the man grunted and shook his head, James felt it safe to tell her what had happened in the penthouse and what he'd found in the diary.

'So,' said Jagua, 'my father meets with MacLean at the Gran Casino tomorrow?'

'That's what was written down,' James confirmed. 'Mean anything to you?'

'The casino is part of a luxury hotel, most exclusive in Havana. Father rents a luxury suite there.' Jagua chewed her lip. 'And MacLean – Chester MacLean – is harbourmaster at the Scolopendra shipyard now. But before that, he was Father's chief enforcer.'

'Enforcer?' James said. 'Makes sense. I don't suppose Scolopendra reached the top of the food chain through fair play and kindness.'

'When Father wanted something to happen, MacLean saw to it. Father did not ask him for details.' Jagua gave a wintry smile. 'It is MacLean I pay extra to get dirt on La Velada for me. He hates her too, you see. Since she comes to court him, Father has no time for his old generals.'

'Seems he's got time for MacLean now,' James said. 'And if your father wants Hardiman to spill what he knows . . .'

'Yes.' Jagua's voice faltered. 'MacLean could make that happen.'

'Can you find out what this "enforcer" has been asked to do?' James put a hand on her arm. 'I mean, if he's agreed to get you this information, you must be close . . .'

'Not close,' she snapped, and shrugged off James's hand as the pump attendant gave her a curious look. 'I pay MacLean for the information and tell him where to leave it, yes? Maritsa should have it by now. But this will not stop him from doing whatever it is my father wants. I hate him. I do not want to see him again, not ever.' Jagua shifted in the saddle, composed herself. 'But for Hardiman's sake, I will contact him.'

'Thank you, Jagua. This is a real lead, you know,' James said encouragingly. 'God knows we need one, if the launch of your father's "operation" is coming forward.' He sighed, frustrated. 'I wish we knew what the hell it was about. That woman, Sarila, died for whatever was in that strongbox, and now it's lost for good.'

'Perhaps . . .' Jagua had grown pensive. 'Or perhaps not.'

'What do you mean?'

She didn't reply as she handed two dollars to the attendant and spoke to him in Spanish. He grunted again and nodded to the main building, a slab of whitewashed concrete with a corrugated-iron roof. 'I will telephone MacLean from here. Wait.'

James raised his eyebrows. 'I'm not likely to go anywhere.'

'I think you are very likely to go everywhere.' Jagua turned and walked slowly into the garage building. James noted the slump to her shoulders.

The pump attendant replaced the petrol tank's cap before retreating back to his stall. James waited in the sidecar, feeling conspicuous, until Jagua returned.

'He already left the office for meetings.' She swung herself back onto the motorcycle. 'His secretary does not expect him back today.'

'Perfect timing,' James muttered. 'Well, we should head back to the apartment to meet Hugo and Maritsa, see if they've got MacLean's evidence . . .'

'Not yet.' Jagua pushed the crash-hat onto her head. 'There is something else I wish to check.'

'Oh? And what's that?'

'You will see, James Bond. You will see.' She gunned the engine, pulled away from the forecourt and swung back out into the road.

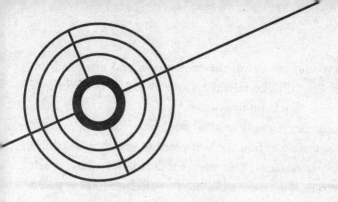

9
Old Life, New Chance

The mystery tour finally brought James to a warehouse in a rundown part of the centre of Havana. Traffic was sparse as Jagua parked the motorcycle out of sight behind the gate of a derelict yard. The sign of the red claw made it clear that the building belonged to Scolopendra Industries.

James climbed stiffly out of the sidecar and eyed the mouldering masonry, high windows and steel shutters over the entrance with little enthusiasm. His bones ached, his fingers and toes burned, but still he itched to do something – anything! – to find Hardiman and release him from his unhappy situation . . . and, yes, to get some payback too. He'd been shot at, hit, nearly killed, all in the name of some 'operation' about which he knew nothing. He wasn't about to give up now and count the hours while the cogs of Scolopendra's enterprise went on turning!

'I'd rather hoped we'd be going to the casino,' he admitted

as Jagua swung herself off the motorcycle and unzipped the leather jacket. 'I'd like to stake it out ahead of your father's meeting with MacLean tomorrow.'

She hung the jacket from the handlebars. 'Stake it out?'

'Yes – you know: find the best place to watch who comes in and out,' James said. 'Get a feel for the layout – how much cover there is, where the exits are . . . If Hardiman *is* taken there, perhaps we'll have a chance to get him out.'

'Perhaps.' She started off towards the warehouse. 'Or perhaps El Puño's fist, or the knife of Ramón, or La Velada's bullet – perhaps they find you this time, yes?'

'There's risk in everything if you look hard enough.'

Jagua glanced back, a thin smile on her face. 'I think you always look hard.'

James shrugged and followed her over. 'Why are we here? What's inside?'

'Equipment.' She walked round to the metal shutters at the side of the building; a padlocked chain secured the door handles to a rusty ring set in the crumbling concrete floor. 'Spare parts for the logging machines, the bulldozers, the cranes . . .'

'The Hugo.'

The voice startled James, and Jagua let loose a flurry of Spanish. Then the shutters rose up a few inches until the securing chain grew taut, and Hugo's familiar rumpled features poked out through the narrow gap.

'Please remain calm,' he deadpanned. 'There is no robbery in progress. Largely because there's nothing worth pinching.'

'Hugo.' James crouched down beside him with relief. He saw that Hugo was lying in a sort of shallow trench that ran below the doorway, allowing him and Maritsa to squeeze through the gap. 'Are you all right?'

'Tired and profoundly disappointed.' Hugo looked apologetic. 'We've looked at every place on the list. No sign of Hardiman. No sign of this evidence Maritsa's meant to collect, either.'

'What?' Jagua frowned as she knelt beside him. 'Move, please. I am coming in.'

'No need. Maritsa and I are coming out. There's only junk in here.'

'This is not so. Let me in, Hugo.'

'Well, since you ask so nicely.' Hugo wormed his way back out of sight. Jagua lay down in the hollow and squirmed awkwardly through the narrow space between concrete and metal. Checking first that there was no one in sight, James lay down flat on his front and tried to do the same. Since he was brawnier than the others, it was a struggle, even with Hugo pulling at his aching arms.

Finally he was inside, the smell of oil and grease thick in his nostrils. Dusty light passed reluctantly through the high windows, and he saw workbenches strewn with spare parts in the shadows; the arm of a crane lying in pieces against a wall. Jagua and Maritsa stood beside a stack of rusting crates, talking quietly and seriously amidst the clutter.

'We shouldn't hang around here,' Hugo fretted. 'Maritsa and I were almost caught by security at the last place.'

'How's your day with her been?' James asked.

'Well, we're both still here. Maritsa doesn't say much, but by God she can run.'

Abruptly, Maritsa broke away from Jagua and came over

to James, talking animatedly and looking him up and down. James could only return her stare blankly.

'She says that to escape El Puño twice is a miracle,' Hugo translated, 'and she wants to touch you for luck like the pilgrims touch the statue of St Lazarus at Rincón.'

James frowned at Maritsa's eager but lopsided smile. '*Where* does she want to touch me for luck?'

'Here in the warehouse,' said Hugo dryly.

Maritsa cupped James's cheeks in both hands and laughed, then went back to help Jagua, who was crouching over the crates, sorting through the contents.

'So much for Maritsa,' said Hugo. 'How's your alliance with Jagua?'

'She handles herself well, though I'm not always sure what she's up to. She plays her cards very close to her chest.' James looked over at Jagua and called hoarsely, 'If you told us what you were looking for, we could help.'

'No need,' she replied.

'See what I mean?' James shrugged. 'Let's start our own hunt – for something to cut through the chain holding the shutters closed. I've had a bellyful of forced entries and exits today.'

Hugo cupped his hands behind his head. 'Go on. I'm all ears.' Although when James told him what he and Jagua had been through, he was pretty much all eyes as well.

'And there was me feeling bold and dangerous after my ordeals! You had to trump me, of course.' He leaned back against a workbench. 'Bloody hell, James, these people don't fool about, do they? I can't believe this La Velada woman actually fired a gun at you!'

'I think Jagua's right – La Velada's more than just the boss of a pharmaceutical company.'

'On the plus side, once she's shot you she can offer a really first-class antiseptic.' Frowning, Hugo lowered his voice. 'Don't you think we're in this a bit deep?'

'Hardiman's in it deeper—' James broke off. 'I'm sorry, Hugo. You barely know Hardiman, and here I am expecting you to make this your fight. If you'd rather sit this out back at the apartment, I understand. There'd be no hard feelings.'

'Oh, James, I can't just hide in the apartment,' Hugo said quietly. 'Not now that this Fist character's seen you, anyway – chances are he'll come looking for you there and pulverize me instead!'

James smiled ruefully. 'That's a good point.'

'So I'll just have to stick with you, won't I? For safety's sake.' Hugo pointed to a large set of bolt-cutters propped up in a cobwebbed corner. 'By the way, is that the sort of thing you're after?'

'Yes!' James took the bolt-cutters' long solid handles and hefted them experimentally. 'What would I do without you, Hugo?'

'Walk faster?'

'No need – we've a motorcycle and sidecar outside.' James positioned the steel jaws of the bolt-cutters round a link in the chain and squeezed. With a dusty jangle, the chain broke and skittered across the concrete. 'It's a bit of a squeeze for all of us, but—'

'I am sorry to say,' called Jagua, 'that we need the sidecar to carry *this*.'

James turned to find her bending over a dark box the size

83

of an accordion – and was promptly dazzled by three blazing lights set inside it.

Hugo flung an arm across his eyes. 'What in God's name is that?'

'It is a submarine lamp. Used for salvage, under the water.' Jagua switched off the lights and laid the cumbersome machine on its side while Maritsa went on rummaging through some other crates. 'Father wanted all my diving things destroyed. Hardiman hid them away for me.'

James frowned. 'Diving things?'

'In the village where we grew up, some of us – we make a club,' Jagua explained. 'A club for diving. *Sociedad Suicidio.*'

'The Suicide Club,' Hugo translated. 'That's sweet.'

'There are dangers' – Jagua shrugged – 'but also rewards.'

James's eyes grew wide with excitement. 'You rarely find one without the other.'

'*¡Lo he encontrado!*' Maritsa heaved an extraordinary contraption out of a crate and placed it over her head. It was a large metal cylinder that looked like a water-heater, with lengths of hosepipe extending from the top. The base was fringed with thick rubber; the inner tube of a car tyre, James guessed, folded and riveted to the metal. The bizarre helmet made her look like a space invader from a Buck Rogers cartoon strip; only the area from forehead to nose was visible through the rectangular glass screen.

'You go underwater in that?' Hugo pulled a face. '*Suicide* sounds about right. But why take the equipment now?'

'She thinks she can dive down to Sarila's shipwreck and find Scolopendra's strongbox,' James said. 'That's it, isn't it?'

'Yes.' Jagua thrust out her chin. 'I watched the cruiser go down. I know where it lies.'

James looked doubtful. 'Surely the ocean is too deep for you to dive to the bottom.'

'With so many little islands in the Gulf, there are shelves of coral beneath the sea.' Jagua gave a sly smile. 'So you see, the wreck can be reached. With the treasure *and* my evidence, Father will have to listen to us.'

Hugo shook his head, despairing. 'But what will you sound like, with your lungs full of seawater?'

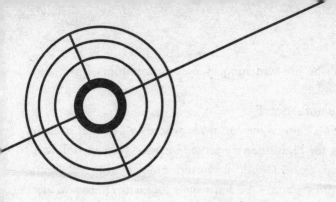

10
Suicide Club: Now Recruiting

Four-thirty in the afternoon, and James was sweating on another crowded motor bus, this time with Hugo. They were travelling through Havana's outlying districts and into the lowlands, towards the little beach village of Celimar. The rutted road ahead shimmered in the heat haze. Here and there plantations rose from the seas of wild green; islands where tobacco and sugarcane were cultivated. James saw *vaqueros*, or cowboys, on their little horses, herding livestock into crude corrals made of rope and tree branches.

He envied Jagua and Maritsa, who were taking the motor-cycle. The sidecar was loaded up with the submarine lantern, the crude diving helmet, and the bellows and pipes that carried air to the diver.

Hugo turned to James. 'So the girls need to practise killing themselves in the water while we watch.'

'I won't be just watching,' James assured him. 'I'm going to dive too.'

'You're not serious!'

'There's a chance we can trade whatever's in that sunken strongbox for Hardiman's release. Then, if we can only get him away from Cuba, it would play merry hell with Scolopendra's plans – perhaps give Jagua a chance to get through to her father . . .'

'So we can all live happily ever after?' Hugo sighed. 'James, you and Jagua are set on a course of action based on nothing but conjecture and wishful thinking.'

'We have to do something. And if there are risks involved, I'll share them.' James sucked on his sore fingers. 'Sounds like Jagua's dived at Celimar before. She and Maritsa will know the waters. It'll be good practice for the main event.'

'I suppose so.' Hugo smiled suddenly. 'Resourceful girl, isn't she? You have only to look at the way she introduced herself at the apartment . . .' He mimed swinging a pan, smiled, then paused. 'I, er . . . did you and she get on well?'

James raised an eyebrow. 'Excuse me?'

'I suppose you did.'

'Do you?'

'Did you?' Hugo shot him a sideways look. 'I mean, she's a lovely . . . that is to say, a most pleasant— Well, you know . . .' He sighed. 'Never mind.'

James raised an eyebrow.

'I just don't want to see her – or anyone – drowning in the deeps in search of unknown sunken treasure.' Hugo wiped sweat-soaked hair off his forehead. 'I mean, your aunt Charmian will be here in three days. She sounds a formidable character. The police will *have* to take her seriously.'

'Even if she fares better than us, Hardiman's in trouble right now. If he's being interrogated tomorrow . . .' James trailed off. 'The thing is, Hugo, right now we're all he's got. Believe me, I don't like it any more than you do.'

'I think perhaps you do.' Hugo sighed. 'But I've told you, I'm not about to run off weeping to my mother . . .' He considered. 'Chiefly because she's nearly five thousand miles away.'

The bus rattled to a stop and the driver coughed. '*Para Celimar*,' he announced.

James signalled his thanks, then he and Hugo pushed their way off and watched the bus chug away into the distance. They saw a narrow track snaking down from the main road through lush, palm-filled greenery that was dense with the whirr of crickets. Beyond, James could see a grey strip of beach and then the sea. There was a sultry stillness in the air that the ocean couldn't cool.

As he led the way down to the dirty beach, James brushed a comma of hair back from his forehead. Men and women were fishing, while sand-caked urchins fought over their castles and moats. With his fair skin, long shorts and white shirt, James felt horribly conspicuous. If Scolopendra's men should come by searching for them now . . .

Scanning the beach, James saw tyre marks leading to a cave; two youngsters were kicking at the sand, obliterating the tracks. Noticing the older boys, they stopped, and one ran off towards the low cliffs at the far end of the beach, where two figures crouched beside what looked like a pile of junk. James recognized them by the way they moved – Jagua graceful, Maritsa more hesitant in her movements. The boy pointed out James and Hugo, and Jagua rose and nodded, sent him racing back to his friend.

'I think we just observed Jagua's security system in operation,' said Hugo. 'Those tyre tracks – from the motorcycle and sidecar, do you suppose?'

'I do.' James took off his shoes and trailed his sore feet in the warm shallows. 'Leaving it out of sight makes good sense.'

'Better sense than do-it-yourself hard-hat diving, for sure.'

Maritsa waved as James and Hugo approached; Jagua simply watched them.

'Hello again, ladies!' Hugo bounded up. 'Behold, we still live.'

'*¡Hombre pequeño!*' Maritsa ruffled Hugo's hair and pinched James's cheek. '*Usted todavía tiene suerte.*'

'She says you're still lucky,' Hugo explained.

'My cheek disagrees.' James gave a nod of acknowledgement to Maritsa and she beamed, then turned to Jagua. Her dress lay neatly folded on the rocks, and now she wore a blue bathing suit. The thick straps couldn't hide the scars on her tanned shoulders; James tried not to look, but few things escaped Jagua's notice. 'The motorcycle . . . is it safe in that cave?'

'The tracks will soon be hidden,' Jagua said matter-of-factly. 'I buried my evidence there too. Do not fear – I paid some children to warn us if they see strangers.'

'Don't you think it's good of us to test them for you?' Hugo spoke with forced brightness. 'Sounds like the motorcycle is safer than we are.'

'So it does,' James muttered, surveying the diving

equipment laid out on the rock: two copper-nosed wooden bellows, with an air-pipe snaking from each into twin wooden boxes, and from there into well-secured inlets drilled into the water-heater helmet. 'This is all you need to go deep down and stay down?'

'The world under the sea is so beautiful,' said Jagua. 'Peaceful. It is filled with life.'

'But how do you preserve your own life down there?'

Jagua tapped the bellows with her foot. 'The bellows pump the fresh air down through the water. The second box increases the pressure. Without it, the air could never reach the diver and . . .' She mimed a knife across her slender throat.

Maritsa shrugged, looked James straight in the eyes. '*La vida es lo que hacemos mientras esperamos la muerte.*'

Hugo translated glumly: 'Life is what we do while we wait to die . . .'

James nodded, and Maritsa smiled at him. He looked at Jagua. 'Is diving worth the risk?'

She shrugged. 'Our village is called Sabana de Robles, in the south of Cuba. The people there have little. Father built a sisal factory, so now the adults support themselves by making rope. Before that, they farmed . . .' A proud smile softened her face. 'We children helped to earn money too – used junk to make the things we need to dive; found small treasures in the sea – jewellery, pottery, coloured glass . . . things we can sell to tourists. That is why we practised the dives here, close by Havana, to sell quickly at market. They are not worth much, but every little helps us—' Jagua bit her lip. 'Helps *them*. Since Father took me away . . . I do not belong. I miss my old life

91

very much.' She looked at Maritsa and there was sadness in her smile. 'Dr Hardiman told me many times, one day I will find another, better life.'

'We all have to believe that,' James said firmly.

'And we have much to find.' She turned to Maritsa. '¿Estás listo, Maritsa?'

Maritsa raised a thumb. Without ceremony she pulled off her top and shorts to reveal a threadbare black swimsuit underneath. Then she scooped up the oversized helmet. Jagua checked the seals and helped her prepare to dive.

James felt a thrill of excitement as he stared into the water. Here at the edge it was turquoise, glimmering in the sunlight, but only a few feet out it darkened to a deep indigo. He longed to know what lay beneath.

'How long have you been doing this?' Hugo wondered.

'Many years. An older boy started the club when I was only seven. He drowned, though.' Jagua shrugged and knelt beside the bellows. 'Our name is well earned. It is not a *deliberate* suicide, but . . .' She trailed off as Maritsa gave her a further thumbs–up. Jagua nodded and returned the gesture.

Maritsa walked to the edge of the low cliff, turned and lowered herself into the water. She sank with barely a splash and quickly vanished beneath the surface. James watched, breath held, as the hose connected to Maritsa's helmet snaked along the rock and followed her down into the water. He counted ninety seconds, and then the air-hose moved further away from the shore.

'She is walking out to where the water is deeper.' Jagua clasped the handles of one of the bellows and pressed them together firmly before pulling them apart and repeating the action on the second set. Then she returned to the first and began again.

The air-pipes unravelled further and further before slowing and stopping with just a few coils left. James marvelled. 'Just how deep is it down there?'

'Twenty feet close to shore. Deeper further out,' Jagua told him. 'It is safe to go down to thirty-five feet. More than that is possible for short times – but there is risk of the bends.'

'Bubbles in the blood . . .' Hugo shivered.

James hardly heard them. He'd swum underwater before, of course, many times, but this – this was different. This was a chance to descend through the depths into an alien world.

He turned to Jagua. 'I'd like to dive myself.'

'Dear Lord, you meant it!' Hugo gripped James's arm. 'You're seriously going to put your head inside a water-heater and sink on *purpose*?'

'Hugo is right, perhaps.' Jagua looked amused as she worked the bellows. 'Don't you have your nice safe life to go back to?'

James suppressed a laugh. 'You really don't know me.'

'Maritsa is right, then.' Jagua seemed pleased. 'She said you are crazy enough for the Suicide Club!'

Hugo rolled his eyes. 'No arguments from me.'

Maritsa's dive lasted about twenty minutes; then she broke the surface some way out, hugging the helmet with both scrawny arms.

As she swam back towards them, Jagua rose to check some arcane markings on the air-pipe. 'She went a long way down. It is not easy, keeping upright.'

'It's like that experiment at Dartington where we placed a

glass upside down in a tub of water,' said James. 'The water can't get in because of the air in the glass.'

'Until the glass is tipped sideways,' Hugo added, 'and then the water floods inside.'

Jagua took the helmet from Maritsa, set it down and then helped her out of the water. They embraced, and Maritsa sat on the rocks, panting. She looked over at James once more and gave her wonky smile.

'She's probably working out what she'll get for your clothes when you drown,' Hugo said darkly. 'Are you sure about going down there, James?'

'You should be pleased,' James teased him. 'It'll give you time alone with your reluctant goddess. You can pump bellows together in perfect harmony.'

Hugo blushed. 'Stop it.'

James grinned as he went over to examine the helmet properly. The air-pipes leading into it were kinked in places but otherwise sound.

Soon Maritsa was miming how to walk on the seabed: using a kind of slow, controlled shuffle, constantly testing the ground ahead. Then she showed him how to clear the pressure in his ears by giving a kind of forced yawn while swallowing hard. Meanwhile Jagua stressed the importance of not bending over; on his first dive, she would work the pump for him while Hugo watched and learned.

James gave Queensmarsh to Hugo for safekeeping and stripped to his undershorts before struggling into the helmet. It was hot and his field of vision was reduced to little more than a letterbox, the sound of his breathing amplified by the metal cage. Even through the rubber collar, the metal edges dug painfully into his collarbone. He bent over so Jagua could check the seals.

'There is a rope attached to the cliff beneath the water,' she said as she steered him towards the edge. 'Use it to pull yourself down to the seabed.'

James quickly found that getting off the rocks was hard when you could only see straight in front of you; and the weight of the helmet threw him off balance. Finally he sat down and swung his legs over the edge.

'Good luck, James,' Hugo called tersely.

James eased himself down into the water. His sore toes stung, then slowly grew numb. He held onto the rocky ledge with both hands, his last safe contact with the world above.

Then he dropped down into blue oblivion.

He felt behind him for the steadying rope, slimy and thick, bracketed to the rock. Each hiss of air that shushed into the helmet was pushed out in a bubbling rush. It was such an alien experience that he found himself gripping the rope tightly, arresting his descent.

Relax, he told himself, and let the rope slide through his fingers again. The harsh rasp of the air was friendly, reassuring, he realized. While it continued, and while he kept himself upright, he was safe.

As he sank deeper, his ears threatened to pop; he attempted to clear them as Maritsa had demonstrated, with limited success. The sun left strange luminous patterns trailing through the water after him. It was growing colder.

Finally, with a gentle jolt, his feet sank into soft sand.

James stood there for a moment, gripping the rope, checking his balance. The water tugged at him, moving him this way and that, but the weight of the helmet on his shoulders kept him centred. Air from the surface, tangy with salt, flowed around his head, and he pictured Hugo and Jagua up above, working busily on the bellows.

Down here, the turquoise depths were speared by fingers of sunlight, sparking through each tiny suspended molecule. His visor was slightly misted, but he could see pink anemones nudging yellow coral; green weed tangled with brown; tiny red trees that stretched and swayed in the swirl of the current. James was almost overwhelmed; it was like discovering a new world.

Captivated, he began to move, lifting and lowering each foot slowly and carefully so as not to slip. When James glanced round, the cliff wall seemed a long way distant, but he carried on.

He laughed, the sound hollow and metallic in his blocked ears, and knew that this dive would be the first of many.

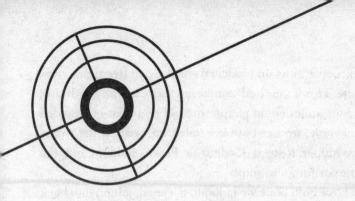

11
Stories Like Old Wounds

Under the tutelage of Jagua and Maritsa, James made two more dives that evening, and felt his confidence and skills increase. Hugo had worked the bellows till his arms were ready to fall off, and as a reward Jagua bought a six-pack of Coca-Cola and a round of *churros* from a seller on the beach. Accompanied by fresh guava, the fried dough pastries were truly delicious, and they all tore into them as if they hadn't eaten in days.

James stretched out in the shade, longing to switch off for a moment, to relax, though he couldn't help scanning the beach for El Puño or Ramón – or the veiled woman, gun arm outstretched, striding implacably across the sand towards him.

He swigged his warm Coke and sighed. How different this was from his childhood seaside holidays in England! He remembered the wet scrape of sand between the toes, the pad-dling in rockpools, the smuggling of shells into his trunk and the bloom of freckles on reddened cheeks; carefree times, now long gone. Hardiman had sometimes met up with the Bonds on holiday; James could picture the old boy now – sprawled in a deckchair, trouser bottoms rolled up, tearing the transparent wrapper from a Cadbury's Flake, holding out the chocolate for James to share . . .

'You have both done well,' Jagua declared, jolting him back to the present. 'Hugo, you pump the bellows so carefully.'

'Such a shame you've only got the one set of gear.' Hugo was reading over Jagua's transcripts of La Velada's telephone conversations. 'With two you could kill yourselves so much faster.'

His sarcasm was lost on Jagua. 'Maritsa has better equipment at the village. We shall collect on the way.'

'When do we dive to find the boat?' James asked. 'Tonight?'

'No. The tides are too high today,' Jagua told him. 'Tomorrow at dawn, when it is quiet, Maritsa and I will take the motorcycle and drive south to our village. We will get more diving gear, go to where I hid the boat at Playa Caimito and wait for the low tide. That will not be until after midnight tomorrow.'

'Midnight?' James knelt up, concerned. 'But MacLean will be at the casino from five in the afternoon. If he *is* there to force the truth from Hardiman, having that strongbox is the only thing that might persuade him to lay off.'

'She's not Queen Canute, James! She can't just roll back the waters and leave the wreck exposed,' Hugo said. 'In any case, doesn't Scolopendra need Dr Hardiman for his grand design? He can't very well hurt him.'

'Oh, I've no doubt Hardiman was quite indispensable,' said James, '*before* the robbery. But La Velada knows that an insider helped Sarila – I heard her say so – and Hardiman's got to be their number one suspect. Who knows what they might do to him!'

'Or to you,' said Jagua, 'when they catch you.'

Maritsa put her hand on Jagua's arm, looking quizzical – until Hugo briefly explained in Spanish. 'Ahh.' She smiled with comprehension, then shot James with her fingers. '¡Pum!'

'I'm not just rushing in where angels fear to tread,' James said with a scowl. 'I told you, Jagua, I want to look around the casino in case there's a chance to get Hardiman out.' He reached into his pocket and slid out Queensmarsh. 'That's where I'll be tomorrow.'

'Very well, James. Get yourself killed with your toy gun.' Jagua turned crossly to Hugo. 'You stay with him, I suppose?'

'I can't leave James on his own.' Hugo gave a nervous laugh. 'He gets into the most terrible trouble without me.'

'I am sure of this,' she said. 'Well, then, you follow us down later tomorrow, yes? You, James and Hardiman all together, perhaps.'

'I'll drink to that.' James raised his Coke bottle. Jagua and Maritsa reached over and clinked theirs against his. Hugo had drained his dry already, so he tapped a dog-eared corner of Jagua's 'evidence' against the glass.

'You can read my writing?' Jagua asked him.

'Mostly.' Hugo smiled. 'What does the "I" before a section mean?'

'Inglés,' Jagua explained. 'She spoke in English, but I record in Spanish. The "R" is for when she speaks *Ruso*, yes? Russian. I think, anyway. I speak very little of this.'

'Don't be modest.' Hugo beamed at her. 'You clearly have a gift for foreign tongues.'

Jagua whispered to Maritsa, and both giggled. Maritsa pushed out her tongue at James, said, 'Gift!' and the giggles became laughter. 'Gift, *chico suerte*!'

James raised an eyebrow and turned to Hugo as the girls went on talking and laughing. 'I think your compliment might be getting lost in translation.'

'It's a hazard.' Hugo held up the piece of paper and lowered his voice. 'Look here – when Jagua doesn't know a word, she writes it down as it sounds. Like here: "Enka Vayday". What's that supposed to mean?'

James shrugged. 'Sounds a bit Russian . . .'

'It appears in both the Russian and the English transcripts. A codename, perhaps? In any case, La Velada is arranging for something to be dismantled at the docks. There's talk of setting up a distribution network, being ready to move quickly . . . Enka Vayday turns up again . . . "Gaye pay you" is another choice phrase.'

'I do not understand it all.' Jagua sounded defensive. 'But La Velada is doing things behind my father's back, I know it.'

'I'm not sure this evidence proves very much on its own,' said James.

Hugo attempted a smile. 'Well, perhaps when we see MacLean tomorrow, we can ask him for the rest.'

The night slipped down, pouring more stars into the sky than James had ever seen. With Jagua still a wanted runaway, they couldn't risk going back to Hardiman's apartment, which would surely be under surveillance. Instead, James suggested they all sleep in the shallow cave where the

100

motorcycle and sidecar lay hidden, taking turns on lookout just in case El Puño or Ramón came looking.

Maritsa offered to take first watch; she sat crosslegged on the sand, her long hair moving in the warm breeze.

James knelt beside her. 'Wake me when you get tired. Say, two, three hours?' She looked at him blankly. 'You wake me then, OK?'

'*Mañana morirás.*' She leaned forward and kissed him quickly on the lips. '*Qué lástima.*'

'She says you're going to die tomorrow,' Hugo called from the back of the cave, 'and it's a shame.'

Maritsa smiled her lopsided smile. James smiled back a little awkwardly, and excused himself.

The cave grew cooler, and darker, the further in you went. For a nightlight, they had the stars winking down through a hole in the ceiling. Jagua lay down on her stolen leather jacket, Hugo opted for the sidecar of the motorcycle and James hollowed out a bed for himself in the sand. It was surprisingly comfortable; or would have been, were it not for the sand fleas that kept landing on his face and hands.

'I was wondering . . .' Hugo's voice was deadened by the stone. 'Who exactly was the goddess Jagua?'

Jagua spoke quietly. 'The Taíno people, who lived in Cuba long ago, believed in her. She taught the people how to hunt and fish and grow crops.'

'Very much of the natural world,' James remarked.

'I think she was also protector of caves. So you should be nice to me.' Jagua was brushing at the insects too. 'My father wanted me to be like a goddess. But all the stories of Jagua are about the men who surrounded her. How she affected them, yes? How they wished her to be. Well, that is not *my* story. A real goddess is free to be herself.'

'What was it like before your father got rich?' James wondered.

'My whole world was Sabana de Robles. A tiny speck in the south near the sea. Shacks to live in. An old well for water . . .' Her voice grew dreamy as the sound of the sea blew in from outside. 'My father wanted more. He had been taught well in the orphanage where he grew up. Always, nature was what he loved. Discovering new things . . . Learning how the world fits together . . . you know? Before he was eight years old he had learned to strain cyanide from cassava. He sold the poison to the pest controllers.'

'Resourceful,' James murmured.

'Clever. He got a . . . what is the word? – a scholarship?'

'To a university, you mean?' Hugo put in.

'Yes, before I was born. He studied natural sciences. He met my mother, who cleaned at the university. Her parents came from Sabana de Robles – that's how they ended up there too . . .'

Jagua was silent for so long, James thought she might've fallen asleep.

'Father knew so much; could recognize new species or variations so easily. But no one respected him. He was just a *mulatto*, after all, a half-breed . . . how could he think himself better than others?'

'Who we are is an accident of birth,' Hugo remarked. 'People can be . . . unforgiving.'

'And wrong.' Jagua paused. 'You understand this, Hugo, I know. Father had always dreamed of making great discoveries, but no one would believe. He could join expeditions only as a porter, carrying bags for *real* scientists. Exploited . . .' Again, she trailed off, the silence filling with the stir of the sea. 'I hardly saw him – he was away so much, for so long. Exploring jungles in Venezuela. Desert in North Africa. Rainforest in Brazil.'

'And he discovered that plant you mentioned,' James said; 'the one that made him rich.'

'Not just that. He discovered he had a daughter who had grown up without him.' Jagua's voice grew harder. 'He discovered that he did not like her. That he needed to change her, yes? To break her.'

'I'm sorry, Jagua,' Hugo said. 'I know what it's like when your parents wish you'd turned out . . . differently.'

'I wish that many things were different.' Jagua sounded bitter. 'And you, James – you wish Hardiman had never met my father, I suppose?'

James pushed out a long breath. 'Of course I do.'

'Well, I wish it more. More than you can know. Gerald Hardiman is the man who changed everything.' There was a quiet tremor to Jagua's voice. 'Five years ago, it was *him* who made my father rich!'

James felt prickles down his back. 'What do you mean?'

'My father told me the story a hundred times. Hardiman was research botanist on the expedition to Brazil. Father helped him find this new plant that makes good medicine. Hardiman said he would share the money with him when they sold it. But Father had waited too long for respect. A share was not enough.'

By now, James was hanging on each word. 'What happened?'

'They returned to Rio. Father knew Hardiman's weakness, and said they must visit a casino to celebrate their good fortune. Father risked everything he had on the roulette wheels; he flipped a silver dollar to choose red or black, odds or evens . . . and he won. He won, won over and over, and each time he would bet all his winnings again. And again, and again . . .'

'And Hardiman?'

'He lost his money as quickly as Father could claim his,' Jagua went on. 'And more – his home and his business too. No luck. No more credit. He could not win it back. Father came to him and said, "I will lend you money to go on playing, so maybe you win in the end . . . but only if you give to me *all* the money you will make from this plant we have found."'

James brushed a flea off his face. 'I suppose Hardiman had no choice . . .'

'It was his only hope. He signed an oath on a napkin. Father had it framed. This was the founding of his empire.' Jagua's voice was now hardly audible over the shushing push of the ocean. 'That money saved Hardiman that night. In the end, he almost broke even. But my father now gets all money from their discovery. Tens of thousands of dollars . . . brought to him by the flipping of a coin.'

James said nothing as he brooded on Jagua's story. Hugo's breathing had grown deeper, soothed by sleep, while Maritsa was humming tunelessly from the cave mouth.

'So much to win, so much to lose,' Jagua said softly. 'Remember this when you reach the casino tomorrow, James.'

James didn't reply. He stared into the darkness, stiff and sore, and waited for sleep to come.

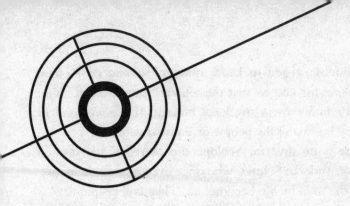

12

The Smell of Sweat in a Casino

It was one of those nights that seem to drag on for ever. James took his turn at the entrance to the cave, Queensmarsh gripped tight in his hands, trying to stay alert. The sky was a magical sight – specks of gold scattered on indigo around a glowing moon. But somehow it only made the beach seem darker and more oppressive.

He could hear Hugo and Jagua talking softly in Spanish. Hugo took over around three in the morning, and James gratefully crawled back to his trench in the sand. He fell asleep with their whispers in his ears and sand fleas skipping over his skin, dreaming of an underwater world like a meadow in bloom beneath the waves.

He woke early, aching all over from sleeping rough as much as from his exertions the day before. Jagua and Maritsa were already packing the diving gear back in the sidecar, ready to head south to Sabana de Robles.

'Is it safe for you to visit the village?' James asked. 'You said your father owns the local factory. If Ramón and El Puño call by, won't the people give you away?'

'There is no love for Scolopendra there,' Jagua assured him. 'For Audacto Solares, who once lived among them, yes. But for the man he has become, no. They will keep quiet.'

Hugo reached out for Jagua's hand, then self-consciously shook it. 'Er, good luck. And goodbye. For now, anyway – but hopefully, maybe . . .' Blushing furiously, he looked at the ground. 'Yes, well. Cheerio.'

'Find us when you can.' Jagua smiled at him, then turned to James. 'I hid the boat at Playa Caimito, ten miles along the coast from the harbour at Batabano. An old fort marks the place.'

James nodded, grateful for the lack of fuss. 'We'll see how the day turns out and hope to see you later.'

'Yes,' Hugo murmured. 'We will.'

Jagua stooped to embrace him. Hugo froze for a moment, then hugged her back. Maritsa caught James's eye with an amused look and said something in Spanish.

Hugo, cheeks red as he pulled away from Jagua, translated: 'Maritsa invites you now to touch *her* for luck, should you wish.'

Again, the cheeky half-smile, and James duly put his palm to her cheek, just as she had done to him. She bit down hard on the side of his thumb, and laughed as he snatched his hand away. 'Luck!' she cried, and made the word sound ridiculous. James supposed it was, and couldn't help but smile as he sucked at his thumb.

A few minutes later the Indian Four's engine faded away across the deserted beach as Jagua turned onto the track that led to the main road. Soon, the two girls and their transport were lost from sight.

Hugo sighed. 'Back on our own again.'

'I'm sorry my company can't compete with Jagua's.' James clapped him on the back. 'The two of you seem to have hit it off.'

'We're just friends,' Hugo said quickly. 'It's always just friends when it comes to me.'

'No such thing as "always",' said James. 'You'll see her again tonight, in any case. And we might just have Hardiman with us by then.'

Hugo nodded without much conviction. 'We might.'

A slow bus back to Havana rolled up at eight o'clock. James stiffened every time a new passenger came aboard. It felt as though danger could strike at any time, particularly as they reached the outskirts of the city.

Hungry and in need of fresh clothes, James decided to chance a return to Hardiman's apartment. He and Hugo kept watch for an hour until satisfied that the place wasn't under surveillance.

But when they got inside, they found that their belongings, and Hardiman's, had gone. Clothes, shoes, books, trunks – everything had been taken. The beds had been made, the crockery, coffee cups and crumbs from yesterday's meal cleared away, the cupboards emptied. It was as if they had never been there.

A tyre-sized wreath of twisted raffia and green foliage,

studded with daisies and marigolds, lay on the kitchen table. Words had been inscribed on a ribbon wound around it: GERALD HARDIMAN AND FRIENDS.

'It's a corona,' said Hugo nervously. 'A sort of Cuban garland. They're left at funerals.'

'Intimidation tactics.' James affected a casual air for his friend's sake. 'If they were really after us, they'd leave someone here to get us instead of playing mind games. They're just trying to scare us away. It . . . it shows we're getting to them.'

'Getting to them. Of course.' Hugo nodded half-heartedly. 'And getting the hell out of here, I trust.'

'What's to keep us?' James muttered.

It was back to walking around town, keeping to the busiest streets. Back to trying not to stand out, keeping close to the crowded shop fronts, even while peering past the tourists for possible threats. Damn Scolopendra! James had been longing to clean his teeth and bathe and change; at this rate MacLean the Enforcer would smell him coming before he got anywhere near the casino.

Pawning Hugo's watch got them two precious dollars; they shared a *mixto*, a Cuban sandwich of pork, ham, Swiss cheese, pickles and mustard, in a cheap café favoured by American tourists. After eating, James headed for the WC. He leaned over the sink and splashed himself with soap and cold water, rubbed fur from his teeth with a finger, and finally felt a little more human.

A portly middle-aged man with a camera round his neck watched James dry his face on a grubby towel. 'Messy eater, huh?'

James spared him the briefest of smiles and rejoined Hugo, who was counting their money.

'Hope we have enough left for train tickets south for our rendezvous with the girls.' Hugo forced a smile. 'Especially if there'll be three of us.'

'Hugo, you know I'm lucky at cards. I'll double that at the casino, no question.'

'In between daring rescues, of course.'

'Of course.' James's smile faltered as he looked at Hugo. 'It's time to go.'

They left the café, returning to the crowded streets to make their way to the Gran Casino. As he walked, James absently tapped Queensmarsh. He'd won the weapon in a fight against the odds, emerging victorious. How many times had he cheated chance before? But luck had no memory, he knew, and the comfort of past success was cold as a gun barrel.

They turned right onto 23rd Street. At the end of the palm-lined avenue, shimmering in the heat on its pedestal of rock, a shining white hotel faced out over the Florida Strait. On they went along the Malecón; James hadn't anticipated the walk would take so long.

Finally, thirsty and sweating, they reached a white marble fountain as big as a swimming pool – the approach to the Gran Casino. It was an impressive building: white stucco and sandstone with luxuriant palms stretching up to the red-tiled roof. It was close to three p.m. but the place was still busy with lunch-time customers. Prestigious motorcars stood out-side, waiting to be parked by valets in grey uniforms. The outer wall of the lobby was glass, so approaching guests could see the opulence inside. At night, lit by spotlights, James supposed the place would look more impressive still.

Hugo was standing behind him. 'See anything?'

'No. But I suppose we're hardly likely to spy hired hoods hanging out of the windows with tommy guns.' James did up a shirt button, smoothed his hands through his hair and approached the revolving door set into the great glass wall. 'Let's go in.'

The lobby was large and thickly carpeted in red; there were touches of gold leaf on the rear wall. The chime and clang of slot machines reverberated across the crystal chandeliers and vaulted ceilings. A concierge took the keys to the automobiles from his valet staff, hanging them from tiny hooks behind his desk.

'What now?' Hugo looked edgy; his small stature was attracting more than his fair share of stares. 'We don't know where the *interrogatorio* will take place, do we?'

'Jagua told me that Scolopendra has a suite here,' James said. 'I suppose the VIP gaming rooms will be private too, but they'll still have croupiers, or waiters coming in and out, and I imagine MacLean will want to work without witnesses.'

'Or interruptions,' Hugo agreed. 'But how do we even find out which suite is Scolopendra's? We can't knock on every door. And we can't ask every new arrival, "Excuse me, are you here to torture a Scotsman?"'

James gave him a sharp look. 'For now, let's just keep our eyes and ears open, and get a feel for the place.' He led the way past three polished mahogany booths, just off reception: the house telephones. *A good vantage point for clocking who goes past*, he thought. Ahead he saw two sets of huge bronze double doors built into the marble walls – lifts to the luxurious accommodation above. A young bell boy, dressed in a smart blue uniform trimmed with gold braid, stood guard outside. James noted a mahogany door to the left: *Must lead to the stairs.*

From the lift area, a carpeted corridor led off to the right. James and Hugo headed along it. Doors inset with crimson leather panels studded the walls at intervals, each a gateway to the gaming tables. James paused beside one, gazing in at an immense, elegant salon with thick carpets and brocade curtains; the smart clientele milled around beneath chandeliers that hung from the high ceilings like layers of glowing glass jellyfish. James drank it all in: the glamorous people and their fine surroundings, the seductive patter of the croupiers, the rattle and spin of the roulette wheels, the clatter of dice in a cup, anticipation ending in alarm as chips were swept cleanly and neatly across the baize.

One of the croupiers glanced over, and James quickly led Hugo on, following the corridor round. It opened into a grand cabaret hall, the walls swathed in ruffled pink taffeta, like a fairy-tale big top. Tables fringed a dance floor and stage, upon which cabaret acts performed. A bar at the rear of the room served beautifully dressed customers, and waiters picked their way through the throng with platters of food.

'The kitchens must be over there' – James pointed to a set of double doors behind the bar – 'wouldn't you say?'

'I suppose so.' Hugo frowned. 'But what has that to do with the price of . . .'

He trailed off, and James prepared to do battle as a bald man, immaculate in a dinner suit, loomed over them. It was one of the casino staff; he spoke in Spanish, his manner as hushed and refined as the deep-pile carpet, but failing to keep the disdain from his face. Hugo answered, arms raised in appeal. The man pointed firmly towards the reception.

'Minors aren't allowed here unaccompanied,' Hugo told James. 'In particular, ragtag, scruffy minors such as ourselves.' He turned James round and steered him back down the passage. 'I said we were looking for our guardian. He said someone at the front desk would ask about for them.' Hugo turned and raised a hand in satirical thanks to the man, who glared after them until they had walked round the corner. 'Now what? We're not going to leave, I take it?'

'You're going to use the house telephones.' James looked at him. 'Pretend you're in Scolopendra's suite – and that you're hungry. Put through an internal call for room service and tell them you want something sent up.'

'Won't they ask me for the room number?'

'He's no ordinary guest; he has his own VIP suite here – the staff ought to know that,' James reasoned. 'If they do ask, act outraged and tell them to find out for themselves.'

'But why am I . . . ?' Understanding dawned on Hugo's face. 'You wily goat, James! If they take the order, we can wait here until a waiter comes with the food, and follow him up!'

'Provided we're not thrown out on our ears first,' James agreed. He glanced around to check that no one was paying attention, then opened the mahogany door of the last telephone booth. He and Hugo slipped inside.

James looked up the number for the kitchens in the hotel telephone directory, and Hugo put through the call, lowering his voice and thickening his Spanish accent. He gave James a thumbs-up and carried on speaking with a kind of macho confidence. Only after hanging up did he collapse against the wall as if his legs were failing him.

'Well?' James demanded.

'They bought it! Or rather, Scolopendra's bought it on his account – a chicken and avocado club sandwich and an ice-cold ginger ale, to be precise.'

'Good work, Hugo.' James felt his senses sharpen despite his fatigue. 'Just think, Hardiman might already be in the suite, shipped here for his session with MacLean.'

'How do we get past the bell boy to find out?'

'We'll need a distraction when the food comes. And we'll have just one shot at getting it right.' James checked the clock above the lift doors: it was twenty past three; an hour and forty minutes before Scolopendra was due and the questioning began.

One shot . . . he thought, an idea forming.

Minutes ticked past. James's stomach felt tight with nerves. He outlined his plan to Hugo, who reluctantly nodded his understanding.

Finally a waiter came into sight, pushing a wheeled trolley towards the lifts. It bore a covered silver platter and a bottle of ginger ale with a glass full of ice.

'That's our man.' James cocked Queensmarsh, ready to fire, and pushed Hugo out of the phone booth. 'Here goes.'

While Hugo followed the waiter towards the bronze lift doors, James went quickly back to the gaming room, heart pounding. He stood just beside the doorway, watching. As the waiter pushed his trolley into one of the lifts, James aimed Queensmarsh at the nearest chandelier and fired.

The *phut* of air was followed by a tinkling crash as the ball bearing found its target and the chandelier shattered, showering the party below with glass. Amid the gamblers' shrieks of alarm, James pocketed his gun. The bell boy looked over from the lifts and James gestured frantically. The boy came running and was quickly collared by a frowning floor-walker to help clear the area.

James sprinted over to the lifts, where Hugo was hopping from one foot to the other in excitement. 'Eighth floor,' he reported; 'that's where the waiter's headed.'

'We'd better get after him.' James stabbed the call button on the other lift and the bronze doors slid open. He dashed inside and punched the '8' as Hugo followed, and the doors closed with agonizing slowness. Finally, with a lurch, the lift got underway, humming upwards. James loaded a further metal pellet into Queensmarsh. Neither he nor Hugo spoke as the lift rumbled on its way.

The doors opened with a soft chime. James looked out, saw the waiter and his trolley disappearing round the corner. With a nod to Hugo, he followed.

The waiter stopped outside a door at the end of the corridor and knocked. James kept well back, heart in his mouth as the door clicked open.

A dark-skinned man in a badly fitting suit stepped out of the room. A pink scar bisected his lips from just under the nose to his chin.

'It's Ramón,' James whispered to Hugo. 'Scolopendra's man. Tried to kidnap Maritsa.'

Hugo grimaced. 'Are you sure? He looks such an angel.'

Ramón pointed to the food and shook his head. The waiter

lingered, puzzled, and Ramón shoved him backwards and kicked the trolley; he waved him away before ducking back inside and slamming the door behind him.

'Didn't seem to want that, did he?' Hugo said with a smile. 'Perhaps I should've ordered him the *hamburguesa con queso*.'

'Come on,' James whispered, heading back towards the lifts. He went through the door to the stairwell and Hugo hurried after him. James didn't let the heavy door close completely; through the gap he watched the waiter push his trolley back into the lift, muttering angrily. Then the doors slid shut again, the lift rumbled away, and James led the way back out onto the opulent hush of the eighth floor.

'What now?' Hugo said as James made for Scolopendra's suite. 'You going to offer friend Ramón some dessert?'

'I'm going to offer him *something*, anyway,' James hissed, banging on the door.

The door was yanked open again. Ramón resumed his angry tirade where he'd left off – but it died on his scarred lips as James swung the butt of Queensmarsh into his temple. Ramón staggered backwards, recognition flaring in his eyes as his mouth puckered grotesquely; James pushed his way into the room and punched the man on the side of the neck.

Ramón fell to his knees and James knew a moment's elation. *I've won*, he thought, and quickly checked for any other opponents. But Ramón was shamming. He pivoted round, kicked out with both legs and caught James in the small of the back. James was sent flying against the wall, and Queensmarsh was jarred from his grip. A fist smashed into his ribs and he shouted out, tried to turn, but Ramón's knee drove up into his groin. Gasping, James fell to the floor.

In a moment Ramón was astride him, knees crushing James's forearms. 'I told you in that alley, boy,' he hissed. 'I gonna make you bleed bad.'

James cried out as Ramón grabbed his face, callused thumbs gouging into his eyes.

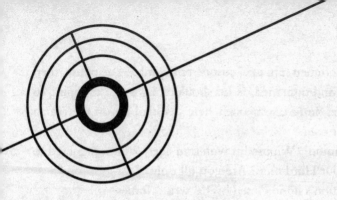

13

Scolopendra and the Silver Dollar

James writhed and bucked, pain lancing through him. He couldn't free his arms, couldn't shift Ramón. That bellowed threat from the alleyway rose from his memory: *I will open your face!* His eyes felt ready to burst.

Then James heard a thump that was almost musical. The pressure on his eyes was gone, but he still couldn't see anything, his vision an angry smear of light and dark. He twisted round and threw Ramón clear. There was a thud, the slam of a door, and then quiet.

'James?' Hugo was at his side, helping him to sit up. 'God, are you all right?'

James nodded, blinking furiously. 'What about—?'

'Ramón's out cold. I clobbered him with an ashtray, and you threw him head first into the door.'

'Thanks for the help.'

'You softened him up. I just crept in and . . .' A pause, then Hugo's hand tightened on his shoulder, his voice dropping to a whisper. 'James, someone's here . . . tied up on the couch – he's out cold.'

'Hardiman?' Wiping his watering eyes, James staggered to his feet. 'Dr Hardiman? Are you all right . . . ?'

But Hugo's hand closed on his wrist. 'James . . .'

'What is it?'

'It's not him.'

'It's not . . . ?' James's stomach clenched. His sight was returning now, and he saw that he was in a spacious, modern room. The man lying on the couch was in his mid-forties, stocky, with short blond hair greying at his temples. Livid contusions on the side of his face looked like dying flowers pushing through the skin. His wrists were bound with thin rope.

James stared. 'Who the hell is this?'

Hugo searched quickly through the man's pockets, pulled out a wallet and checked his ID. 'This . . . is Chester MacLean.'

'Scolopendra's enforcer?'

'Judging by the rope, he's not here for tender loving care. Looks like Scolopendra's done the enforcing on *him*.'

'Jagua couldn't get hold of him yesterday,' James remembered. 'His secretary said he was out of the office.'

'Yes, and out cold in a casino.' Hugo put the wallet back in MacLean's pocket. 'I suppose that's why he didn't leave Jagua's evidence as arranged . . .'

'He must've been found out.' James rubbed his burning eyes and swore. 'I almost lost my sight trying to rescue this thug!'

'I'm sure MacLean would thank you, if he hadn't been beaten into a coma,' Hugo said with a shudder. 'Now what?'

'Well, right now, any enemy of Scolopendra is a friend of ours.' James scooped up Queensmarsh from the floor. 'Chances are he can tell us about Hardiman.'

'And give us the lowdown on La Velada.' Hugo raised his eyebrows. 'So, how do you suggest we get him out?'

James had already gone over to Ramón's prone body and was rifling through his pockets. 'When I first saw our friend here, he was driving a Hispano-Suiza Coupé de Ville in crimson and black.' He fished out two keys on a fob that bore the familiar winged logo, and pocketed them. 'There. We'll get MacLean away in style.'

'Ah, of course. Splendid. Then we'll be arrested for abduction *and* theft at the same time.' Hugo was wringing his hands. 'For God's sake, James, how do you expect to even reach the car park? This man is unconscious, and I'm hardly built for carrying.'

Ramón stirred, eyelids flickering, one hand twitching to the back of his head.

The boys both froze and fell silent. As they did so, James heard the distant chime of the lift arriving on their floor, and the rattle of its opening doors.

'We've got to get out of here!' Hugo scurried over to the door and was about to open it when James stopped him, peering out through the peephole. The glass was blurred, but he saw two men and a woman in a black veil heading towards them.

'La Velada,' he breathed. 'El Puño's with her – and someone else.'

'Scolopendra? But it's barely four o'clock.' Hugo looked panic-stricken. 'You said the appointment was for five!'

'Do you want to ask them to come back later, or should we try to stay alive?' James shoved Hugo back into the living room and saw that the sliding door to the opulent bedroom was wide open. 'Quickly – get under the bed.'

'Oh, the indignity . . .' Hugo was already wriggling out of sight.

There was a sharp *rat-tat-tat* on the door. Ramón groaned again. James got down and pushed himself under the bed beside Hugo. It was a narrow squeeze but good cover: the silk counterpane hung down almost to the soft pale carpet, yet below it, James had a fair view of the living room, and the couch where MacLean lay.

Hugo sniffed and stifled a groan. 'Wish we'd been able to wash now.'

'You're not alone.'

The same pattern of knocks came louder, and James heard Ramón get up and open the door, start to talk in Spanish – only to be steamrollered by deep, commanding tones.

Ramón broke in: '*¡Lo siento, Scolopendra!*'

So – the big man himself had indeed arrived! James's heart started to thump so fiercely, he feared it would give away their hiding place. But the commotion went on, and James wished he could make sense of it. Ramón wouldn't know where his attackers had gone; if he decided to search the place now, James knew that he and Hugo would be sitting ducks . . .

'What's happening?' James whispered.

'Scolopendra isn't happy – thinks Ramón was asleep,'

Hugo hissed back, his mouth close to James's ear. 'Ramón's not arguing – if he and El Puño don't buck their ideas up, they could go the same way as MacLean.'

Small wonder Ramón's not owning up to his beating, James thought, *Scolopendra doesn't seem the type to tolerate many failures*. Then his mouth dried as the talking stopped and he saw movement in the full-length mirror on the living-room wall. Ramón, glancing about sulkily, was laying out a tarpaulin on the floor in front of the couch. El Puño, eyes shining in his sweaty, impassive face, took hold of MacLean's collar and hauled him to his feet. Then La Velada, slender and sinister in her mourning black, came into sight; she was holding a syringe, and she injected something into a vein in MacLean's arm.

James watched grimly as MacLean twitched, then shuddered, drool spilling from his lips onto the tarp – until suddenly he shocked properly awake. La Velada retreated back across the room while El Puño changed his grip on MacLean's neck.

'What the . . . hell?' MacLean spoke in a midwestern American drawl. 'What have you . . . done to me . . . Scolopendra?'

James felt a bead of sweat run down his brow as a giant stepped into sight – a towering man of mixed ancestry. His long hair, panther-black, was slicked back from his forehead. He looked immaculate in a steel-grey suit; the double-breasted six-button jacket had broad, pointed lapels and square shoulders to emphasize his powerful frame. James could see traces of Jagua in the strong, proud features, but there was a fierce, sensual hunger about Scolopendra's face. He might

121

have come late to the feast of the rich man, but it seemed that had only left him more determined to take all he desired.

'It's quite simple, MacLean. Quite simple.' Scolopendra's deep voice had grown softer and slower now that he was speaking English, but it was no less arresting. 'El Puño's blow put you to sleep, and my new drug has restored you to a waking state.'

MacLean wiped his wet mouth with the back of his hand. 'I feel . . . real sick.'

'At present nausea and an excess of saliva are side effects. Further trials of the drug should eliminate the problem.' Scolopendra's grin did little to reassure; it reminded James of a predator which had found its next meal. 'I regret that action against you was necessary.'

MacLean tried to break free of El Puño, but froze as the great granite fist was placed on his shoulder.

'Hey, look. I found something in the parking lot outside.' Scolopendra stepped closer, a small creature cradled in his hands; it made a rasping, clicking noise as its legs flailed help-lessly. '*Rhopalurus junceus*. One of the thirty-six different types of scorpion to be found on Cuba. You've lived here for some time, now, do you happen to know what is unusual about this creature?'

MacLean shook his head impatiently.

'It's known as the Red Scorpion – and also as the *Blue* Scorpion. Red on account of these patches on its body, and blue for the patches on its stinger. That's confusing, isn't it? Red *and* blue?' Scolopendra held out the squirming arachnid as if for closer inspection; MacLean flinched as its pincers brushed his nose. 'You should know that I don't like confusion.

I like to know all creatures as one thing or another. Ally or enemy. Safe or dangerous. Then I can deal with them accordingly.' Abruptly he dropped the scorpion and ground it under his heel; the body cracked open over the cream carpet. 'Do you understand me?'

MacLean looked down at the floor. 'What is all this?'

'Scolopendra monitors the bank accounts of his employees . . .' La Velada said. 'A large amount of money was paid into your bank account two days ago.'

'What?' Even from across the room, James could see the panic on MacLean's face. 'Well, so what? I . . . I inherited some money, is all. My cousin in Iowa died out of the blue.'

'Ah. I see.' La Velada's voice was an insinuating purr. 'The payment's not a bribe, then?'

'A bribe? Are you crazy? A bribe from who?' MacLean's wide eyes moved past the woman in black to Scolopendra. 'This is why you turn the muscle on me? I thought we were a team . . .'

'When I started out, you helped me to acquire so much, so quickly. Such a professional.' The unnerving shark-like smile didn't change. 'You know, MacLean, I remember . . . you used to say that during one of your, ah, *persuasions*, you could always tell when a man was going to break, just by the look in his eyes.'

'It is true, my love,' La Velada agreed. 'When the victim comes to see that the lies and the pleading won't stop his pain, the truth is all he has left.'

'And you didn't lift that detail out of a fortune cookie, did you?' MacLean gave her a small, tight smile. 'This lady of yours is a real catch, Scolopendra. Glamorous, rich, sophisticated. And that mysterious past, of course.'

James held his breath. *The evidence*, he thought. *What did MacLean find out?*

'You know she has links to the NKVD back in Russkyland, right?' MacLean nodded smugly. 'That's NKVD as in the People's Commissariat for Internal Affairs – responsible for espionage, political repression, torture and execution of enemies of the state—'

Ramón stepped forward and grabbed hold of MacLean's throat, restricting his speech to thick glottal chokes.

'Scolopendra knows that as a Russian aristocrat I was considered an enemy of the Soviet state myself,' La Velada said calmly. 'He knows that ten years ago I was recruited by the NKVD to gather intelligence on White Russians – my husband included – and that he and many others were put to death as a result.'

Scolopendra nodded calmly. 'But you escaped from your past.'

'As you escaped yours.' She took his hand. 'My proud, proud love.'

MacLean's face had reddened, his eyes were bulging, each breath a battle. Finally Scolopendra signalled to Ramón, who relinquished his hold. MacLean was left gasping for breath, El Puño's hand still on the back of his neck. James watched, both repulsed and spellbound.

'So you see, MacLean' – Scolopendra placed a hand upon La Velada's shoulder – 'my partner and I both know what it is to be trapped by circumstance. We understand the need to do whatever it takes to escape.' James caught the wide, bright smile in the mirror. 'Why, look at me! I was even forced to ally myself with the likes of you.'

MacLean's voice was hoarse. 'But . . . I don't understand . . .'

'We know you've been snooping around for information on La Velada,' Scolopendra snapped. 'She found the files in your briefcase.'

'I – I was only worried for you.' MacLean coughed. 'You're my employer, my friend—'

'Also in your case was jewellery I gave to Jagua on her sixteenth birthday,' Scolopendra continued. 'So either you stole it, or you accepted it as payment for a particular service. Which is it?'

'I . . . I found the jewellery in your yacht at the shipyard,' MacLean said desperately. 'I was going to return it.'

'Was she paying you for the information,' La Velada wondered, 'or paying for you to help her escape?'

MacLean's expression was caught somewhere between shell-shocked and terrified. 'Come on, Scolopendra. You've got no right—'

'Oh, now you truly disappoint me, MacLean. Bleating about rights?' Scolopendra shook his head as if bemused. 'Human beings go to such lengths, trying to impose restrictions on others. In the natural world there is only one right that matters: the right of the strongest to dominate all others.'

'Look, Scolopendra—'

'Did you make a deal with Sarila Karatan?'

'Who?'

'An arms dealer and thief for hire,' La Velada elaborated, 'willing to work for anyone if the price was right.'

MacLean was sweating. 'I've never heard of her.'

'You're certain of that?' Scolopendra sounded like a teacher working with a dull pupil. 'Only, the day you came into all that money, Sarila Karatan was able to remove some extremely confidential items from my private lab. Now, is that a coincidence?'

'Hardiman told her,' MacLean said quickly. 'Come on, it's got to be Hardiman, right? He's always been a weak link . . .'

Sweat was pouring now down James's face.

'Gerald Hardiman is back under my control,' Scolopendra informed him, 'and will soon resume his important work.' (*He's still alive*, James thought, with a silent prayer of thanks.) 'But weak links are dangerous, I agree. Sarila gained access to my estate in a Scolopendra Industries delivery truck. A truck registered to the main shipyard.'

'Then she must've stolen it.'

'I interviewed your office junior,' La Velada said calmly, 'who told me he parked it outside the shipyard gates – on your instruction.'

'What . . . ?' MacLean's face looked bloodless. 'That – that must've been for a delivery.'

Scolopendra's smile had gone. 'Tell me why construction of the log raft fell so far behind schedule.'

'You brought the deadline for launch forward by three months! And we lost so much timber when that storm hit back in April—'

'No,' Scolopendra snarled. '*I* lost so much timber. You faked its loss and sold it cheap to a competitor. A sloppy scam I suspect you have been running on and off for years.' He paced slowly towards MacLean. 'Sarila Karatan was a professional, she did her research. She checked out the staff and reckoned you'd most likely take the bribe. Am I right?'

'You're crazy if you think I've got anything to do with—'

'*Shut up.*' In a rush of movement, Scolopendra pulled a pistol from inside his jacket – it looked like a Colt Woodsman fitted with a silencer – and jammed the barrel between MacLean's teeth. 'Don't take me for a fool. Not ever.' Scolopendra's voice dropped lower still, like the warning hiss of a poisonous snake. 'I know what you thought, MacLean. Educated white American like you, doing a *mulatto*'s dirty work . . . working for a savage who got lucky. How degrading for you, huh, MacLean – taking orders from me?'

MacLean tried to shake his head, to form words around the barrel of the gun. El Puño let go of him, took a step back, left him standing on the tarp. MacLean held up his hands, clearly terrified.

'You know, all that wealth and success came to me from a single silver dollar. I have it still.' Scolopendra smiled; he seemed calmer now as he reached into his jacket pocket and held up the coin. 'It's my lucky dollar. It helps me reach certain decisions – such as letting you live so that you can try to make amends . . . or killing you like the weak little runt you are.' He flipped the coin with his free hand, catching it neatly without looking. 'You like that?' He laughed, nodding his head encouragingly as MacLean attempted to nod. 'Like the gangster in *Scarface*, you see that movie? You think it's a good trick? Hey, you want to guess heads or tails and see what it is I decide?'

MacLean closed his eyes; he was shaking, his teeth clattering against the barrel.

'*Do you?*' Scolopendra shouted.

His thumb flicked the silver dollar higher, and he caught it in his big palm. He looked down at it.

Slowly, almost reluctantly, Scolopendra pulled the Colt Woodsman from between MacLean's lips. He turned and paced silently over the carpet.

MacLean opened his eyes again.

'We can't argue with the coin, Mr MacLean.' Scolopendra turned and fired – and MacLean's left eye burst open as the bullet went into his brain.

James felt bile rise in his throat as the man dropped to his knees on the tarpaulin, then flopped backwards.

'See that?' Scolopendra held the silver dollar up to MacLean's one still-staring eye. 'Heads you die.'

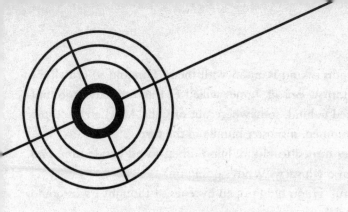

14
Breakout

James tried not to look at the lifeless body on the floor. After killing MacLean, Scolopendra passed the gun to El Puño, went over to La Velada and embraced her tightly. Ramón and El Puño busied themselves with wrapping MacLean's corpse in the tarpaulin, drowning out Scolopendra's conversation with his woman. James was fed up with not understanding the language, which sounded more and more like the angry buzzing of wasps in his ears.

One thought kept spinning around in his head: *If La Velada's bullet had hit me yesterday, I'd be a corpse on the floor myself.* Now Scolopendra had executed a man, and she hadn't even flinched; clearly they were two of a kind. James shuddered. To shoot a man dead in cold blood, at point-blank range . . .

I could never do that.

Finally Scolopendra and La Velada left the apartment,

apparently taking Ramón with them. Longing to crawl out of his narrow prison, James willed El Puño to leave too, but he stayed behind, somewhere out of sight. MacLean's corpse also remained, a sinister bundle in the tarp.

James turned to Hugo, lying ashen-faced beside him, and spoke in a whisper: 'What's going on?'

'Sorry.' Hugo didn't open his eyes. 'I thought I was going to be sick.'

'I mean, what are they saying?'

'Ah. I understand a bogus laundry truck is coming to collect the body at five o'clock.'

'So *that's* why "five p.m." was written in the diary,' James muttered. 'This appointment was always going to end the same way.'

'Ramón's escorting his bosses down to the casino, then collecting a linen trolley on the way back so they can get MacLean out of here.'

Like rubbish, James thought.

'Well, at least we know Hardiman's all right,' Hugo added. 'For now, at least.'

'If only we knew where he was being held. Scolopendra didn't say anything?'

'It was a little hard to hear. La Velada said something about Hardiman having to finish a cure.'

'A cure for what?' James pondered. 'Do you think he's at Scolopendra's estate on the Isla de Pinos after all?'

'Could be. Although she also mentioned research centres for tests of some sort.'

James laid his cheek against the carpet. 'After all we've been through, we're still no closer to finding Hardiman.'

'Scolopendra thinks the operation has been compromised. Says, the sooner they get out of Cuba the better—'

James shushed him quietly as El Puño came back into the living room, grabbed the edge of the tarpaulin and dragged MacLean's corpse towards the hallway. 'Must be getting ready to go. And so should we.'

'Can't we tell the manager about this fake laundry pick-up?' Hugo pleaded. 'If the police were to see MacLean's body . . .'

'Scolopendra would bribe them to forget, know that someone's spying on him and be more careful in future.' James shook his head. 'We have to go and meet Jagua and Maritsa. Finding that strongbox and using it to barter for Hardiman is our best chance now.'

Hugo closed his eyes. 'If that's our best chance, God help us.'

Around ten to five there was a bang on the door. El Puño opened it silently, and Ramón entered. There was a dragging sound, and muttering as MacLean's body was manhandled into the trolley. Then the door clicked shut.

'I think they've gone,' Hugo whispered.

Slowly James crawled out from under the bed and stretched. 'We'll give them a couple of minutes to get clear.' He checked that Ramón's car key was still in his pocket, then went to the bathroom, splashed water on his face and drank thirstily from the tap. Hugo did the same, and then, heart in mouth, James carefully opened the door. The corridor was empty.

'We'll take the stairs this time.' James led the way to the stairwell and ran down towards the lobby, pausing at the base of every second flight for Hugo to catch up, until they'd reached the ground floor.

James opened the door to check that the way was clear;

when there was no sign of Ramón and El Puño, he led the way outside.

'¡Eh!' The bell boy spotted them at once; he called for help and grabbed hold of James's arm. James quickly twisted round, tripping him up. As he fell, Hugo grabbed his cap and pulled it down over his eyes.

'Come on, Hugo!' James dashed for the lobby, but the bell boy's shouts had brought two huge bouncers running. James stopped, held up his hands as if to say he'd come quietly. The first man reached out to grab him, but at the last moment James shoved him aside, sent him sprawling across the marble. The other bouncer caught James around the neck. Hugo kicked him in the back of the knee and knocked him off-balance. James elbowed the man in the stomach and broke free.

'Hugo, quick!' James turned and pelted across the lobby to the revolving door. But he was forced to change course as staff moved to block the exit.

'We're trapped!' Hugo shouted.

Desperately James pulled out Queensmarsh and waved it around wildly. People screamed, mistaking it for a real gun, and his pursuers dived to the floor. He thrust the pistol into Hugo's hand, hefted an elegant ashtray on a long, solid brass pedestal and charged towards the wall of windows like a knight with a jousting pole. The impact jolted his arms and shoulders, but the glass shattered; James closed his eyes and burst out into sunlight in a shower of glittering shrapnel.

Hugo hared out just behind him, panting for breath. 'And now?'

'Let's find Ramón's Hispano-Suiza and get out of here. Move!'

The concierge emerged through the revolving doors, and James rolled the ashtray towards his ankles, tripping him up. Then he turned and chased after Hugo towards the car park at the rear of the building.

'Is that it?' Hugo pointed Queensmarsh at a familiar black-and-scarlet automobile.

'Must be.' James vaulted the door and landed on the hard-sprung leather of the driver's seat. He reached across and unlocked the passenger door for Hugo and pulled the keys out of his pocket.

'That was quite an escape, James!' Hugo said, sliding into the seat. 'We're like those gangsters, Bonnie and Clyde! Not sure which of us is Bonnie, mind, but . . .'

While Hugo babbled in shocked excitement, James surveyed the packed dashboard. It held a dizzying spread of quality Lenvex dials – a rev counter, speedometer, thermometer, amp meter and petrol gauge showing half-full – and a Jaeger clock that showed it was close to five. James checked the fuel/air blend and turned the starter switch. At once the hefty six-cylinder engine grunted into life.

'Do you know what you're doing?' asked Hugo.

'I hope so.' James found the gear lever to his right, along with the handbrake. The three-speed gate had reverse on the outside-rear slot; he engaged it and pressed down on the accelerator. The heavy car shot backwards, and James slammed on the brake before he rear-ended the car behind. The Hispano-Suiza jerked to a halt and almost stalled.

'Oh God.' Hugo had turned to see casino staff racing over the tarmac towards them. 'They're not giving up!'

James grappled with the gear lever. 'Come on . . .' How

many cars had he driven since Uncle Max first taught him in his old black-and-white Bamford and Martin? 'Come on!' He slid the lever across and forward into second, and this time the Hispano-Suiza had no problem pulling away. James turned the wheel hard; the steering was heavy and required both hands, but as soon as he dared, he used his right hand to slide the gear lever into third and stamped on the accelerator. James and Hugo were thrown back in their seats as the automobile shot from a crawl to a gallop in a matter of seconds. Smartly dressed figures leaped out of the way as the Hispano-Suiza roared through them. He headed for the exit and swung the wheel hard right onto the main road.

'Jagua said she'd hidden her boat at Playa Caimito . . .' Hugo held on as James took a corner too fast and they almost skidded into bushes lining the road. His euphoria seemed to be fading. 'It's on the south side of the island, isn't it? How far is that? How will we ever find it?'

'We head for that harbour . . . what was it called?'

'Batabano,' said Hugo. 'But we're in a stolen car, and after assaulting staff and waving a gun about while smashing our way out of a casino, well . . .'

James nodded grimly. 'The police will be out in force.'

'I can see the newspaper headline now: DANGEROUS FUGITIVES SPARK MANHUNT.' Hugo dropped Queensmarsh as if it were red-hot. 'And if we're caught . . .'

Gripping the wheel in terse silence, James floored the accelerator and headed south.

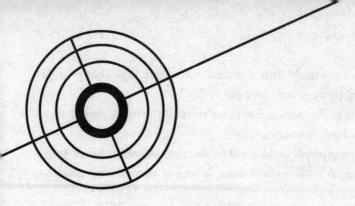

15
Mission into Night

The journey was long and frustrating. Signposts were few and far between, even on the major roads, and James was wary of sticking to the obvious route as the stolen Hispano-Suiza would be so easy to spot.

With no map and no real clue where to head – and with Jagua primed to dive down to the stolen boat as soon as the tides allowed – they needed to reach Playa Caimito as quickly as possible. Again and again James had to stop so that Hugo could ask for directions. Unsurprisingly, two grimy youths driving an expensive car met with suspicious stares and pointed questions. One woman hurried away as soon as they stopped, shouting in Spanish to others down the street.

Hugo turned to James, white-faced. 'She says we're the casino robbers the police warned about on the wireless. Armed and dangerous.'

'We're what?' James pulled away quickly. 'They've put our descriptions out over the radio?'

'And if the police think we're really armed, they'll shoot first and ask questions later!'

All these people we've asked for directions will remember us, James realized. *It's like we're drawing a map of our route for anyone to follow.*

'Shouldn't we ditch the car?' said Hugo.

'And get caught stealing another?' James shook his head. 'We need to reach Jagua and Maritsa as soon as we can.'

At eight o'clock the sun was setting, and James and Hugo approached the elegant outskirts of a town called Melena del Sur. There was an air of quiet decline about its spacious streets, as once-fine villas slowly shed their paintwork to the salt breezes. Papery shreds of burned sugarcane blew about from the surrounding fields.

James stopped the car near a small grocery store, so that he and Hugo could stretch their legs and get something to eat. With the Hispano-Suiza out of sight, the owner was friendly; she told James that Playa Caimito was maybe twenty-five miles cross-country to the east.

Night came, and the road shone black in the glare of the headlamps. The countryside beyond looked grey in the light of the gibbous moon, and the way grew more and more treacherous. The Hispano-Suiza's servo-assisted brakes were a godsend; when James almost ran into an old pick-up truck blocking the road, the car stopped the moment he stamped on the pedal, as if grabbed by a giant hand. James didn't like the way the bearded driver was looking at the automobile; he wrote something in the dust on his windscreen before trundling away. Had he heard the radio bulletin? James wondered.

He tried to concentrate on the road. His arms ached and his eyes felt dry from the wind in his face, and the petrol gauge was dangerously low. Barely a mile on from the pick-up James found the road blocked by another obstacle: rice had been laid out to dry on one side. Mounting the grassy verge, James steered the car past – and almost smashed into a weathered signpost leaning drunkenly into a dusty T-junction. He braked hard, and saw carved letters lit by the headlights: CAIMITO.

'I don't believe it.' Hugo looked at James. 'Are we actually on the right track?'

'Which way now, though? Hard to know where that sign's pointing.' Putting the car into first gear, James turned left and bumped up the hill towards the summit. 'Perhaps we'll have a clearer view from higher ground.'

At the top, James pulled on the handbrake and killed the motor and the lights. The engine clinked and tapped as the metal cooled, and somewhere in the darkness the sea swept its lullaby hush against an invisible shore.

'What's that?' Hugo pointed to a rugged silhouette a half-mile or so across the headland, black against the star-flecked indigo sky. 'A castle?'

'Or a fort . . .' James's eyes widened. 'Hugo, that must be it – the landmark Jagua mentioned.'

'This close to Caimito, it's got to be!'

'We can hear the sea. Perhaps there's a way down to the beach . . .' James let off the handbrake and the Hispano-Suiza trundled down the other side of the hill. He veered off the track, over the long grass, until the automobile was at least partially concealed. In these wild surroundings and at this time of night, he reasoned, passers-by ought to be few and far between.

James climbed out of the car and waited for Hugo to do the same. Then they rejoined the track and hurried on down the hill. The sound of the sea grew louder. James scanned the narrow strip of beach that edged the shadows far below at the foot of the cliffs. There was no sign of movement.

'Anything?' Hugo called.

'I think we need to take a closer look.'

A quick reconnaissance revealed a route down the steep hillside. It was not the kindest of paths, twisting snakelike, but in the grassy dunes the going was easier.

Keeping the fort in sight, James and Hugo trudged towards a pebbled stretch of beach with a rotting wooden slipway and a tumbledown jetty.

'Well, you did it.' Hugo looked up at James as they walked. 'Defied the odds yet again, and brought us to the right spot – very nearly in one piece.'

James smiled. 'I'm as surprised as you are.'

'I'm sure the girls will thrill to the story of it all too.' Hugo sighed.

They reached the slipway that led down to the jetty. Crested with silver, the black waters of the Gulf stretched out before them. A tall palm grew almost horizontally out of the slope, its broad leaves splayed like a shield against the endless ocean. There was no noise but the steady whoosh of the tide and the hum of cicadas. A distant birdcall rose like a flare.

'We must've got here first,' said Hugo. 'Do you mind if I tell Jagua what we learned about La Velada's background with the Soviet secret police . . . ?'

'The secret police are the OGPU,' James said. 'They're now part of the NKVD, which includes all law-enforcement agencies, I think.'

Hugo groaned. 'You're an expert, then.'

'Hardly. I've had some first-hand experience of Russian Intelligence, that's all.' James shuddered as he thought back to his run-ins with Babushka, the Soviet spymaster. Both times they'd met, he'd barely survived.

'*Had some first-hand experience of Russian Intelligence,*' Hugo parroted. 'Honestly, what chance does a little boy like me have with a natural hero like you around? All the girls love you, James. You're a modern-day St George, ready and willing to slay their dragons.'

'Is . . . this about Jagua?' James stopped and put a hand on his friend's arm. 'Hugo, remember, we wouldn't be here now if you hadn't clobbered Ramón like that. Without you, I'd most likely be dead or blind.'

'I suppose that's true . . .' Hugo managed a wry smile. 'Although I'm afraid saving you may have been in vain. You know what happened to the real St George, don't you?'

'He killed the dragon and rescued the maiden?'

'No. He was tortured on a wheel of swords and his head chopped off.'

'Is that all?' James smiled. He knew Hugo couldn't stay sullen for long.

'Hey, James – look.' Hugo pointed to the long grass that led to the cliffs. 'There's the motorcycle.'

James followed his gaze and caught the faint glint of moonlight on chrome. 'It's been separated from the sidecar . . .'

A dark wraith rose up beside it. 'To hide both more easily.'

James jumped as Hugo shouted, 'Jagua?'

'Glad to see you still live.' She was wearing a black swimming costume and black shorts. 'Although this is thanks to Hugo, yes?'

Hugo looked mortified. 'You – you heard what I . . . ?'

Jagua smiled. 'Most of it.'

James tensed at sudden movement behind the sidecar, buried in the grass twenty yards away – but it was only Maritsa. She was holding another diving helmet; this one was made of clear glass – a large cookie jar perhaps. She blew James a kiss and gave her lopsided smile, and James smiled back.

'Now, you say that *bruja* La Velada had "background" with the Russian police?' Jagua was frowning. 'What does this mean?'

'It was in the 1920s,' said Hugo. 'They threatened to kill her if she didn't betray her countrymen, so she did as they asked. Your father said he'd seen MacLean's evidence . . .'

She swore softly. 'Well, he may trust her past, but I do not trust what she does now.'

'You get Hardiman?' called Maritsa.

James shook his head. 'At least we know he's alive. Unlike Chester MacLean . . .'

He gave the girls a brief outline of what had happened in Scolopendra's suite at the Gran Casino. Maritsa looked lost for the most part, but Jagua's hands were soon clutched over her stomach.

'My father killed MacLean himself?' In the moonlight, Jagua's eyes looked coal-black.

James nodded slowly. 'On the toss of a coin.'

'Was this because Father found my jewels in his case? You must be truthful.'

'MacLean was cheating Scolopendra before you approached him. Before Sarila approached him.' Hugo looked uncomfortable. 'I get the impression that your father prizes loyalty.'

'Loyalty and belief. This is why he listens to La Velada,' Jagua said. 'Always, Father believes in survival of the strongest. Always he is fascinated by predator and prey. But now, egged on by *her* . . . it is like he must live these things.'

Maritsa looked up from unspooling the lengths of breathing hose. When she saw Jagua's face, she called over in Spanish, concerned. Jagua shook her head, trying to regain her composure. Hugo reached out a tentative hand to offer comfort, then snatched it back when she turned round to face James.

'So. All we can do now is fetch my father's treasure from the sea.' Jagua tried to sound matter-of-fact. 'Perhaps we will learn then what it is, this "great task" he kills for, yes?'

'If we could only get a hold over *him* for a change,' said Hugo.

'He might trade Hardiman for our silence . . .' James desperately wanted to believe there was a chance. 'Well, first, we'd better damn well find this strongbox.'

'The tides are at their lowest now,' said Jagua. 'We got Maritsa's diving things from the village, so if four of us go, two may dive at once.'

James felt excitement prickle along his spine. 'We can take turns?'

'It will be dangerous. Maritsa and me, we shall be too busy minding our own skins to spend time minding yours.'

'Understood,' James said quietly.

'So.' Jagua looked at Hugo. 'You will help me launch the boat . . . my champion?'

'I can't see how you'll do it without me,' Hugo quipped, but James saw the blush on his friend's cheeks.

James stripped down to his shorts and shoes, and carefully folded his shirt around Queensmarsh. Then he stowed the bundle in the motorcycle sidecar. Jagua's boat, a sixteen-foot Dodge runabout, lay concealed by driftwood and palm leaves close to the Indian Four. At its highest, the tide clearly covered most of the surrounding beach; unable to use the slipway single-handed, Jagua had grounded the boat on the shallow dunes – hardly recommended procedure, but James supposed she had no choice, and in any case, the hull seemed to have survived. The Scolopendra insignia glared out from both sides.

The four of them were able to drag and manhandle the runabout along the slipway and into the sea. It was a fine boat made of polished African mahogany, with room for four – cockpits fore and aft, separated by a hinged wooden casing that concealed the powerful Packard engine. Hugo sat up front with Jagua. Maritsa sat with the lamp, helmets and pumps, eyes closed, catnapping. James perched on the engine hatch, the air-pipes coiled about him like sleeping snakes.

Jagua took the helm and piloted them out towards the charcoal line of the horizon. The thrust controls were simple, with a lever for forward and reverse. As the runabout chugged away from the shore, low in the black water, James felt dwarfed, insignificant; the dark sea seemed as boundless as space, and their boat the tiniest speck of starlight.

He watched Jagua gauge their distance from the shoreline, gazing to port and starboard and up at the sky. 'Sometimes,' she announced, 'when I was small, my father would take me night fishing. He was not always a monster. When my mother was dying, he was so gentle with her; he tried so very hard to save her.'

'What was wrong?' asked Hugo.

'Something in her blood, Father said.' Jagua shrugged. 'He did not trust the hospitals and could not afford the bills. He was certain his cures would work. But they did not.' She paused. 'I think this was the biggest hurt for him. He could not prove himself.'

'Hardiman's been working on a cure of some kind for Scolopendra,' Hugo noted. 'Could it be linked to that?'

'I doubt it. Why would Hardiman have a problem working on something good, like that?' James pondered Jagua's story in the cave. 'It sounds like your father still has a chip on his shoulder over how others see him.'

'You are surprised?' She raised an eyebrow. 'You, who are white-skinned and from a rich background, accepted wherever you go . . .'

'Besides casinos,' joked Hugo awkwardly, trying to lighten the mood.

Maritsa had woken and was now pointing at something in the thick, pitching gloom. '*¿Qué es eso?*'

'What is what?' Hugo peered in the direction of her stabbing finger. 'Hard to tell . . .'

'I think it's a buoy,' said James.

'Yes. And this is the place I think the cruiser went down.' Jagua stared out. 'The buoy there? It is an old smuggler's trick. You have a little buoy on a rope inside a heavy block of salt, yes? You tie it to whatever you want to lose for a time, and throw it overboard. The harbour patrol finds nothing bad on your boat and must let you go. Then, later, the salt dissolves, the buoy rises—'

'And you've a handy marker showing you just where your illicit cargo lies,' Hugo concluded. 'All you have to do is haul it back up.'

'Sarila came prepared, all right.' James was itching to reel in the possible prize. 'Let's find out what she was smuggling.'

Maritsa lifted a steel anchor from the bottom of the boat and dropped it over the side, where it was swallowed by darkness. The rope uncoiled rapidly; she let it trail through her palms.

'Is there enough to reach the bottom?' Hugo wondered.

As he spoke, with just a few feet left slack, the rope stopped unwinding. The anchor had struck the coral far below.

'Almost forty feet down,' Jagua murmured. 'Cold too. This will not be easy.'

James reached over the side and grasped the buoy. He gathered in the thick rope, muscles straining, sweat flowing – but then the rope would come no further. He pulled harder, but almost overbalanced the boat.

'It is caught on something, perhaps.' Jagua rose from her seat. 'I shall dive down and see.'

'I'll come with you,' said James.

'Very well.' Jagua spoke briefly to Maritsa, who looked at James and shrugged. 'At this depth we work in short shifts, to stop risk of the bends. Say, twenty minutes. You and I go first, James. Then Maritsa and I will work. Then you go with Maritsa.'

James nodded his understanding. 'Hugo, you do still remember how to work those bellows . . . ?'

'As if it were yesterday. Which it was.' Hugo set about uncoiling the air-hoses. 'I know what I have to do.'

'No arguments?'

'No. Because I know this is what *you* have to do.'

James helped Maritsa lift up the submarine lamp and balance it on the side of the boat. She pulled roughly at a stubborn control and it blazed into radiance. James shut his eyes, blinded, tried to blink the glare away.

'How long will the batteries last?' he asked.

'We do not know,' said Jagua simply.

The boat rocked alarmingly as Hugo helped Maritsa lower the lamp on its old, slimy rope over the edge of the boat. James leaned over to track the phosphorescent glow as it dwindled. Hugo struggled to keep his balance as he helped lower the home-made helmet over James's head and smooth out kinks in the hoses. Maritsa did the same for Jagua.

The rocking of the boat lessened as everyone took up their positions – Maritsa and Hugo at the pumps, Jagua and James on opposite sides, ready to drop over the edge.

'Wait.' Hugo's voice carried faintly through James's helmet. 'I hear something.'

Everyone froze. James listened but could only hear his own breathing, amplified around him. 'What is it?'

145

'Not sure. Might've been an engine. But it's stopped now.'

Maritsa said something that sounded dismissive. Jagua spoke more softly. 'The sea plays with sound, Hugo . . .'

'I'm sure you're right, but . . .' Hugo peered keenly into the darkness about them, then sighed. 'Sorry. Well, sooner you're down, sooner you'll be back, eh?'

'That's right.' With a surge of adrenalin, James felt for the buoy rope.

'We return when I signal,' Jagua told him. 'To be sure we beat the bends, do not rise too quickly. Wait some way below the surface for three minutes to let your body adjust to the different pressure.'

James nodded. 'I'll do my best.'

'You would be wise to.'

Holding the rope securely in one hand, James eased himself off the side of the boat into the water.

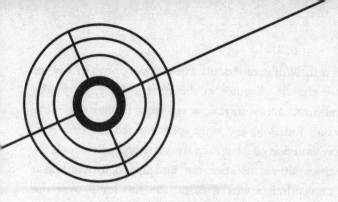

16

A Struggle of Shadows

Down James went, ramrod straight, into the shock of the deep black water. The cold made him tense, tighten his grip on the rope with hands and feet. He paused, breathed deeply, the now familiar shush of the fresh air joined by the bubbling as breath escaped. His vision was little more than a rectangle of blackness as he pulled on the rope to lower himself down. An image of bait on a crab-line came into his head, and he did his best to push it away, to stay upright as his descent continued. He swallowed hard, forcing a yawn to clear his ears. Even now, as the pressure increased, nitrogen would be seeping into his tissues and blood. How deep could he go before the air pressure could no longer compete with the pressure of the sea and the life-giving hiss of air sputtered and died? His every muscle tensed, James wondered what else was down here with him, besides Jagua, besides . . . ?

Scolopendra's cruiser.

He felt a thrill of excitement. There it was, way below, its pale hull a distant glimmer in the electric light. A spindly shadow billowed across it; that was Jagua, further down the rope, leading James to the right spot. He felt his ears pop, every nerve on edge as he slowly sank towards the wreck.

The cruiser lay on its keel, but had tipped forward at a drunken angle. Jagua was walking the sub lamp over the coral-clad shelf, shifting it closer to the boat; the mahogany sides were illuminated in ghostly white light that emphasized the darkness beyond. Unknown creatures drifted at the edges of the glare. James focused on the cruiser and, with a shiver, saw the scores of bullet-holes in the elegant sweep of the hull, through the sign of the Scolopendra claw.

But the buoy rope led to . . . nothing.

James felt a twist of disappointment as he saw that the rope had simply snagged on a broken window-frame. No treasure lay attached.

It's come loose, he realized. *Or was that me, pulling too hard on it?*

Jagua turned to James, the light reflecting off the glass of her visor; pointing to the cruiser, she pressed her helmet against his. 'We search.' Her voice sounded tinny and hollow, barely audible through the hoarse rush of air pumped down from above. 'Upright always.'

James gave Jagua a thumbs-up, watched as she carefully hauled herself up over the remains of the side-rail, which had splintered against the coral. She padded slowly along the deck towards the stern. Through the inky gloom he saw her kneel carefully in front of a bench seat, keeping her upper body vertical. The seat lifted to reveal storage underneath, and she began to sort through it.

James climbed aboard cautiously, his movements clumsy; it was hard to judge things this deep underwater. His limbs ached, and he felt rushes of dizziness. The pumped air was like an old man's breath rasping in his ears; he prayed that the light stayed working, that Hugo and Maritsa kept the oxygen coming. How long had they been down here, forty feet below the surface?

Rather than following Jagua to the stern of the boat, James made for the cockpit. There were further bullet-holes blasted into the interior wall – Scolopendra's men must have come alongside the cruiser and really let rip. The light wasn't so strong back here; it was hard to see anything. What a primitive expedition this was!

Something dark floated ahead of him, like some eerie deep-sea phantom. It was a backpack of some sort, its strap caught around a wooden spoke protruding from the steering wheel. He watched, revolted, as something pale and stringy, like an eel, came undulating out of the bag. Then he realized it was only a guy rope, the end severed; before the line snagged and severed on the broken window-frame, it must have been attached to the backpack . . .

Gripping hold of the flap, James opened the bag and reached inside. His fingers brushed something sharp-edged and heavy. Trapped air bubbles floated up, obscuring his vision, but once the flurry had cleared his eyes zeroed in on the object: a metal strongbox marked with the red claw, INDUSTRIAS SCOLOPENDRA embossed beneath it.

James's heart pounded against his ribs. This was it – the treasure they sought.

Carefully he straightened, turned to summon Jagua, pleased and proud that he had found it first.

But the dark figure beside him wasn't Jagua.

A torch beam played about the shattered cabin. In broken flashes James made out a facemask, dark skin, a pressurized canister strapped to the man's side . . .

Someone else had come treasure hunting.

In the giddy light of the man's torch, James took in the breathing apparatus connecting the facemask to the canister. State-of-the-art equipment. This diver was a professional; clearly he'd been waiting for low tide too.

The man brought up a long-bladed knife in his left fist and indicated that James should move away.

James held up his hands to show that he wasn't armed – a sign of surrender, a play for time. He tried to block all sight of the backpack with his body, desperate to keep his discovery a secret. Was this man alone? he wondered. Where the hell had he come from?

Desperate for a diversion, James pretended to suffocate. Clutching desperately at the base of his improvised helmet, he flailed around like a clumsy marionette. The diver lowered his knife for a moment, and James grabbed hold of his wrists and heaved him close. The man's head smashed against James's metal helmet with a dull clang. At the same time, James kicked out hard at his leg, catching the kneecap dead-on. The diver fell away from him, dropping the knife as he did so.

Quick! James acted on instinct to snatch up the knife – but his moment of exultation was short-lived. His precious air-pipes were now hooked under his enemy's arm; and the man pulled hard as he fell.

James felt the helmet lifting off his head and took a huge

gulp of air – just as it scraped off his shoulders entirely and his face was pulled into dark water. Blinded for a moment, he felt a foot kick into his ribs and gasped, precious air wasted as he tumbled off the deck of the boat, keeping hold of the knife. In the eerie light, he saw a struggle of shadows on the hull. Jagua was in the grip of a second diver. She'd lost her helmet too.

More nimble now that he was unencumbered, James twisted in the water and powered astern with the knife. Ignoring the pressure building in his lungs, he attacked the second diver from behind.

James slashed at the man's breathing tube with the knife. Bubbles blossomed from the split. The man's hands flew automatically to his mouth, and Jagua slammed his head against the cruiser's hull. James snatched the severed tube and took a deep breath of the pressurized air as it escaped. *The treasure*, he thought. *Is there time to get . . . ?*

No. The first diver was already swimming towards them.

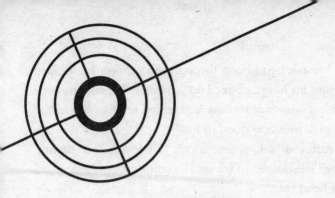

17

A Darkling Shore

There was no time for delay. Chest aching, temples prickling, James grabbed Jagua's wrist, planted both feet on the side of the hull and propelled himself away, pulling her with him.

Jagua snatched back her arm and swam alongside as they raced upward. Down below, the light was fading. Was that suffocation robbing him of his sight, James wondered, or simple distance? He turned to check that Jagua was still beside him, but there was only a black soup of nothingness. His head started to pound and desperation clawed at his chest. How far to go now? Was he still swimming upwards? There was no reference point. The knife slipped out of his hand. His lungs were on fire. His arms and legs were cramping. He felt sick. His whole body was screaming at him to breathe in, but blind, stupid defiance drove his arms into a final wild windmill – until—

At last James's head burst through the surface. He gulped air down into his lungs, choked on seawater. He remembered Jagua's safety warning: to stay submerged ten feet below the surface – well, that had gone to hell!

Jagua surfaced a few feet away, whooping for breath. 'Boat gone!' she gasped. 'Helmet . . . came away. Almost . . . pulled my head off.'

'Hugo?' James tried to shout, treading water, looking around desperately.

'They left,' Jagua hissed.

James retched up water, realized there was a noise behind the roar of adrenalin in his ears. 'Listen!' It was the drone of an engine rolling out across the ocean, growing louder. 'They're coming back for us!' He turned through 360 degrees but couldn't pinpoint the source – until powerful headlights torched the water around them. A motorboat was approaching. Behind the blinding haze, incomprehensible words squawked through a loudhailer.

'That must be the boat that brought the divers!' James shouted. Hugo had heard an engine after all; the newcomers must have rowed closer to the dive site in order to take them by surprise, but now the need for stealth had passed.

Jagua was already striking out for shore. James powered after her, forcing his arms into a furious front crawl. He heard the chilling crack of gunfire, risked a look behind, glimpsed a silhouette standing in the boat, firing into the darkness. Jagua had got off to a good start but was slowing down now.

'Come on!' James tried to goad her. 'You going to let me beat you?'

'Go to hell!' she panted, pain pinching her face as she forced herself to swim harder.

James used his anger to fuel his strength. If only he and Jagua had made it to the site just five minutes earlier! Then they might have won the prize they'd risked so much for. If only the divers had stayed away longer, they'd have found nothing of interest . . .

The swell lifted James again, and he fought to keep going. His legs were cramping; he felt light-headed. The tower on the headland was his marker, the muddy beach of Playa Caimito not far now. Fifty yards, maybe? It seemed so much further! The water tasted foul. His arms burned. *Just keep going*, he told himself. *Find the strength for one more stroke and make it last for two. Keep going!*

Finally the surf threw James against rocks beneath the surface, grazing his knees. He tried to stand but his legs would not support him, and he fell on his side in the shallows not far from the old slipway. He lay there as foam broke over his face. His shoulder ached . . . decompression sickness, or overwrought muscles? Jagua crawled out of the sea beside him, head bowed, shaking as she retched and gasped.

There was no sign of Hugo, Maritsa or the little motorboat.

Where are you? What happened? James gazed out to sea, shivering with shock and cold. *Whose boat is that?*

Jagua shook him gently. 'Uh-oh,' she whispered. 'Look.'

James turned his head and caught movement further along the dark beach. He lay down flat and held as still as he could beside Jagua. The moon dabbed silver onto a figure in a diving mask, who was climbing slowly out of the sea . . . And on the strongbox marked INDUSTRIAS SCOLOPENDRA that he was clutching under one arm.

'That's the treasure,' James whispered. 'I found it in the wreck before that man attacked me.'

'Why didn't the boat pick him up?' Jagua wondered.

'It wasn't there when we surfaced, remember?' James shrugged. 'In any case, this is our chance to get the strongbox back from him!'

The man fell forward, breathing heavily, clutching the box to his side. Whatever was in it was worth killing for. James was determined to get hold of it himself.

'If I win back that strongbox, we'll need to make a fast getaway,' he hissed to Jagua, 'but the Hispano-Suiza's running on fumes. Is the motorcycle fuelled up?'

'Quarter of a tank,' she said. 'But we took off the sidecar, so it will be faster. I'll clear away the cover.'

'Do that.' James thought of Queensmarsh in the sidecar, hidden in his clothes. There was no time to make use of either now. While Jagua flitted soundlessly up the beach towards the dunes, he used his elbows to pull himself along on his belly, forcing a little shield of sand ahead of him.

The man stirred, looked up, and his eyes widened.

James hurled sand into those eyes. With his last reserves of energy he jumped up and sprinted towards his would-be killer, then kicked him in the shoulder. The man clutched the box to his chest and rolled with the blow – but then gasped and staggered as he tried to get up. There was blood on the sand where he had been lying, and a gash in his right leg; he must have been injured in the underwater fight.

James hesitated but knew he mustn't waste his advantage:

he aimed a kick at the diver's injured leg. The man howled, dropped the strongbox and collapsed on the sand.

James snatched up the treasure and ran. He heard Jagua start up the Indian's engine: it spluttered, backfired with a sound like a pistol crack, then grew steadier.

'No!' the diver screamed after him. 'Give it back!'

He speaks English? The accent sounded American. James was so surprised he actually stopped running and turned round. But the man had drawn a knife.

Terrified, James felt the blade whistle past his ear as he resumed his sprint towards Jagua. It struck the wet sand while he ran on and jumped into the saddle behind her, wedged the box between them and clasped his arms around her waist.

Jagua engaged the gears, the four-cylinder engine roared and the rear wheel spun in the sand, edging them sideways until the tyres got purchase. Then, as the motorcycle lurched away, she slammed it into third and they surged over the beach.

We did it! For a few moments James felt invincible. *We've got away with Scolopendra's treasure.*

But when he looked down, his confidence ebbed away. The Indian had little clearance, and with both James and Jagua on board they were practically scraping the sand. The questions came one after the other as he clung to Jagua in the bone-jarring darkness. Who were the divers? Had they been sent by Scolopendra? Or were they friends of Sarila watching out for the smugglers' buoy – in which case, who did they work for?

Most important, what had happened to Hugo and Maritsa?

Dimly James saw a track leading up into the foothills. 'Turn right,' he yelled in Jagua's ear. 'Harder for them to follow.'

She sent the Indian swerving uphill. The terrain swiftly changed from sandy mud to tussocks of grass that slashed at their bare legs. James glanced back at the moonlit beach, straining to catch sight of the man with the American accent.

But as he did so, the front tyre hit a large stone. The jolt knocked Jagua off balance, the Indian twisted underneath them, and she, James and the strongbox were thrown onto the hard ground. Left on its side, the motorcycle's rear wheel spun in the sand, throwing grit over them until the engine spluttered and stalled.

'*¡Ay Dios!*' Jagua muttered as she shook off the sand and tried to hold back tears.

Spitting grit, James scrambled up to right the Indian and climbed into the saddle himself. 'Come on!' he urged Jagua.

'*Me duele la muñeca.*' She was clutching her wrist. 'I landed badly.'

James kicked down the stand, dismounted and led her round in front of the headlamp: he couldn't see much swelling. 'I don't think it's broken.' He looked at her. 'I can drive if you can still hold on?'

'Let me get the strongbox.' She gasped with pain as she tried to pick it up. 'Wait. James – the lid. It has loosened in the fall.'

James came over and bent down, his fingers scrabbling at the box. The top, though loose, still wouldn't give, so he tried hammering at it with a stone. Finally the warped metal jumped on its steel hinges.

His fingers hesitated before he lifted the lid . . . *Treasure worth dying for?*

Jagua put her fingers beside his and they opened the strongbox . . .

Inside was another box, wrapped in oilskins, sealed with wax to keep it waterproof.

James almost laughed out loud at the anticlimax. 'What is this, pass the parcel?' He pulled at the thick protective covering, but it was too strong. 'We need that diver's knife—'

'Wait.' Jagua held up her good hand for silence.

The growl of a motorcar had stolen into the noise of the surf. Men's voices too. James scrambled to the top of the rise to look down . . .

He swore.

Two police patrol cars had appeared on the hillside, not far from the Hispano-Suiza. Men in uniforms and peaked caps, guns in their hands, were fanning out, heading towards James and Jagua.

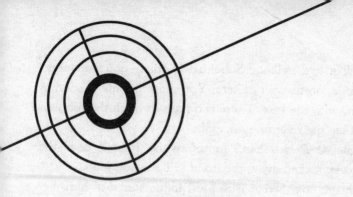

18
The Route of All Evil

'Hugo and I passed a man in a pick-up on the way down here. I knew he recognized the Hispano-Suiza from its description on the radio . . .' James felt sick as a familiar sense of unending nightmare came over him. 'He must've got to a telephone, called the police . . .'

'And when they get here, they hear the motorcycle and come looking.' Jagua looked at James steadily. 'If they catch us now . . .'

James returned to the Indian Four, placed the oilskin package back in the strongbox and wedged it between the saddle and the front axle. 'If we go up there at full revs, perhaps we can surprise them . . .'

'The ground is too bad – it rides too low. With my wrist, I make your balance harder.' Jagua looked up at him. 'Take the strongbox and go. You'll be faster alone.'

James glanced down at her hand. 'You're sure?' he asked.

'I shall go to the village. Sabana de Robles – you remember? Seven miles north-west of here. You must find me as soon as you can, with the box. There is a path through the tobacco fields. Keep the river on your right.'

'*Sabana de Robles*. Yes.' James swung himself onto the motorcycle, kicked away the stand. 'I'll see you soon.'

'With the box! Swear it to me?' Jagua stared at him, her eyes wet now. 'I can trust you?'

He gave her a crooked smile. 'My word's my bond.'

She pressed a kiss to his cheek, and James felt fleeting guilt for the missing Hugo. Then his thoughts turned to his own predicament as he kick-started the engine and accelerated up the rise. Without meaning to, James pulled the motorcycle up into a wheelstand as he went over the brow, and almost mowed down a cop who was diving for cover. The motor-cycle's front wheel hit the ground with a heavy jolt but James stayed upright, checked the strongbox was still jammed in position, and powered away along a narrow dirt track. He heard shouts and gunfire, and the zing of a bullet bouncing off chrome.

Ahead, a patrol vehicle and the Hispano-Suiza blocked the track and there was barely room to get past. James put the motorcycle into third gear, twisted hard on the throttle and aimed straight down the middle. He smashed the patrol car wing mirror with his handlebar and clung on as he accelerated away.

James stared down at the strongbox. Whatever was inside might hold lives in the balance, he reflected. Or it might just kill him outright. Right here, tonight.

A corner showed in the hard, juddering light of the

headlamp and James took it at forty, wheels skidding and churning dust all around him. He had no crash-hat, no protective clothes – a fall would most likely kill him, but he didn't dare slow down. It wouldn't take the coppers long to get back to their patrol cars . . .

The track twisted to and fro, but James took the corners as fast as he dared. On the fifth hairpin bend he skidded and almost came off the bike.

Still he couldn't slow. The angry growl of an engine was building behind him. James swore as the police car came screeching round the corner, headlamps glaring like the eyes of a wild beast charging him down.

The road widened and the patrol vehicle strained forward, seeking to get past him – or to ram the Indian off the road. James opened the throttle further. He weaved left and right in front of the car, making himself a tougher target as he pulled away.

But as he rounded the next turn, he recognized the tree-branch barrier guarding the drying rice. James couldn't brake in time, swerved violently, almost lost control, then veered wildly up the bumpy embankment in a cloud of dust.

The strongbox was shaken free.

'No!' he bellowed, braking hard as he reached the top of the rise. He saw the box tumble down the slope and into the road with a heavy clatter.

Moments later, with a thick metallic *thunk*, the patrol car drove straight over it. A tyre blew and sent the automobile slewing into a spin that stopped only when the front ploughed into the mud-bank on the opposite side of the road.

Using the dust and darkness as cover, his heart thumping a

nauseous rhythm, James wheeled the Indian into a thicket of trees over the top of the rise. With any luck, the policeman would think he had driven on ahead; that they stood no chance of catching him now. Then he doubled back on foot to spy on the three officers climbing out of their beat-up patrol car.

Perhaps they won't find the strongbox, James thought. *Perhaps they won't realize it caused the blow-out, or—*

His cautious hopes were dashed as he heard the words '*Industrias Scolopendra*'. One of the policemen set the battered strongbox down on the road in front of the headlights, then opened it up. Another pulled out a penknife and started stabbing and sawing at the oilskins. His colleague helped him unwrap the bundle inside.

Feeling sick, James watched their progress. *This was a good night's work*, he thought bitterly. *Hugo and Maritsa are missing. Jagua's injured and on the run cross-country. And after all you've put yourself through, you've just given away your last hope of helping Hardiman* . . . Breathing deeply, he forced himself to shrug off the self-pity. *Thought, not feelings – that's your only chance to change things.*

Inside the oilskins, gleaming in the bright lights, was a clear glass box. Its metal lid seemed to be secured with some sort of resin, an airtight seal. One of the patrolmen sliced through the seal, prised off the lid. James's heart pumped faster. People had robbed and chased and killed and died for this mystery box. Now he could see . . .

The box was full of money.

The policeman picked up a wad of banknotes, whooped and waved it around. '¡Miralos! ¡Billetes de cien dólares!' His colleague shook his head, snatched it away – then waved it around himself.

Hundred-dollar bills? James felt confused, cheated somehow. Why would Sarila go to such lengths to break into Scolopendra's private estate just to steal some money? It didn't add up. Had they found the wrong box? Could there be something special about the wrapping, the oilskins . . . ?

The third officer was not joining in with the celebrations; he directed them to put the money back. James caught the words 'Scolopendra' and '*recompensa*'. Of course, with such powerful friends, Scolopendra was not someone you fooled around with; better to please him with the news of recovery, and angle for a reward.

Shivering in the night air, James crept back to the motorcycle, heaved it upright and wheeled it through the trees. *Keep on going*, he told himself, though he wondered how he was going to find Jagua's village – and how he was going to face her when he did.

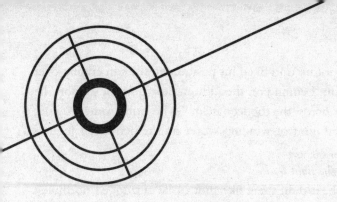

19
House Calls

Around three a.m., too wary of the police to ride the Indian out on the road and too exhausted to push it any further, James came to a stop in the middle of a tobacco field. The plants came up to his chest, the leaves thick and waxy with a heavy, earthy scent. They would offer good cover. He lay down in the dirt beside the motorcycle, longing for a blanket or even just his shirt. Even so, he was asleep in moments.

He awoke from confused dreams of hiding in his old room at Eton and found himself wet with dew; above him a dark grey sky was just beginning to bleed pink. As memories of last night came back to him, James rubbed the sleep from his eyes. Everything hurt. As a young child he'd harboured romantic notions of an outlaw's life, camping out under the stars with just a tuft of grass for his pillow. The reality was, he felt like he'd been stretched on a rack.

James got up and fixed his position by the sun edging over the horizon. Leaning on the filthy motorcycle for support, he struck out across the tobacco field. To his right, some way off, he saw the glint of winding water and remembered Jagua's directions.

I'm on the right track.

In truth, it didn't feel like that as he zigzagged northwest through the fields. His head tumbled with worries for Hugo and Maritsa – and Jagua too; had she found her way back safely?

He found no answers in the trilling of the birds and hum of insects. Tobacco gave way to bristling sisal plants, the broad, spiky leaves like armour plating for the ground. In a neighbouring valley, James saw outbuildings of concrete and corrugated metal: some sort of factory. Men and women laboured in the fields; some hacked at the sisal with machetes, while others fed their harvest into the smoky machinery, a noisy, whirring sacrifice. Higher up the hill stood a small settlement, like a drab stain on paradise.

Jagua said that her village depended on the sisal factory. Surely this had to be it? Benevolent Scolopendra, granting his former neighbours the means to scratch out a living while he sat at the head of his own empire. Had he been prompted by compassion, or was this a salve to his wounded pride? *No, I never saved my wife, but I'm keeping all of you alive . . .*

Arms fit to drop off, James decided to hide the motorcycle near the edge of the sisal field and come back for it later. Then he climbed the hillside track towards the settlement. The sun was baking his shoulders; they felt tight and sore. Halfway up the hill stood a conical hut like a sentry box. An old man sat outside, a pile of unripe plantains beside him, a cigar stub clamped in his mouth. Skinny chickens pecked at the dirt about his feet. He stared at James, dull-eyed.

'Sabana de Robles?' James asked. '¡Por favor?'

The old man went on staring.

James tried again. 'Maritsa? Jagua?'

Finally a wizened hand waved further up the hill.

James thanked him and climbed to the brow, looking down into the valley. Sabana de Robles, it seemed, was little more than a street of shacks marking time before their final collapse. James remembered the upmarket cool of Scolopendra's penthouse in town; it was hard to believe that he and Jagua had lived for years in such an environment.

A larger rectangular building with concrete walls, wooden doors and a gabled roof stood at the end of the dusty street; it looked like the centre of the community. The excited chatter of young children drifted out from within; James guessed that they stayed here with the older villagers while the able men and women went to work.

Deciding to start his enquiries there, James headed towards the big hall. But as he passed a small thatched house on his right, a shout made him jump. 'James?'

'Hugo?' For a few seconds James forgot everything as his diminutive friend came out to greet him. 'Hugo, I don't believe it!'

'You're alive!' Hugo gripped James's hand like he meant to stop the circulation. 'I've been worried sick. Look at you, without even the shirt on your back! Are you all right?'

'Never mind me – what happened to you? Are Maritsa and Jagua—?'

'I am here.' Jagua followed Hugo out. She was dressed in a faded blue cotton dress. The skin around her eyes was as dark as her braided hair, and by daylight her wrist looked bruised and swollen. 'We do not know where Maritsa is,' she said, then studied him searchingly. 'And the strongbox . . . ?'

'I'm . . . I'm sorry.' James broke the news bluntly. 'It fell off the motorcycle, Jagua.'

She physically flinched from the news, then stared into his eyes. 'It is lost?'

'The police have it now.'

Jagua's face hardened. 'All the long walk here last night, afraid and hurting . . . I thought of that box. I thought of how so much depends on what is inside it: Dr Hardiman's future, Father's future, *my* future . . .'

'I saw what was inside it. Money.' James saw her face cloud in confusion, and nodded. 'I saw the patrolmen pull out notes and wave them about. Hundred-dollar bills. Must have been at least ten thousand there.'

Hugo whistled. 'A lot of dough.'

'But this money would not mean so much to my father . . .' Jagua looked suspicious. 'And why would the notes be sealed in oilskins?'

'Waterproofing?' James suggested.

'Perhaps Sarila got away with the wrong box altogether,' said Hugo. 'Or that diver did.'

'I found it in a backpack. But I was interrupted before I could look any further.' James put a hand to his hot shoulder and nodded to the tumbledown shack. 'Can we go in?'

Jagua nodded, clearly still troubled. 'There are old clothes in the group hut. I will fetch something.'

'Come on, then.' Hugo steered James inside. 'You look fit to drop. And that's before *my* story knocks you off your feet.'

James followed him into an oppressively hot living-room-cum-bedroom, with wooden crates for furniture and little more than dirty straw mats on the hard-packed earth floor. The kitchen at the back was bigger. It had a wood-burning stove, a table and simple chairs made of wood and rawhide.

Hugo fetched a tin cup and poured out some coconut milk. It was warm and tasted brackish, but James gulped it down gratefully. 'Thanks. You've made yourself at home, then?'

'I arrived a little after dawn,' Hugo told him, 'though I was sensible and came by taxi, with the last of my watch money.'

James raised his eyebrows. 'A taxi from where?'

'I'd best start at the beginning.' Hugo perched on a crate, kicking his feet against the old wood. 'You'd been down in the wreck a while. Suddenly this bloody boat came out of nowhere! I heard someone shout, "Murderers!" in Spanish . . . Next thing, we're being shot at.'

'*Murderers?*' James echoed.

'There were bullets flying everywhere.' Hugo hugged himself at the memory. 'I ducked down flat, but I kept pumping at the bellows. Only, next thing I knew, the engine had started up. Maritsa had stopped pumping. She'd hacked through the anchor rope and was starting the engine. Suddenly we were off! I tried to stop her, but she said we would die if we stayed.'

'Maritsa was right.' Jagua had returned; she dropped threadbare grey trousers and a blue calico shirt at James's feet. 'I would have left also.'

James nodded his thanks and pulled on the clothes; they weren't a bad fit, but reeked of tobacco smoke. 'Where is Maritsa now?'

'I'm coming to that.' Hugo looked downcast. 'The boat chased after us for quite a way before it gave up. It doubled back towards the dive site . . . Maritsa said it was hopeless to go after it and try to find you. Said you'd swim for it.'

'She was right,' said Jagua.

'So we followed the coastline till we reached the harbour at Batabano. But those damned red claws on the side of the boat stood out a mile, of course, and brought the harbour police running. Maritsa jumped ship, tried to swim for it.' He shrugged forlornly. 'I heard lots of shouting, much of it from her. I think they caught her.'

'Sounds bad.' James's sore fingertips stung as he fumbled with the shirt's few buttons. 'How did you get away?'

'I hid beneath the bellows and hoses in the rear compartment.' Hugo looked sheepish. 'I cowered there until the harbour police had moored the boat and left, fighting over which of them would call Scolopendra . . . I sneaked away the moment the coast was clear.'

'It's a good news day for Scolopendra,' James muttered. 'He'll have his Hispano-Suiza back, his motorboat, the strongbox . . . All his missing property recovered.'

'Not so,' said Jagua quietly. 'He has not recovered me.'

'But how do we keep it that way?' asked Hugo. 'What's our next step?'

'To remove La Velada?' There was a curl to Jagua's lip. 'With his dream of wealth come true, Father might have found peace . . . But to win her, he needed status too. She fed that desire – told him how to be, who to meet, who to beat . . .'

'How to become a player in the world of the rich,' James murmured. 'But it's not only business she knows, is it? The way she turned and fired at me . . . That wasn't from fear or anger. That was training.'

'You heard her, James,' Hugo said. 'She used to help the NKVD, or whoever they were—'

'Wait.' Jagua got up and quickly pulled a rug aside. A board was wedged into the earthen floor; it lifted up to reveal a small coffin-shaped space.

'What's that?' James asked. 'Storage, or . . . ?'

'Maritsa's father hid stolen things in here,' Jagua said simply. 'No one knows of this place outside their family.' Inside the hiding place lay sheets of crumpled paper – the transcripts of La Velada's phone conversations. 'Hugo, when you spoke just now, it made me think.'

'I'm a natural born orator,' he said.

'And I am a fool.' Jagua tapped her finger on the paper and handed it to him. 'NKVD – you said each letter as an Englishman would. But in Russian, the letters sound different, yes? *En, Kah, Veh, Deh* . . .'

'She was talking about the NKVD,' James realized. 'Or . . . *to* them?'

'Good grief.' Hugo started poring over the papers. 'You think she's still involved?'

'James said she acts with training,' Jagua said. 'And I know she talks to people behind Father's back.'

'She might just be phoning friends in Russia to talk about

173

the old days,' Hugo cautioned. 'But this bit here, "Gaye pay you" . . .'

'*Geh, peh, oo.*' Jagua started pacing the floor. 'GPU!'

'From OGPU. The secret police.' James felt a shiver prickle along his spine. 'Perhaps we're wrong, or reading too much into this.'

'Maybe. But this does not matter. Father believes that La Velada and him, they are alike,' Jagua said, her eyes narrowing. 'Trapped by their circumstances, they did what they had to do in order to survive. Fate favoured them with luck enough to start over and make a prosperous life.'

James understood where she was going. 'So if Scolopendra starts to think it wasn't fate that brought La Velada to him but the Soviet People's Commissariat for Internal Affairs . . .'

'Loyalty is so important to my father. He demands it above all else.' Jagua's hand brushed against her scarred shoulder. 'And he punishes disloyalty. Hard.'

'So we've seen.' Hugo went over to Jagua and put his hands on hers – squeezing the wrist she'd hurt. She cried out in pain and Hugo snatched his fingers away as if he'd been burned. 'I'm sorry! Sorry!'

Jagua cuffed him lightly round the head with her good hand, and James couldn't help but laugh at his friend's mortified expression.

'Wait.' Jagua held up her hand for silence; silence invaded by the approaching growl of a finely-tuned engine.

James jumped up, crossed to the window and peered out into the glare of the sun. The noise had brought children dancing out of the communal hut. The old and the lame of Sabana de Robles followed them out, looking less happy – as a scratched and dented black-and-scarlet Hispano-Suiza Coupé de Ville came crawling through the squalor.

Hugo swore. 'I hoped I'd never see that damned motorcar again.'

James pushed the comma of hair off his sweating forehead. 'Scolopendra's men . . .'

Jagua's fingers fumbled for the cross at her throat. 'They have come for me.'

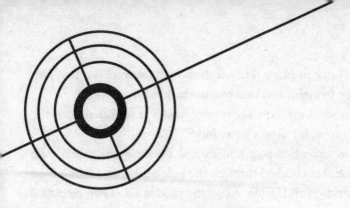

20

A Circus of Betrayal

For a moment Jagua looked like a small scared child; then the mask of resolve was back. 'Father's scum have come looking here before and never found me.' She took the pages of evidence and pushed them inside her dress, then pointed at the shallow trench in the floor. 'I hide there, but the two of you . . .'

'Hugo' – James glanced into the kitchen – 'there's a stove, can you fit inside?'

'I'll try.' He was helping Jagua curl up inside her hole in the floor. Her dark braids fell over her face and he brushed them aside. 'Are you able to get out again?'

'Yes,' she said. 'If I lie in the right place, I can.'

'Go on, Hugo, I'll cover her.' James looked down at Jagua. 'Ready?'

She nodded calmly, but James could see the fear in her eyes. He sealed her in with the covering board and then put the rug back in place. He felt as though he were burying her. Then he straightened and ran to the kitchen. 'Hugo?'

'Nobody here by that name,' came a whisper from the stove. 'Now, for God's sake, hide!'

James smiled grimly and turned his thoughts to his own salvation. He climbed through the hole in the wall that passed for a window and balanced on the muddy sill. Then he pulled himself up onto the thick straw of the conical roof, clinging there, pressed flat against the thatch, as the Hispano-Suiza pulled up outside, hidden from view.

There was a clunk as the door opened, and the deep rasp of a voice: '*¡Los niños adentro!*'

Not just his men, then. Scolopendra himself was here, braving the dust of Sabana de Robles in person! James held perfectly still. He glimpsed the children being herded back inside the larger building – the mock-cheery tones of their guardians at odds with the grave faces glancing back – and wondered why Scolopendra was clearing the area. He wanted no witnesses, perhaps? But witnesses to what?

Slowly, silently, James began to scale the thatched roof so he could peep out at what was happening. Then he heard a familiar voice.

'*Jagua!*'

It was Maritsa. James tensed, sweat soaking his back. So, Maritsa *had* been caught by the harbour police, and handed over to Scolopendra along with his boat. And, of course, she knew all about Jagua's 'secret' hiding place.

Maritsa called again to her friend: '*¡Jagua! ¡Por favor, sal de la casa! Me van a hacer daño si no sales . . .*'

She sounded terrified, and though James didn't understand

the words, the desperation came through loud and clear. There was the sound of a smack, and Maritsa shrieked. James heard uncertain singing from the children in the hall – some kind of nursery rhyme – their guardians were hoping to drown out the noise, perhaps.

I have to burst out and create a distraction, James thought; *give Maritsa a chance to break free.* He peered over the roof to see what was happening, fearing the worst.

His sweat ran cold when he saw that Maritsa was not in pain at all.

There she was, simply standing behind the car. Scolopendra waited beside her while Ramón sat in the driver's seat, smiling. El Puño crept towards the doorway, ready to grab Jagua as she came out.

It's a trap, James realized helplessly.

Scolopendra clapped his hands, and Maritsa cried out again as if she'd been struck. 'Jagua!' Then she gazed down at the ground, her eyes troubled.

There was a clatter of wood from inside the hut; unable to bear her friend's distress, Jagua must be crawling out from her hiding place to give herself up, James thought.

'*¡No dañar Maritsa!*' Jagua called from inside, and James closed his eyes in despair. If only he could warn her! But he knew that even if he did, there was no way she could escape now. Scolopendra could've dragged her out, kicking and screaming, but that would deny him the chance to assert his superiority, to demonstrate his control over Jagua's oldest, closest friend, repaying her betrayal of him with treachery that would cut so much deeper.

James knew he needed a plan, but his mind was blank and

he was so damned tired. He snapped open his eyes, determined to think of something.

That was when he saw the spider on the back of his right hand, barely a foot from his face. It looked like a tarantula, but with stubbier, hairier legs. The creature must have felt the vibrations and come crawling out of the thatch.

James held absolutely still. Besides their bite, he knew that certain tarantulas could shed toxic bristles to warn off predators; if the hairs got in your eyes, they could leave you blind. Was this bloated horror one of those?

Scolopendra would know, he thought darkly. *Want to ask him?*

The weathered door squealed as it opened and Jagua emerged. James swore under his breath. The spider squatted down on his hand, eight black eyes fixed on his face. The smallest movement and it might strike.

El Puño stepped forward and grabbed Jagua as she came out, his big hand closing on her wrist.

When she saw Maritsa standing there unharmed, looking shamefaced at the ground, Jagua lunged for her, shouting angrily, almost breaking free of El Puño. Scolopendra strode forward and took his daughter by the shoulders.

'How much did you pay her?' Jagua spoke English, as she always did to her father, this time through gritted teeth. 'How much for her to betray me?'

'Very little, I'm afraid.' Scolopendra nodded to El Puño, who turned and went inside the hut. James heard him crash about inside. If he opened the door to the stove . . .

Thankfully, the inspection was brief. '*Estaba sola*,' El Puño said, his voice unexpectedly soft.

'Alone, huh.' Scolopendra tightened his grip, and Jagua squirmed as the huge fingers dug into her flesh. 'The boys who helped you, who came with Hardiman – where are they?'

'Gone,' Jagua hissed. 'Where . . . is Hardiman?'

'Ah, the good doctor.' Scolopendra smiled down at her. 'He waits for us at home.'

'Your home, not mine.' Jagua shook her head. 'I will not stay there. Let me go.'

'Let you go? My darling girl, whenever I let you go, you *know* what happens . . .' With a sudden, brutal sweep of his arms, Scolopendra dashed her to the ground. 'You fall.'

Seeing Jagua sprawling in the dust, James burned to try and even the score. *You can't fight the lot of them*; he knew that. But anger is the enemy of reason, and if it hadn't been for the tarantula still testing his flesh with its quivering legs, James might well have thrown himself into the ring.

El Puño hauled Jagua back to her feet. She groaned, her head hanging down.

'You will come with me, Jagua. You will not disappoint your friend, Dr Hardiman, I think?' Scolopendra placed his hand around her neck. 'Although if you disappoint *me* again . . . he dies.'

She shook her head. 'You need him.'

'Not for much longer. Soon we will be gone from here. And there will be nowhere for you to run.'

James held his breath. The spider was crawling slowly up his forearm. If he tried to move or shake it off, the noise would attract the attention of Scolopendra's men, and not only his men. The back door of the Hispano-Suiza swung open, and a familiar veiled figure stepped out.

La Velada. James felt an instinctive jolt of fear and disgust at the very sight of her, worse than the spider. He watched her walk to Maritsa, who stood alone and forgotten. The girl looked up fearfully, her face streaked with tears, but the woman only handed her a manila envelope, then returned to the automobile. She held the door to the private compartment open while El Puño carried the half-conscious Jagua inside. James could only watch helplessly as she climbed in after them and the door swung shut. He looked down and saw that the tarantula was rocking to and fro as if getting ready to jump.

Maritsa stared dumbly at the envelope. '*Lo has hecho bien,*' Scolopendra told her. '*Quédate con el dinero. Nunca vuelvas a hablar con Jagua . . .*'

He went on talking; James picked out 'Batabano' from the surge of Spanish. Then, at last, the Hispano-Suiza's door slammed as Scolopendra got in. Ramón blew Maritsa a grotesque kiss with his scarred lips and switched on the engine; it hammered into life, then warmed to a purr.

James couldn't wait any longer. He shook off the spider – so violently that he lost his grip and fell, slithering down the roof before tumbling onto the baked earth behind the house. His ankle went over as he landed, but he kept still, praying he hadn't been noticed. As the automobile pulled away, thick dust falling like a veil in its wake, James warily circled the house.

Maritsa looked up and saw him. Her eyes widened and she made as if to run, but Hugo had emerged from the stove and grabbed her arm, then pulled her into the house, berating her in Spanish.

James followed them inside, his muscles cramped from clinging on for so long.

'She sold Jagua!' There was a rawness to Hugo's voice that James had not heard before. 'Scolopendra said he'd squared things for her with the harbour police and given her five hundred dollars never to see Jagua again.'

Maritsa pulled away and fell to her knees, muttering fiercely, the envelope clutched to her chest.

'If she *did* see Jagua again,' Hugo told James, 'Ramón said he would give her lips like his.'

The girl looked up at James, her eyes wet. Then she tore open the envelope, fingers scrabbling at the bundle of notes inside. 'Share,' she pleaded, pulling out the bills – but as she did so, there was a sharp crack and they burst into flames. Maritsa shrieked and dropped the envelope, staring as it charred and blackened.

'Booby-trapped,' James breathed. 'Must've been a tiny incendiary charge in the package.'

'I suppose Scolopendra thinks that betrayal brings its own reward.' Hugo snorted. 'Maritsa, you just sold Jagua down the river for nothing. *¡Todo para nada!*'

Maritsa sucked on her burned fingers, rocking on her haunches as the last of the money smouldered and curled. Then she spoke quietly in Spanish, and Hugo's frown soon deepened.

'What is it?' said James.

'She says that La Velada asked her about you and me . . . Why we're here. How well we know Hardiman.' Hugo looked at him. 'She was . . . very interested.'

'I don't much like the idea of that.' James turned to go,

then hesitated in the doorway. He glanced at the scrawny girl kneeling on the floor amongst the ashes. Alone, outnumbered, threatened with disfigurement or worse, offered more money than she'd ever seen in her life . . . was it any surprise that Maritsa had chosen to betray her closest friend?

Perhaps not. But right now James couldn't find it in himself to forgive.

'You really shouldn't have touched me for luck,' he said quietly.

Then he turned and strode outside, ignoring the people drifting warily out of the hall, forcing his aching legs into a jog back up the hill.

'And then there were two,' Hugo said, scurrying after him. 'What the hell are we going to do, James?'

'The objectives haven't changed.' James glanced back at him. 'Jagua chose to speak to her father in English; I don't think that was just to help him practise. She wanted to make sure we both understood what was being said.'

'So if I'd been found and flattened by El Puño,' puffed Hugo, 'you'd still be able to understand.'

'Correct,' James agreed. 'We know that Hardiman's at Scolopendra's estate, that Jagua will be joining them – and that they'll all be moving on somewhere soon.'

'I don't know what Scolopendra meant when he said she'd have nowhere to run,' Hugo fretted, 'but I don't like the sound of it.'

'So it's time to choose.' James kept striding ahead. 'Aunt Charmian will be here in two days – we can wait for her to arrive. Our passage home is booked: we can sail away from Cuba, get back to safety and school and all the rest. If the

Bolsheviks' spy network *is* involved, we can contact Agent Elmhirst when we're back and tell him all we know; try to convince him that a British subject is in danger; hope that he'll know someone who can do something about it—'

'But Hardiman could be dead by the time we cut through all the red tape,' Hugo said. 'Jagua will be a prisoner some-place, and Scolopendra's "great task" will carry on unchecked.'

'Right,' James agreed. 'You know the old saying: *Bad men need no better opportunity than when good men look on and do nothing*. So we do something.'

Hugo grabbed hold of his arm, stopping him a moment. 'And this "something" would be . . . ?'

'I heard Scolopendra mention Batabano.'

'Yes, he said they're collecting something on the way to the harbour there. Must be where he keeps his boat.'

'I'm going to stow away on it,' James said, 'and cadge a ride to where Hardiman's being held prisoner.'

'You can't be serious!'

'Now, I can remember how to contact Agent Elmhirst's office. Use your powers of persuasion, get them to wire a message to Elmhirst on his liner. Then, wait for my aunt—'

'So I'm the good man who does nothing? No, it's not on.' As they reached the brow of the hill, Hugo looked up at him. 'I can't walk away from this, James. Not after all we've been through these last forty-eight hours. Not after . . . Well, you know I like Jagua . . . That is to say . . .' He cleared his throat. 'In any case, St George needs his squire, doesn't he? I'll help you get on board if I can, then try to get on to Elmhirst's office . . . Though can you imagine how long it will take to place an international call to England from Cuba? I've seen enough money go up in smoke today . . .'

'Thanks, Hugo.' James half smiled, scanned the landscape. Though the roads were hidden amongst fields of sisal and tobacco, plumes of displaced dust still rose lazily from Scolopendra's automobile. 'I'll go and get the motorcycle ready. You catch me up.' He ran full pelt down the hill. 'Next stop, Batabano!'

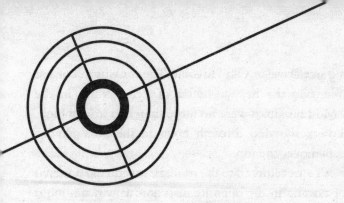

21
Human Wrecks

The chase was on. James pushed the motorcycle as hard as he dared, and Hugo spotted the occasional sign to Batabano that kept them on the right road. But the going was rough and the journey a bone-juddering ordeal. For long, agonizing minutes they had to trail along behind five mules hitched to a lumber cart. The petrol gauge was tracking empty, and James knew the feeling. The sweat poured off him as the sun beat down. His head buzzed, his throat had dried, he felt sick.

After what seemed like an age, they came to the outskirts of the quaint seaport. James was grateful for the sultry breeze blowing in off the ocean.

'The harbour's this way,' Hugo shouted in James's ear, pointing. 'I think it is, anyway.'

'We're running on nothing,' James reported, looking around for signs. The streets of Batabano were long and undulating like those in Old Havana. The air was full of salt and smoke, and the hectic chatter of steam trains in the distance. Most buildings were no more than two storeys high, old brickwork showing through holes in the pink plaster. Palms peeped over the top.

As James's eyes returned to the road, he saw an old battered police car passing in the opposite direction. It was missing a wing mirror.

He kept looking dead ahead, praying he hadn't been seen. *It was dark last night*, he told himself, *and the Indian's so covered in dirt and dust it's barely recognizable—*

The patrol car turned through 180 degrees, and suddenly it was right on their tail.

'Hold on!' James opened up the throttle and the Indian thrummed forward.

Hugo groaned. 'Of all the luck! If they catch us now . . .'

James pushed the motorcycle faster and overtook a horse and cart; the animal reared up in alarm, and the cart toppled sideways. The police car jammed on its brakes, and James swung the Indian hard left, over a bridge and onto another street. When he was out of sight, he slowed down.

'Jump off,' he told Hugo. 'Get to the harbour – I'll lead them away.'

Hugo leaped down. 'But you're almost out of fuel. Come with me!'

'On foot, together, we'll be picked up in no time.' James saw the police car appear round the corner, revved the engine, spoke faster. 'Go and find Scolopendra's boat. I'll join you as soon as I can.'

Tearing away in a haze of exhaust fumes, James turned

right down another street. It was choked with traffic; a truck had stalled at the junction. He tried to worm his way through the gridlocked cars and buses, but the engine was choking on its last gasps of fuel – and then it died. Leaving the motorcycle where it dropped, James jumped off, cut through the traffic on foot and dodged down a side alley.

You can't get caught now.

The next street was less busy, and lined with boarded-up buildings. *No way in. Nowhere to hide.* Desperate now, James dashed along the cracked concrete pavement. He heard the squeal of tyres on tarmac as the patrol car swung round the corner in pursuit. Surely there was an alleyway, a parking garage – someplace that could hide him?

The police car pulled past him, slewed round and mounted the pavement ahead. James didn't stop: he used the rear of the car as a vaulting horse and flew clear over it. But he landed badly; his leg buckled and he crashed down on the concrete.

Rolling over, he got to his feet, panting for breath, ready to run again.

'*¡Alto!*'

James turned to find both cops out of their car, guns trained on his legs.

Sorry, Hugo. Slowly, James raised his arms. *Sorry, Jagua.*

The policemen advanced in a cloud of stale body odour. They were stocky, dressed in grey, sweat-stained shirts, navy slacks and peaked caps, their expressions stern. The shorter one, who wore spectacles, addressed James in Spanish.

'Speak English?' James panted. 'Please – someone is being kidnapped. You must help.'

'Shut up,' said the cop with the glasses. He looked to his colleague for approval. 'Good English, huh?'

'Good,' the other agreed with a smile, before turning back to James. 'You under arrest, boy.'

James shook his head. 'There isn't time for this. A girl is going to be taken—'

'Shut up,' said Spectacles again, and slipped cuffs onto James's wrists.

'We look for you all night and this morning.' The other cop pushed him inside the patrol car and slid alongside. 'Trouble for you.'

James looked at his handcuffs in despair.

The patrol car rattled along a busy street called Calle Maceo, and James noticed a canal running parallel to the road – there were barges laden with goods, along with canoes ferrying messages to and fro. *The canal must feed into the harbour,* he thought. What would happen to Hugo, waiting there alone? *And what do I do now?* James had no doubt that Aunt Charmian would get him out of this in the end, somehow, but in the meantime . . .

He recognized a familiar sign on a whitewashed building across the street: POLICÍA. The car drew to a stop outside, and the cop with glasses pulled him out onto the pavement. Suddenly James realized: *If the police from last night are based at this station, did they bring Scolopendra's strongbox here for safe-keeping too?*

With a shiver of fear, he remembered what Hugo had said about Scolopendra needing to collect something en route to the harbour.

The strongbox.

He might be here right now.

James was pushed into the coolness of the station. The reception was large and whitewashed. The duty officer stood behind a well-worn oak counter; he was deep in conversation with a colleague and didn't look up when the cops brought James inside. In the waiting area opposite, people sat slumped, listless; some eyed the new arrival. James ignored them, and continued to survey his surroundings. A tiled corridor led off towards a T-junction . . .

Suddenly, from the left, a woman in black appeared, her features hidden by a lace veil, the battered strongbox in her hands. James quickly turned his back, stepping behind his arresting officer. *She's got the money and she's walking away*, he thought grimly, *while I'm the one who'll wind up behind bars—*

All at once there was a cry of horror from a girl in the waiting area, sparking further screams and exclamations. James turned to see why – and froze.

A policeman was staggering up the corridor towards them. His face looked raw, as if the skin were peeling away, and his hands were a mass of blisters; he held them out in front of him as if he were blind or sleepwalking, and his breaths came with a hoarse, bubbling rasp. His red eyes were wide with fear and wept bloody tears; James detected the sickly stink of putrefaction as he approached.

James felt sick. *What's happened? What's wrong with him?*

The cops who'd arrested him turned to their colleague in shock, and the waiting people backed away. The duty officer shouted and pointed. 'L-Luis,' Spectacles stammered, hands held up to his advancing colleague. '*Vuelve la cama . . .*'

Luis didn't hear; he suddenly lurched forward and stumbled

into the counter, his hands bleeding freely now. The duty officer recoiled with a shout. There were more screams as everyone surged for the exit. Once they were through, Spectacles slammed the heavy door shut and bolted it behind them. Luis fell to the floor; his body had gone into spasm, and the stench of rotting flesh was overpowering. Half-formed words fell from his lips in a red foam.

Overlooked in the sudden crisis, James slipped away down the corridor. He wanted to see where La Velada had been. He soon came to an open door, and smelled putrefaction. Bracing himself, he looked inside.

Another policeman lay on a stretcher on the floor, his head held at an unnatural angle, blood and spittle coating his twisted face. He was dead.

James recognized the man. He'd seen him last night, dancing and laughing with his fellow officers in the headlights of the patrol car, waving the banknotes. *Here's your reward for telling Scolopendra you recovered his property, boys.*

But why? What had these men done to earn such retribution? Thoughts whirled around James's head: La Velada – had she done this somehow – and if so, why? At the casino she'd injected MacLean with some experimental drug; had she been testing something on these men here? *La Velada said that Hardiman was supposed to finish a cure*, James remembered. Was this some kind of test? A test that had failed . . . ?

He was about to turn and run on down the corridor when, over the noise from reception, he heard a commotion some-where up ahead – a challenge in Spanish, then a hollow thump, like a rock striking the wall.

'Get me out of here!' came a shout in English that sparked

flashbacks to last night. 'What the hell is happening?'

'The diver . . .' James breathed, his mind racing. The expert with the latest diving technology who'd reclaimed the strongbox – and who'd nearly killed James on the beach. The same police officers must have found the wounded diver and brought him here to the cells. Could that be the purpose of these gruesome deaths – a deadly distraction, under cover of which La Velada could get the man out? *But if the police are in Scolopendra's pocket*, James reasoned, *surely they'd release the man without charge?*

The diver had fallen silent now. He'd sounded so desperate . . . or delirious, perhaps . . .

James's thoughts were interrupted by the approach of heavy footsteps. He quickly ducked back into the office and peered through the gap between door and doorjamb.

El Puño was approaching with a large petrol can.

James looked down at his cuffed hands, and knew with certain horror that if he was discovered now, he wouldn't stand a chance.

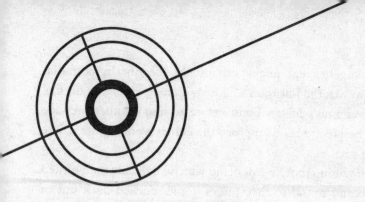

22
Unfinished Business

James held his breath as El Puño barged into the office, upended the petrol can and doused the corpse in fuel. He splashed it over the desk, the walls and floor. Then he put down the can and pulled a couple of what looked like metal pineapples from his jacket pocket. He placed one on the dead cop's belly and one beside the door.

Hand grenades, James realized with a shudder. Whatever the motive for this attack, with the strongbox back in Scolopendra's hands and the poisoned bodies burned and blown to bits, no evidence would survive.

He tensed as El Puño pulled a Colt Police Positive Special from the dead officer's shoulder holster and strode out into the corridor towards the reception. There were more screams, silenced by two gunshots. Spectacles shouted what might have been a cry for help. James heard the whump of shattering stone and wood. Then silence.

Shaken, he crept quickly out into the corridor. In reception, El Puño was the last man standing, already emptying his fuel can over Luis's lifeless body before tossing another grenade down beside it; James supposed the flames would ignite it, like a time fuse.

As if sensing that he was being watched, the big man turned and swung round to face James. James ducked back out of sight, but he wasn't quick enough. Without hesitation, El Puño raised his great fist and started to charge.

A surge of adrenalin sent James sprinting down the corridor. He splashed through puddles of petrol, burst through a loose-hinged door, swung round to the right – and then stumbled over the body of another policeman. James went sprawling; the cuffs cut into his wrists as he struggled to his feet.

Pounding footsteps told him that El Puño was fast approaching.

What if I charge straight into La Velada? James thought. It couldn't be helped. Running on, he reached the cells – a row of cement cubicles with rusting metal bars running from dirty floor to cracked ceiling. All were empty, but in one there were signs of a struggle – a dirty plate broken, a pail of water kicked over, the cell door wide open.

He pressed on, passing a small canteen with coffee urns and a gas stove that had been left on. The smell of gas was overpowering; at the slightest spark, the whole place would become an inferno.

Every instinct screamed, *Get out!* There had to be a back exit, an escape route for El Puño when he blew this place to kingdom come. James stumbled upon it almost immediately

– a locker room with a battered door in the wall opposite. A small glass panel above it let in sunlight.

There, slumped on the floor, was the diver. His leg had been neatly bandaged, but he was unconscious, a trail of blood seeping from a lump on his temple.

Then the diver can't be Scolopendra's man, James realized. *Not if he's being taken by force.*

He tried the door. It was locked. El Puño – or La Velada – must have the key. But he had run out of time: heavy footsteps were approaching.

The wooden lockers weren't large, but James managed to quickly wedge himself inside one, face jammed up to his knees, arms over his legs. The door was warped so he could only pull it to; he felt horribly vulnerable.

Through the gap, James saw El Puño step into the room, peering around like a bogeyman from a child's story, his chipped stone fist raised. He stepped closer to James's locker.

Then the diver stirred weakly. El Puño turned towards him. James couldn't see any more, but heard a dull crack, and the turn of a key in the lock. The door creaked open, and misshapen shadows showed as a slant of sunlight swept into the room.

He's gone, James thought breathlessly, *and taken the diver with him*.

Almost as an afterthought, another grenade was tossed in from outside. It rolled into the corridor, closer to the gas stove.

James imagined the initial explosion, then the fierce rush of flames as the gasoline on the floor ignited, a further blast as the gas from the stove went up. Would the locker act as a shield or become his coffin . . . ?

He couldn't chance it. James burst out, hitting the floor hard, then launched himself towards the door. The fuse wouldn't burn for more than a few seconds . . . He flung the door open, found himself in the station yard—

The air shifted around him with the suck and punch of the explosion: behind him, doors and windows shattered in a blast that threw him off his feet and into a pile of garbage. The only sound was a high-pitched whine in his ears and he stared, thoughts tangled in shock. The police station was ablaze. Everyone trapped inside . . .

James rolled over, got painfully to his feet. Thick smoke pumped out from inside the station. Crouching, breath held, eyes streaming, James glimpsed a cop crawling across the blackened, ravaged locker room.

Swearing, he forced himself back inside. The heat was intense – he could hardly breathe. Retching and choking, he managed to drag the cop outside and laid him down on his back. The man looked up through broken spectacles, shivering with shock, and James saw that it was the cop who'd arrested him.

He sorted through the man's keyring for the one to his handcuffs. Shouts now pierced through the ringing in his ears as people began to gather in the street beyond the yard. Coughing, eyes stinging, James finally found the right key and the cuffs sprang open. He jumped up, massaging his wrists, and called for help – one of the few Spanish phrases he knew: '¡Ayuadame!' Two men came running into the yard, and James helped them move the policeman to safer ground.

Please let him live, James thought. *He can identify El Puño as* his attacker – and confirm that *La Velada came for the strongbox.* Then, there would be a proven trail leading from the murder and violence back to Scolopendra; surely the authorities, however corrupt, would have to move against him then . . .

My case against you's building, Scolopendra.

James wiped soot and sweat off his face and started to walk away. But almost immediately his legs buckled, his balance thrown by the blast. He shook his head, trying to clear it – then fell to his knees as the ground shook and another explosion came from the front of the building. *Those grenades must have detonated,* James supposed. He looked around. The fire had provided a smokescreen for El Puño: leaving the burning precinct house with the diver slung over his shoulder, he must've seemed like one more rescuer carrying a survivor to safety . . . Presumably La Velada, having made her discreet exit with the strongbox, had already been picked up by one of Scolopendra's team. But just what had she done to those poor policemen – and why?

Ahead of him, James saw fire-fighting volunteers cordoning off the street so that their colleagues could cross the road to the canal for water to throw on the blaze.

A canal's convenient, he thought – *a direct route to the harbour.* Chances were, Scolopendra wouldn't set sail until his collection had been made. There might still be time to reach the harbour, find Hugo and sneak aboard . . .

Crossing the road to the canal, James saw a sort of gondola approaching on the water. '¡*Ayuadame!*' He waved frantically to the elderly ferryman, pointed to the blazing police building, then to himself. 'Harbour? How do I say it? *Surgidero de Batabano* . . . ?'

Perhaps it was the desperation in James's eyes or his dishevelled air that made the boatman take pity on him. James clambered into the gondola, and sat down next to sides of raw meat that were thick with flies. The man rowed away, firing words at James. '¿Papá? ¿Madre? ¿En el puerto?'

'Yes, I'm meeting them there,' James lied. It was easier. He sat there, his head pounding, lungs burning.

It took perhaps ten minutes before the canal emerged in the busy harbour, where the air tasted of fish and bitumen. Here wooden jetties stuck out from the waterside like long boarded tongues; the sail-lines of the boats moored there pierced the bright blue of the near-noon sky. On the horizon he saw skiffs and steamers and sponge-fishing boats. It took his scattered senses a while to absorb the jigsaw of masts, sprits and sails as he hunted for any sign of Scolopendra or his men, and for Hugo.

The old man steered into a narrow space between fishing boats and helped James onto the wooden jetty. James waved goodbye and hurried along the wide wooden decking that edged the harbour. He was glad of the crowded moorings – they offered cover as he searched for—

'Hugo!' James saw him loitering near a group of men loading sacks of coffee onto a skiff.

'Thank God you made it.' Hugo scurried over, looked him up and down. 'People have been talking about a big fire in town – explosions at the police station. I—' James opened his mouth to answer, but Hugo jumped back in: 'Oh God, it was you, wasn't it? I'll lay odds it was all down to you—'

'Have you found Scolopendra's boat?' James broke in.

'Hard to miss, with Ramón keeping watch outside. El

Puño showed up here a while back, carrying a man who looked decidedly un-shipshape.'

James nodded. 'The diver. He'd been locked up in the station.'

'The station! Explosions and fire!' Hugo groaned. 'I *knew* it was down to you!'

James quickly filled him in on all that had happened.

'So Scolopendra's "great task", and Hardiman's work on a cure, could be linked to the state of those poor policemen,' Hugo mused.

'Their bodies just . . . fell apart.' James shuddered. 'The thought of there being no cure for whatever did that scares the hell out of me.'

'But to kill them in public and then destroy the whole building . . . Why take the risk?' Hugo shook his head. 'It's hardly the most discreet of scientific tests.'

'The policemen who were affected were the ones who found the strongbox last night,' James told him. 'Well, two of them, anyway. The third one—' He broke off, remembering. 'The third one didn't touch the banknotes. The other two did.'

Hugo looked at him uneasily. 'We said that a box of dollar bills was a curious thing to steal from a lab.'

'Unless there was something very special about them . . .' James stared down at him. '*My God*, Hugo. La Velada didn't do that to the officers. I reckon the *banknotes* did. The policemen who touched them were poisoned somehow.'

'So our veiled lady and El Puño went to pick up the notes and destroy all trace of what happened?' Hugo thought it over and nodded slowly. 'Fantastic . . . but it makes a lot of sense.'

'And now they're taking the stuff back to Scolopendra's lair.' James felt himself flushing. 'It's all my fault. If I hadn't dropped that strongbox, let the police get hold of it—'

'Then both you and Jagua would be dead by now,' Hugo pointed out, 'and probably me too. Let's be thankful for small mercies.'

James was not in the mood for reflection. 'Show me Scolopendra's boat,' he said, hurrying Hugo along the quayside. 'There may still be a chance to get aboard.'

'Getting poisoned might be a kinder way to go after all.' Hugo led the way through the crowds for perhaps thirty yards. 'Well, thar she blows.' He pointed out a smart, twin-screw motor yacht, painted white and blue, moored at a private jetty. On the side, in fancy lettering, was written *Estrella de Jagua*. 'Ramón's not on guard any more . . .'

James shook his head as a crewmember appeared and tugged at the mooring rope. 'That's because they're leaving. There's not a damn thing we can do.'

'*Something* you can do . . .' James jerked round at the sound of the familiar sneering voice. 'You let us settle scores.'

Ramón had come up behind them, his distorted smile self-satisfied. Beside him stood La Velada, her miniature Derringer pressed discreetly – so very discreetly – to Hugo's throat.

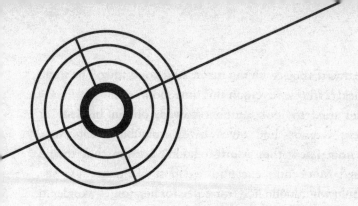

23

A Tour of the Works

Ramón forced James forward along the dockside while, a few yards ahead of them, La Velada held her pistol to the back of Hugo's neck as they walked. James knew he couldn't make a break for it now; couldn't step out of line. Not unless he wanted to see his friend killed.

'El Puño say you dead, boy,' Ramón hissed.

James shrugged. 'He was wrong.'

'No. He just telling future.' Ramón leaned forward, whispered in his ear. 'Say nothing that you saw me in room at casino.'

'When we knocked you out, you mean?'

'You look for Hardiman, I know. But you not find, so you go snooping till chased away.'

James longed to say, *Actually we were hiding under the bed watching everything you did.*

'So, listen.' Ramón leaned closer. 'Say one thing, I will put out the dwarf's eyes with my razor. And yours too.' The smile was back. 'No one save you this time, boy.'

James tried to look suitably cowed, but in his fear of discovery Ramón had given away valuable intelligence. James now knew that Maritsa hadn't let slip that they'd witnessed MacLean's execution – most likely because she knew only what Jagua had translated for her. James wondered how he might best use this knowledge to blackmail Ramón, or to intimidate Scolopendra.

They caught up with La Velada and Hugo at a quieter jetty; moored there was Jagua's stolen runabout – the one they'd taken to the wreck.

'So that's why you're not on board Scolopendra's yacht with the others,' James realized. 'Taking the boss's boat back?'

'I thought this would be a good opportunity to talk.' La Velada motioned for Hugo to climb into the stern, and sat beside him, her gun poking at his ribs. 'We saw the dwarf trying to spy – such anguish on his little face . . . I thought I would have to take him alone. Your survival, Bond, is a bonus.'

James made no reply as Ramón forced him aboard, cast off, and sat next to him behind the wheel.

'No tricks, now,' La Velada said quietly. 'No calls for help. Or I will have to kill you both.'

'Why haven't you already?' James wondered. 'We're no use to you.'

'I disagree.'

Hugo stayed very still. 'Where are we going?'

'To the heart of things,' she said.

Ramón reversed slowly into the busy harbour. At any other time James might've enjoyed the thrill of the ride. As it was, he felt bone weary, wet with sweat from exertion and now fear, the sun's glare and the thrum of the engine doing little to help a growing headache.

The shipping soon thinned out, and the bustle of Batabano was left behind. Now there was just the roll and swell of the waves, and on the horizon the low-lying Cuban cays rising out of the sea.

La Velada was looking at James. It was unsettling, not being able to see her face. 'Why do you wear that thing?' he asked bluntly.

'Perhaps as a mark of mourning for fallen comrades . . . Perhaps I am terribly disfigured . . . or so famous I would be recognized anywhere I go.' She leaned forward. 'There is a power in anonymity, Bond. My nationality, my loyalties, even my expression . . . all my secrets are my own until I choose to share them.' She paused. 'Now, then. You have known Hardiman a long time.'

'Did Maritsa tell you that?'

La Velada said nothing, just looked at him.

'Hardiman's a friend of my aunt's,' James said; he had no veil, but wore his best poker face. 'He's looking after us until she gets here in a couple of days. She's been delayed on a dig in Mexico.'

'How boring for you all.' La Velada tilted her head to one side. 'I think Dr Hardiman is glad to have you here, Bond. He is very fond of you.'

'Did he say so? That's nice.'

'And you are fond of him. You broke into the penthouse

because you hoped to find him there, I think.' She nodded thoughtfully. 'You risked your life.'

'And you nearly took it.' Tired of deflecting questions, James decided to go on the offensive. 'Why are you so worried about Hardiman? Because you need him to find a cure for the poison you put on those banknotes?'

La Velada regarded him for a while before answering, and James wished he could see her face. 'Is that what Hardiman told you?'

'He didn't tell me anything,' he said quickly. 'I know about the notes because I took the strongbox from the sunken ship.'

'Ah, yes.' She sounded amused. 'You and dear, sweet Jagua beat the American diver to it.'

'He's on Scolopendra's yacht now, I suppose?'

La Velada ignored him. 'Maritsa told us how you took the underwater equipment from the lock-up. What a resourceful team the four of you were.'

Were. Past tense. James looked at her. 'Why would you poison money?'

'Don't you know?' she said evenly.

'To kill people, risk-free?' he suggested. 'You can send it through the post, or leave it somewhere you know it will be found. It's easier to deliver than a sniper's bullet.'

Again La Velada seemed amused. 'What colourful books you must have read, Bond.'

James was tired of being patronized and decided to try a bluff. 'You *haven't* got rid of all the evidence, you know. I found one of the banknotes at the police station and hid it.'

La Velada shook her head. 'You did not.'

'Let Hardiman go . . . and Jagua . . . and I'll tell you where it is.'

'That's a child's stratagem, Bond. You are not a child. Do you imagine we would not ensure that each bill was accounted for?' She sat back in her seat beside Hugo. 'The interview is ended. For now.'

For his part, James tried to appear relaxed and confident. He gave Hugo what he hoped was a reassuring smile.

Hugo could only stare back, ashen-faced.

A stiff breeze was blowing and the sea was choppier than the night before. More tiny islands peppered the horizon. The boat passed close to one, a dot of white sandy shore and sickly-looking palms. Next to a small wooden jetty was a large sign for Scolopendra Industries and some words in Spanish.

'*Reserva Natural y Centro de Investigación*,' Hugo read slowly. 'Wildlife sanctuary and research centre.' His attention turned to the placards planted in the beach. '*Riesgo de contaminación . . . ?*' He looked sharply at James. 'This is a quarantined area, no entry.'

'Keep boats away,' Ramón said.

'Looks like someone came here.' James saw that the buildings behind the signs were blackened ruins, razed to the ground. 'All evidence destroyed again – is that it?'

'The research has been completed,' said La Velada. 'And the fruits of that research will soon be harvested.'

James watched the ruins dwindling, and felt strangely uneasy. There was something mournful and sinister about the place.

Abruptly, La Velada addressed Ramón in Spanish. He held up his index finger in reply.

'One hour till we reach the shipyard,' Hugo explained.

James raised an eyebrow. 'I thought we were going to Scolopendra's estate . . .'

'The head of shipyard operations has unexpectedly left Scolopendra Industries,' said La Velada. 'I must oversee the final preparations for this project myself.'

Hugo caught James's eye. '*Chester MacLean?*' he mouthed.

James nodded a fraction, kept his face neutral. 'Final preparations?' he said out loud.

'This particular business venture has been a long time in the planning,' she said calmly. 'And, as I said, the harvest will soon be gathered.'

The shipyard was built into a natural harbour, a cove cut into Cuba's Isla de Pinos by millions of years of storms and tides. James had expected it to be the heart of Scolopendra's timber operation, a bustling place with traffic coming and going. But as they skirted the coast, he saw few signs of industry. Silent mechanical diggers and lifting equipment stood motionless like strange dinosaurs, and the sprawling sawmill was deserted.

Instead, the workers were dotted about a vast floating island of logs, projecting from the shore like an arrow aimed across the Caribbean. James marvelled at the sight: acres of timber, the logs held together by thick lengths of chain and attached to a powerful tugboat. Makeshift tyres protected the tug's white hull from damage; ropes dangled down from each tyre, trailing in the water.

'The log raft.' He glanced at La Velada. 'I saw the plans in Scolopendra's penthouse.'

'A standard way of transporting timber internationally,

isn't it?' Hugo observed. 'I'm surprised the big boss would concern himself with the plans . . .'

'Or that his girlfriend would come all the way out here just to inspect the real thing.' James watched some of the workmen lashing large crates to the top of the raft. 'What are you really doing here?' he asked La Velada.

'What I must,' she replied simply. 'I must be sure we have the right things on board for the work ahead.'

Through the woman's veil, James thought he glimpsed a deep-red smile.

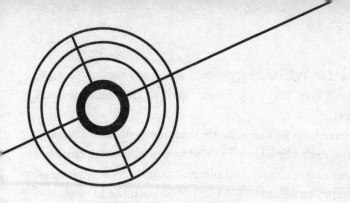

24

The Lair of Scolopendra

While La Velada went about her business on the log raft, Ramón forced James and Hugo into a seaplane moored outside the harbour building. It was a Consolidated Commodore Model 16, and it made a far more comfortable prison than the runabout. It was warm and protected from the elements. Each passenger compartment had its own windows, with seats upholstered in pastel fabric and armrests of polished mahogany.

'All the comforts of home, eh?' said Hugo. 'Apart from him.' He nodded at Ramón, who was covering them with the Derringer.

James noticed some papers on the floor, covered in an inky scrawl. 'Is that Jagua's writing?'

'Looks like it. It's her father's plane, after all.' Hugo leaned forward, but Ramón jabbed the gun at him, warning him back.

When La Velada reappeared, she had a pilot in tow, and soon James felt his stomach lurch as the seaplane took to the air.

He peered out of the window and saw propellers blurring. Below the streamlined landing sled was an untamed, trackless world. A solitary town stood out amongst the vast expanse of green shapes and shadows, while to the west, the logging had carved great scars into the coast. The bare discs of tree stumps stared up like a thousand dead eyes.

James remembered the last time he'd been on a plane, coming in to land over the tobacco fields of Cuba's tiny airport. He'd felt so free. Now here he was, a prisoner. But he wasn't about to give up. *A chance to escape will present itself*, he decided. *The game's not over yet.*

A change in the engines' note stirred him from his thoughts. The plane descended steadily, turning in a wide circle. Now he could see the tops of individual trees . . . as well as something manmade.

Hugo squinted. 'What's that?'

James looked down on a huge building that rose from the trees like a palace. It was modern in design: sharp edges and whitewashed walls, with more supporting pillars than a three-tiered wedding cake. A dense tree canopy shielded the surrounding gardens from view; it came as no surprise to James that Scolopendra valued privacy. It was as if some elegant Hollywood estate had been transplanted to the jungle and hidden from the world; a secret dream made reality where you least expected it.

Winding through the trees was a river, which came up to meet them as they landed. The Commodore skimmed the surface like a dragonfly, and James heard the engines throttle right back, the drag of the water acting as a natural brake.

Ramón got up and gestured with the gun that James and Hugo should do the same. The seaplane ploughed through the glistening water until it reached a long, finely crafted jetty. Through the window, James surveyed the lie of the land. A paved track led up a gentle slope to a road, where two bright red roadsters waited. If they could hijack one of the automobiles, perhaps he and Hugo might make it to that town.

But no – of course, the only roads would run through Scolopendra's estate; the township had to be tens of miles from here. He and Hugo had no supplies, only the clothes they stood in. Even if they could make it away, they wouldn't make it far.

They had to go through the cockpit to reach the exit doors. La Velada was in the co-pilot's seat, adjusting her veil. 'Scolopendra is expecting you,' she said coolly. 'In the main laboratory.'

James and Hugo were marched up the slope and pushed into the back of one of the roadsters. Ramón watched them as their chauffeur drove along a winding path into dense forest.

Ten minutes later, the car stopped at a set of sturdy gates, gleaming bronze in the dappled light. Peering through the foliage, James saw that a high chain-link fence topped with rolls of barbed wire extended on each side. A muscular guard opened the gates and they continued over a humpbacked bridge across a fast-flowing stream. Then, to his surprise, he saw a rustic stone building built right across the stream; a

213

waterwheel turned busily, churning the water down the channel towards them. It looked like it belonged in the English countryside, not the tropics.

'It's some sort of mill,' James observed.

'Perhaps they make their own bread there,' said Hugo.

Ramón scoffed and rubbed his stomach sarcastically; a reminder to James that he hadn't eaten for an age.

The road wound onward through the grounds of the estate. High above them was a canopy of camouflaging foliage, shielding the grounds from aerial view. Bizarre ornamental streetlamps shed a flat, unnatural light, casting strange shadows over the long grass and swampland, the miniature desert and wooded areas, all teeming with life. James glimpsed tiny frogs, large lizards and spiders, birds with bright plumage; none were native to Cuba, he thought. Although carefully cultivated, these grounds looked authentic: different land-scapes in miniature, captured and contained beneath the canopy. Scolopendra's dominion over nature.

The vehicle slowed as it reached a large brick building shaped like a cross with a dark wooden roof.

'X marks the spot,' said Hugo as they parked beside two more cherry-red roadsters. A figure in a thick rubber suit with protective gauntlets and headwear came out of the door, held up a hand to Ramón and the pilot, then went back inside.

James felt apprehension shift in his stomach like a solid thing. 'I suppose this must be the main lab.'

'Been nice knowing you,' Hugo joked, with fear in his eyes.

'We'll be all right.' Even as the words left his lips, James knew how hollow they sounded. 'I'm . . . sorry, Hugo. I know it's my fault we're here.'

His friend forced a rueful smile. 'You'll be hearing from my solicitors.'

Ramón gestured for James and Hugo to get out of the car. Then the door to the lab swung open again.

Scolopendra filled the doorway. It was James's first proper look at the man. He found himself standing that bit straighter – a reaction to the sheer physical presence before him. Scolopendra's long hair was swept back from the proud face. A black silk kimono emphasized the powerful contours of his body, while his burning eyes suggested a different, deeper kind of strength.

'Well, well.' Scolopendra studied his guests. 'James Bond and Hugo Grande, at last. I took possession of your belongings from Hardiman's apartment.' He laughed suddenly. 'Now I have possession of you too.'

James folded his arms, said nothing, while Hugo stuck his hands in his pockets.

'Do come inside, gentlemen,' Scolopendra went on. 'With Dr Hardiman and my daughter, it should be quite the reunion.'

Ramón motioned for them to follow Scolopendra into the lab. It was cool inside, the thick stone walls painted a clinical white, so the red-on-black claw design stood out all the more boldly.

With every step, James grew more uneasy. Scolopendra opened a wooden door that gave onto another, made of metal. It opened with a hiss. *Airtight seal*, James thought warily. He smelled disinfectant, and a more sinister note beneath: the stink of a sick ward.

He looked around the room they'd entered. Three of the walls were covered with white tiles, with what appeared to be air vents near the top, while ahead of him was a large glass inspection window. James felt a jolt at the sight of Gerald Hardiman, still in his crumpled linen suit, standing behind a long steel cabinet on the other side.

'Dr Hardiman!' James ran forward, heart pounding. 'You're all right?'

'Oh, James, my boy.' Hardiman's voice sounded tinny through the loudspeakers mounted high on the right-hand wall of the room. His smile was strained and he looked pale and tired. 'My dear boy. Why didn't you stay away from all this?'

Another face appeared next to Hardiman's, and it was Hugo's turn to run to the window. 'My God, Jagua, we've been so worried. You've not been hurt?'

She shook her head, touched the glass. Hugo raised his hand to meet hers.

As he watched Jagua and Hardiman through the glass, James suddenly had the feeling that some horrible experiment was about to be performed. 'Why have you been put in there?' he asked.

'James!' Hugo's eyes grew wide. '*They're* the ones looking in on *us* . . .'

'What?' James spun round as Scolopendra left the room, pulling the door shut behind him, sealing them inside. He took in the vents in the tiled wall, the stink of disinfectant, and realized with a sinking heart that Hugo was right. This was some kind of special laboratory – and *they* were the ones being studied.

Scolopendra reappeared on the other side of the glass wall and spoke, the words distorted by the speakers.

'There's no need to be alarmed. Not yet.' James saw that he was tossing his silver dollar up in the air and catching it again. 'The two of you seem determined to take my daughter's affections away from her father.'

'Affections!' Jagua did not look at him. 'For you?' She appeared to be in control, but James spotted a faint tremor in her eyelids.

'To disrupt my business is one thing, but to interfere with my personal affairs . . .' Scolopendra shook his head. 'I cannot tolerate this.'

'For God's sake, let them go,' Hardiman said. 'You've got me. Aren't I doing what you want now?'

'No, Dr Hardiman.' La Velada now appeared in the inspection chamber. 'I believe you are stalling. In the hope of rescue, perhaps?'

'Rescue?' Hardiman gestured to James and Hugo. 'By children?'

'No, Gerald.' Scolopendra gazed at him steadily. 'By whoever has already paid you several hundred dollars for detailed information on the layout of my laboratory.'

'I don't know what you mean—'

'*You're lying!*' The words exploded from Scolopendra's mouth. He flipped the coin faster. 'Should I give you to Ramón? He will extract the truth from you, as a backstreet dentist pulls teeth – painfully, and with much blood.'

'You should give him to *me*,' La Velada said softly. 'My techniques will get the truth from the American diver – and from Hardiman too.'

'Toss a coin for who gets me, if you like.' Hardiman shook his head, pinched the bridge of his nose. 'But you can't hurt me before I've found a way to make your precious cure viable in a suspension of—'

'*Don't tell me what I can or cannot do.*' Scolopendra's whisper curled out of the speakers like smoke on a dragon's breath. His face remained deathly calm. 'What I know is this: when truth is beaten from a soft man like you, it comes out sloppy. A half-truth here, to buy time. A part-confession, to stop the pain. Well, I need to know everything. I need to know it *now*.'

'Please, Father,' said Jagua, 'don't do this. Don't be this person.'

'This *person*?' He rounded on her. 'I am your father!'

'You are *her* lapdog!' Jagua stabbed a finger at La Velada. 'You think she respects you? She has trained you, like an animal!'

Lashing out, Scolopendra slapped her face with the back of his hand. Jagua was thrown against the thick glass, a trickle of blood edging from her nostril.

'Leave her alone!' James shouted as Hugo watched helplessly, wringing his hands.

Scolopendra ignored them, turned to face La Velada, rubbing the silver dollar between thumb and forefinger.

'This is how she repays you for all you do for her, my love.' La Velada's voice was soothing. 'A jealous child spits venom like a serpent. You have greater priorities than her now, and she resents that. She must learn her place.'

Hugo shouted, 'You make her sound like an animal!'

'You can teach me nothing, Father.' Jagua wiped her

bloody nose with the back of her hand. 'You will have to kill me. Or else I will kill you.'

'Or perhaps you'll make young Bond here kill for you, huh?' Scolopendra turned back to James as if sizing him up. 'Yes, he will kill – and kill well, I think . . . He has the fire to fight in him.'

'I . . . I'd fight for her too.' Hugo was trembling. 'I'm not very good, but I would.' He swallowed hard. 'How dare you treat her like this!'

'Well, well.' Scolopendra grinned. 'So many champions, Jagua. From the head of the pack to the runt of the litter, they line up to protect you from your wicked father.' He flipped his silver dollar again, only this time he looked at the outcome, and laughed. 'You know, boys, here in my grounds I keep many rare animals whose biological make-up may one day benefit science, and I breed more in my laboratories. Often, the very smallest can be of the greatest interest.'

'I've always thought so.' Hugo's voice was barely audible.

'Have you heard of *Dermatophria hominis*?' asked Scolopendra.

James glanced uneasily at Hugo. 'No.'

'It is a species of parasite I discovered in Venezuela. A relative of the botfly, it attacks human beings.' Scolopendra paced slowly along the window. 'The flies lay eggs in animal skin. Body heat induces hatching upon contact. The larvae burrow into the skin. They feed on the flesh underneath, and grow fat as they poison their hosts . . . Large numbers will undoubtedly kill.'

'James?' Hugo looked appalled.

'He's bluffing.' James tried to keep calm. 'Just trying to scare us.'

'I have bred these flies specially.' Scolopendra turned to Hardiman. 'If you will not answer my questions, I will release thousands of *Dermatophria hominis* into the lab. They will be drawn straight to the boys and lay eggs in their exposed skin.'

'You cannot do this!' Jagua shouted.

He held up his huge palm to silence her. 'Once more, Dr Hardiman: who organized the raid on my facilities here?'

Hardiman's voice rose angrily. 'I've told you a hundred times – *I don't know!*'

'Too many people know too much of our business. Who have you told about the operation?'

'No one! Can't this diver you've dredged up tell you anything?'

'He has resisted initial questioning,' La Velada said. 'He has received professional training.'

'For the last time,' Scolopendra went on, 'who was running Sarila Karatan?'

'I can't help you!' Hardiman shouted.

'Then I cannot help *them*!' Scolopendra banged his fist against the glass partition, glaring at James and Hugo. '*¡Se me está agotando la paciencia!* I warned you what would happen if you lied.' He dragged Hardiman over to a bank of controls, forced his hand onto a lever.

'Father, no!' Jagua cried.

There was no reprieve. Hardiman yelled as he was made to slide the lever home. James held his breath at the metallic clang that came from the vents; moments later, a thick cloud of brown flies – hundreds and hundreds of them, the size of honeybees – exploded into the lab.

James cried out in disgust, swatting the flies helplessly as they swarmed around him. He ducked down and curled into a ball, his skin already a seething mass of botflies. Rolling around to try and crush the insects, he felt them crawling into his ears and nose, brushing at his eyes and lips, as Hugo began to scream.

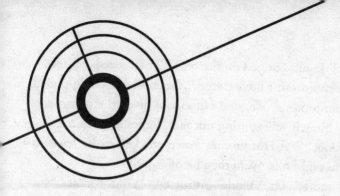

25
Confessions

Hugo's cries were drowned by a piercing whistle of feed-back from the speakers. 'All right!' James heard Hardiman bellow. 'Yes, I talked. I told the CIP all I knew about your plans. Now, for God's sake, get the boys out of there!'

CIP? The word echoed uselessly through James's mind. He couldn't think, couldn't breathe; the flies were every-where . . .

Then the metal door hissed open and the man in the protective suit ran in with what looked like a yellow fire extinguisher. A foul-smelling thick white smoke poured out, and the flies dropped to the floor and lay still. James retched, his nose running as he spat out botfly carcasses. A rubber mask was pressed to his nose and mouth, and James glimpsed a white cylinder behind it. Pure oxygen? Head spinning, nausea tightening his throat, he suddenly found that he could breathe again.

'Hugo!' Jagua banged on the glass. 'Hugo needs air too.'

Scolopendra must have agreed; the mask was duly pulled away from James's face, and Hugo was given the treatment. Hugging himself, still spitting out flies, James drew in air.

'The boys . . .' Hardiman's voice cracked as he tried to control his emotions. 'Will they be all right?'

'Talk more,' La Velada instructed. 'Your tongue was clearly loose enough for the Corps of Intelligence Police.'

Of course, James realized. *The CIP – America's foreign intelligence service.* He pushed himself up onto his elbows and looked through the glass.

'A CIP agent approached me,' Hardiman said miserably; 'wanted to know how to get into your laboratories.'

'What was the agent's name?' asked La Velada.

'Valentine Barbey. He had a sister who worked at one of the research centres. A girl you killed in your poison trials, right there on the other side of this glass. But Barbey didn't buy your "tragically lost at sea" excuses and started looking into things more closely.'

James thought back to the ruined remains of the research centre; to the broken, bloody bodies at the police station in Batabano. *Yes*, he thought. *All evidence destroyed once again.* How many other research centres had been used in experiments? How many more lives lost?

'How did they know about the money?' Scolopendra said quietly.

'I don't know. They were talking to Chester MacLean at the shipyard too – perhaps he knew something . . . ?'

He did, James thought grimly.

'So Sarila Karatan stole from the lab on CIP orders?' La

Velada said. 'And when she failed to deliver the strongbox . . . Valentine Barbey got a specialist dive team to reclaim the samples.'

James turned as Hugo groaned and rolled over, shedding dead botflies, brought back hard to his own dismal situation. Then Hardiman spoke again.

'I don't know anything else,' he insisted. 'Now for God's sake, you must get treatment for James and Hugo.'

'Must I?' Scolopendra scoffed. 'As a matter of fact, that species of botfly is harmful only to sheep, not meddling little boys. The most valuable specimens in my private collection have been temporarily rehoused at the university labs in Havana.'

James almost wept with relief. He caught hold of Hugo's wrist. 'You . . . all right?'

'Think so, James.' Hugo squeezed his forearm in relief. 'It . . . it was being called a meddling little boy that really hurt.'

As he spoke, something clicked into place in James's head. According to Hugo, the CIP divers had shouted, 'Murderers!' before opening fire. Of course – Jagua's motorboat was marked with the red claw; in the dark, the divers must have thought they were Scolopendra's guards, perhaps the very ones who had killed Sarila . . .

Almost killed by the good guys. James shook his head at the irony. What a bloody mess this affair had been! If he and Jagua hadn't risked their lives on the dive, the strongbox would be in the hands of the CIP by now – giving them the evidence they needed to bring down Scolopendra and his woman. Instead . . .

Scolopendra had turned back to Hardiman. 'We are close to pulling off the biggest deal in the world. The largest headline in history. And now, at the last minute, thanks to *you*—'

'The CIP don't have evidence,' La Velada told him, 'so they can't move against you.'

Scolopendra looked unconvinced, but then the conversation switched abruptly to Spanish – and James could no longer follow it. As La Velada took the big man's hand and spoke reassuringly, James saw Jagua staring at them, while Hardiman looked helplessly at the floor.

The telephone transcripts! James wanted to yell. *Show your father; drive a wedge between them . . .*

Perhaps she already had, and to no effect. James felt a sense of despair. Perhaps, all told, it was too late to do anything now.

Scolopendra beat his fist on the glass again. '*Bueno, sácalos de ahí.*'

The man in the protective suit came over and pressed the rubber mask to James's face. James gulped greedily at the oxygen . . . Too late he realized that the white canister had been swapped for one that was red – and that the world was turning black . . .

James woke on a soft, narrow bed feeling surprisingly refreshed. For a few blissful moments he thought he was safe in Hardiman's apartment, that Aunt Charmian would be arriving any moment, and that everything would be back to normal.

Then he caught a faint tang of chemicals and remembered

the smothering flies. He jumped up, felt the tiles under his bare feet, stumbled against another bed.

He coughed, his throat dry; the room was oppressively warm. So much for his dream of safety. Charmian's arrival was still two days off, and when she finally did reach Cuba, she would find no trace of Hardiman – apart from the wreath on the kitchen table . . . James couldn't bear to think of it.

On the other bed, Hugo stirred, his eyes opening sleepily. 'Who's there . . . ?'

'Only me, I'm afraid.'

'Well, well, James. Back in the land of the living, are we?' He sat up and rubbed his hair. 'Or rather, the land of the won't-be-living-much-longer.'

'Don't say that. There's got to be a way out.' James looked around. 'Starting with this place.'

They were in a sparsely furnished room: twin beds separated by a chest of drawers, a small round table, a chair and a wardrobe. Saloon doors led to a dressing room and en suite bathroom.

How long had they been asleep? It was night; a clock on the chest of drawers read eight-fifteen. James tried the handles of the French windows that looked out over floodlit tropical grounds, but they were locked, and so was the door. He noted that their belongings from Hardiman's apartment had been neatly laid out at the foot of each bed.

'At least we can have a change of clothes now.' James's grubby shirt stank of chemicals and he pulled it off. 'And a bath too.'

'Definitely. Those disgusting flies! Can you believe what Scolopendra did to us – and to Jagua?' Hugo put his head in his hands. 'Although I suppose it's what he's *going* to do to us that we should worry about.'

'What do you suppose he meant when he said he was close to making "the largest headline in history"?'

'Not a clue. But if he's rehoused his specimens, he must plan on being away for some time.'

James noticed a note left on the chest of drawers and picked it up. 'Perhaps we can ask him. This says dinner is at nine p.m. sharp.'

'Oh? I had a mouthful of botflies not long ago – not sure I could eat another thing.' Hugo sighed. 'What are we going to do, James? I shouldn't even be here. I'm a fool, not a hero.'

'In the end, I'm not sure there's much difference between the two.' James prowled restlessly about the room, pulling open drawers and cupboards. Then he noticed something tucked in a corner of the wardrobe. It was a large bound notebook with a blue cover; a journal of some kind. A looping cursive script had been crammed between the narrow lines. 'It's a diary or something.' James sat down on the chair with it, flicking through the pages. 'Written in Spanish. Here.'

He handed it to Hugo, who turned to the first page. 'Belongs to Lana Barbey.' He looked at James. 'Barbey. Do you think she's the sister of the CIP agent – what was his name . . . ?'

'Valentine Barbey. Yes, it must be hers. Perhaps she was kept here . . .' James took the book again, scanning the pages with renewed interest. 'Not like Scolopendra to leave evidence lying around for anyone to find.'

'It's his house. And the diary's in Spanish, of course. Perhaps he hasn't reckoned on my immense linguistic gifts.' Hugo shrugged his shoulders. 'Or, more likely, there's nothing worth reading in it . . .'

'We may as well check. Look, there's something about Scolopendra here . . .' James pointed: the name appeared several times.

'Reading someone's diary – I don't know . . .' Hugo took the book from him, sat on the bed and pored over the words. 'These mentions of *Scolopendra* refer to the centipede variety. *Scolopendra deltadromeus.*'

'Scolopendra's new species?'

'Right. I think that's what they were researching at one of these island sanctuaries.' Hugo frowned, muttering as he worked his way through the scrawl. 'She talks about how sick they're getting.'

'Sick?' James sat beside him and flicked over a page. 'What sort of sick?'

'People . . . have died: rashes on the skin . . . bleeding . . .' He frowned. 'I don't understand it all, but it's like the skin went . . . *wrong*. Hot and red. Blisters.'

James looked at him. 'That sounds like the policemen I saw at the station.'

'Bleeding . . . ? *Internal* bleeding, I think that says . . .' Hugo went on reading.

James waited impatiently. 'No mention of banknotes?'

'Can't see any. Even when they played cards – which was often – it looks like they only played for buttons.' Hugo handed James the journal. '*Baraja* means "pack of cards". See how often that word comes up . . . even when she was feeling very bad.'

229

James tracked a finger over the lines, scanning through to the last page. 'How does it end?'

Hugo blinked. 'She hopes she'll feel better tomorrow.'

'She never knew she was being poisoned?'

'No. The team destroyed all the centipede specimens as a precaution, but . . .' Hugo looked up from the book. 'Scolopendra prevented them from going to the mainland. Got them medical help at his own expense.'

'Generous of him,' James said sarcastically. 'I bet he only did that to see if conventional cures would have any effect. And since Hardiman's still working on an antidote, I suppose they didn't.' He drummed his fingers on the pages. 'The policemen at Batabano died within twelve hours of touching the notes, but poor Lana lived for days. What does that suggest to you?'

'That she had a strong constitution . . . or that Scolopendra's made the poison stronger.'

'Perhaps it comes in different strengths,' said James, 'depending on whether you want to inflict a quick death or a slow, lingering one.'

'These are not issues I want to think about right now,' Hugo muttered. 'I stink of chemicals. All right if I have a bath?'

'Be my guest.'

'Except we're guests of Scolopendra's. The bath taps most probably run hot and cold anacondas . . .'

James tried to muster a smile, but he knew that in less than an hour they'd be facing Scolopendra again. What awaited them next?

He heard movement on the other side of the door. An

eavesdropper? Cautiously he crossed and put his eye to the keyhole.

There was no one there now, but James could hear the click of high heels on tiles and the swish of tassels as La Velada walked away.

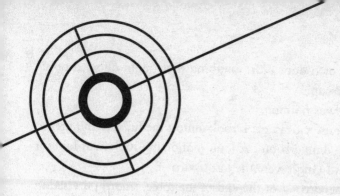

26
Death at All Costs

At five minutes to nine James heard a heavy bolt being thrown back. The door handle jumped and El Puño stepped inside. He grunted, gestured that they should follow him.

James felt a jolt of apprehension as he looked at Hugo. 'Dinner is served.'

'*El diario.*' El Puño's voice was a strangled growl. He held out his gloved hand, expectant.

'Someone's realized their mistake,' Hugo murmured.

'I thought La Velada must've been listening.' James went over to his bed and removed the book from under the cover. 'It was very interesting . . . I think more people should have the chance to read it.'

El Puño took the journal with a sneer and marched them along cool white corridors. James guessed they'd be brought back this way; he looked for any lapses in security – an open window, or a door ajar; anything that might allow a possibility of escape.

There was nothing.

The house was large; it took almost the full five minutes to reach the dining room. A long mahogany table was laid for six; he and Hugo were the last to arrive.

Scolopendra sat at the end of the table, smartly dressed in a white tuxedo, though his hair looked wild, and his shirt gaped where his massive barrel chest pulled at the buttons. He inclined his head, his dark eyes brooding.

Jagua, in a high-necked blue dress patterned with tiny white flowers, sat on her father's right; she smiled weakly at them. La Velada sat on Scolopendra's left, her face still veiled.

Hardiman rose from his seat next to Jagua as James and Hugo approached. 'Boys!' He reached out, embracing each of them, gazing into their faces. 'Are you all right?'

'We're fine, sir.' James shook his hand and drew some small comfort from the contact.

He made to sit next to Hardiman, but Scolopendra shook his head, pointed to the seat beside La Velada. 'You'll sit here, please.'

James hesitated, but Hardiman forced an encouraging smile and nodded. Hugo took his place at Hardiman's side, while James walked slowly round the table and sat beside La Velada. She turned towards him; he caught the aristocratic sweep of her profile and a glimpse of pale skin, but the details were lost.

As he looked away, an antique ormolu clock chimed nine. Before the chimes had finished, Ramón had entered the room with a large trolley laden with serving platters and tureens. James's stomach felt hollow – but while the roast fowl, cold meats, and seafood on glistening beds of ice all looked amazing, the sight of Ramón killed his appetite stone dead.

'What's the occasion?' Hardiman asked acidly.

'You could call it a last supper.' Scolopendra's smile did nothing to dissipate the menace of his words. 'La Velada has finished her questioning of the CIP diver.'

'His name is Franklin John Ford. He confirms that he has been gathering evidence on our activities.' She looked at James. 'Ironically, with less success than a determined child.'

Ramón put a plate down beside James, and gave him a venomous look. James longed to tell Scolopendra how he and Hugo had taken Ramón down – but the secret might yet gain them some advantage, however slight.

'In the light of the CIP's involvement – and your betrayal, Hardiman – we are forced to bring forward our great task.' Scolopendra began to pile meat upon his plate. 'We leave in the morning.'

Jagua started. 'What?'

'You will have to pack clothes for colder weather, my darling daughter. But no more questions for now. Eat!'

James found that despite his unease, he was hungry. The iced water soothed his throat, and he tried a mouthful of whatever wild bird it was. It tasted gamy, and was served with a rich stock that was more European than Caribbean. Scolopendra's own stab at sophistication, or La Velada's influence?

'James, Hugo, I hope you have learned from this

afternoon's display.' Scolopendra started on his steak tartare. 'You saw how quickly Dr Hardiman confessed when he thought your lives were in danger. By threatening you, I have control over him.'

'They're children.' Hardiman pushed away his plate. 'This behaviour, it's inhuman.'

'Merely efficient.' Scolopendra calmly chewed his raw steak. 'Your upbringing has given you the luxury of ideals, Hardiman. If you'd fought for every scrap in the slums as I did . . . If you'd raised a child with nothing, spent years fighting for acceptance from people with inferior minds, inferior skills . . . inferior *ambitions* . . .'

'And what are your ambitions, eh, Scolopendra?' Hardiman asked. 'You seem obsessed with creating the perfect antidote for this poison of yours. Do you want to kill people or cure them?'

Scolopendra smiled. 'The power to do both will make me a god. And then they shall see, those great white fools who looked down upon me, who refused to show me respect.' He slammed a fist down on the table. 'They shall see how they were wrong.'

Hardiman shook his head. 'And becoming a millionaire businessman pretty much overnight hasn't proved that?'

'Chance. Blind luck – the toss of a coin. This is something *I* have made happen.' Scolopendra grinned across at Hardiman. 'With a little help from my friends, huh?'

Hardiman turned to James. 'I swear I didn't know about this poison when Scolopendra took me on. He told me I would be neutralizing a toxic element in a new chemical treatment for the pulp and paper industries.'

James wanted to believe it. 'But the strongbox – you must have known what was in it to tell Sarila—'

'I thought there were *notes* hidden in the safe,' Hardiman told him. 'Notes on the poison's composition, not dollar bills.' He looked at Jagua, then nodded to La Velada. 'I got out when I . . . I overheard her briefing somebody about a poison spread through paper. I wanted no part of it.'

'Hence your sudden request for time off to work on projects at the Universidad de Habana. Such high principles.' La Velada seemed amused. 'And yet those principles didn't stop you accepting a retaining fee against future services, so Scolopendra would continue to pay off your debts.'

'I know.' Hardiman looked shamefaced. 'I'm surprised you let me go at all.'

'It was actually convenient,' said Scolopendra. 'I had to perfect the poison's absorption rate before you could continue with your cure. Now that has been determined, you must restart your work.'

'Why Dr Hardiman?' James demanded. 'Why can't you let him go and get someone else?'

'Because he is truly brilliant in his field. Because I have a hold over him.' A cold smile. 'And because it amuses me that after years of carrying his bags through jungle and desert, now he must labour for me.'

'But who does your "business partner" labour for, Father?' Jagua reached down inside the neck of her dress and pulled out the thin sheets of her precious transcript. 'It was I who told Dr Hardiman what La Velada was saying on the telephone. I who listened to her talk when she thought no one heard.'

The voice behind the veil was icy. 'What juvenile foolishness is this?'

'*Papá, lea este.*' Talking quickly in Spanish, Jagua held out the pages to Scolopendra. James made out 'NKVD' and 'OGPU', willing the man's dark face to show anger, for La Velada to start begging for her life. But to his dismay, she looked untroubled, while Scolopendra talked to her with apparent sympathy.

Hugo looked despairing. 'Oh . . .'

'You must let me explain, Bond.' La Velada turned to James. 'As a member of the Russian aristocracy, I was persecuted during the Bolshevik revolution. The NKVD forced me to spy on my friends and feed the information to the secret police.'

James tried to act as if this was news to him. 'Forced?'

'I wear this veil always – am in mourning *always* – for those whose blood is on my hands.' She paused. 'In the end, I ran from the NKVD, escaped them. Even today, my name remains on their death list. Their agents have pursued me halfway across the world. In the penthouse, I thought at first that you were one of their assassins.'

'So why would you be talking to them on the telephone?' asked James.

'We've made a deal with the Bolsheviks,' Scolopendra interrupted. 'She will buy her freedom with the sale of the poison to the NKVD.'

'Buy my freedom, yes.' La Velada inclined her head. 'And a very healthy profit for both our companies.'

Jagua looked crushed. 'Please – you cannot trust her, Father!'

'You dare to speak to me of trust?' Scolopendra's eyes were like stones. 'You, who would stab me in the back the moment I look away!'

But James wasn't finished with La Velada. 'Why did you talk in English?' he said, searching for eyes behind the veil. 'When I was in the penthouse and you were telephoning, you weren't speaking Russian then.'

'The NKVD have agents all over the world.' She was as still as a cat watching its prey. 'I thought you'd be aware of that, Bond.'

James felt a shiver pass through him. Could this woman know more of his past than she was letting on?

Scolopendra clearly thought it was time to regain control of the conversation. 'Soon now, La Velada will lay to rest the ghosts of the revolution – and of her old life,' he said, placing one hand on hers. 'When our great task is achieved, she will be free to start again.'

'Oh, she will indeed,' La Velada purred. 'There at your side as you are courted by the most powerful rulers in the world.'

'Will you tell those rulers how you "perfected" your poison?' James asked, then turned to Jagua. 'Your father tested it on the staff at the research centres. Ran experiments on them.'

'We found the journal of the CIP man's sister, Lana, in our room,' Hugo added.

Jagua turned to Scolopendra, eyes wide. 'Father . . . ?'

'We needed to see the full effect of the poison,' said Scolopendra through another mouthful of steak tartare. 'A controlled trial was a discreet and effective solution.'

'It was murder!' Hardiman started to stand up, but Ramón slapped a hand down on his shoulder, pushing him back into his chair. 'Mass murder!'

'Working at the frontiers of science, on occasion sacrifices must be made.' La Velada laid her cutlery neatly down on the porcelain plate. 'Having read the journal I left out for them, the boys will know what I mean.'

Her calm admission wrong-footed James; he looked at Hugo, who seemed just as taken aback. 'Why leave it for us?'

'It's important that you understand the seriousness of the situation,' La Velada said with a smile. 'And the scale of our great task.'

'*Everyone* here must understand.' Scolopendra took an oyster and tipped it down his throat. 'Understand that today's great powers have already begun the slide towards a new global war. Millions upon millions will perish in this conflict, which will last for many years. But my poison can bring about an *end* to war.'

'Excuse me?' Jagua scoffed. 'Killing your enemy with a box of poisoned money is supposed to bring peace?'

Her father ignored her, took a billfold out of his pocket and tossed it down the table to James. 'Money rescued me when knowledge was not enough. It is fitting now that I make money my weapon.'

James eyed the billfold warily.

'You need not fear.' La Velada picked it up, extricated some notes and fanned them out. 'You see?'

James studied the notes – not American dollars, but British pounds sterling. Three white notes – worth five, ten and twenty pounds – a red ten-shilling note and a green one-pound note. 'British notes? Not dollars?'

'The notes are counterfeit. Scolopendra can create any currency using the paper mill and press in the grounds.'

James tried not to look impressed, but the truth was, the counterfeit notes felt and looked identical to the real thing. He passed them on to Hugo.

Scolopendra's smile faded. 'You know, it is a very violent process, the production of money.' He looked around the table, making sure he had everyone's attention. 'The liquid pulp of cotton and linen is forced out onto great sheets of gauze. They're pounded, sliced and crushed until they reach the proper thickness. Replicas of the original minting plates are used to print the fake money, before it goes on the "name roll" to receive its watermark.' He picked out another oyster and swallowed it down. 'After that, the notes are run through a vat filled with a synthesized biochemical solution.'

Hardiman put it another way: 'You mean they are soaked in your poison.'

La Velada nodded. 'A poison that remains active in the impregnated paper for up to two months, now that Scolopendra has perfected the absorption rate.'

'Millions of poisoned banknotes,' Scolopendra emphasized. 'Scores of millions, introduced to a country's money supply.'

James stared. 'What?'

La Velada rose silently to her feet. 'Do you know how quickly paper currency travels through the economy, Bond?' she asked. 'Thousands of notes changing hands each day . . .

It enters the body through the skin of anyone handling the affected notes. Within hours, the first symptoms appear: red blisters on the hands.'

Scolopendra leaned forward. 'As more and more of the counterfeit notes enter the country and spread out, so more and more people will be afflicted. Hundreds at first, then thousands . . . millions. A mystery illness that strikes without warning. Think of the effect on national morale, the collapse of industry, the confusion. Now imagine how easy it would be to invade such a country. Imagine how much that country would pay to have the cure for that disease.'

'They . . . would give anything.' James felt numb inside. 'Surrender to anyone.'

'After all, we know the difficulties inherent in perfecting a cure,' La Velada said, looking at Hardiman. 'Don't we, Doctor?'

'To plan suffering on such a scale . . .' Hardiman stared back at her. 'It's obscene.'

'No.' Scolopendra held up a finger. 'It is *power*. Power that will command an incredible price.'

'The weapon will soon be offered up for sale.' Was that a thin smile that James glimpsed through the veil? 'That is why I have worked so hard to arrange a demonstration.'

La Velada sounded as if she were planning a family outing; James looked at her with loathing. 'Where's the test to be – here, on Cuba?'

'Oh no, Bond. As an example for the world, and as an advertisement for our power, a more important target is required.'

'You asked why she was talking English on my telephone . . . Have you not guessed?' Scolopendra gestured to the banknotes on the table. 'Great Britain will be the first world power to fall.'

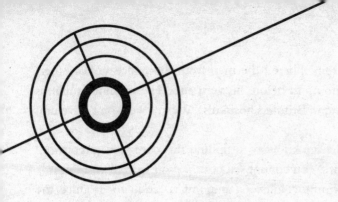

27
Resistance

Silence fell around the table. James couldn't take in the horror of Scolopendra's plan.

'There has been much to arrange with our agents in Britain, as you can imagine,' La Velada confided. 'To smuggle so many banknotes into the country is not without risk; and then to oversee their dispersal through the financial system—'

'Why target Britain?' James broke in.

'The NKVD made that decision. Russia desires a bridge-head in Western Europe. Your country will be given an antidote to the sickness only after signing a binding agree-ment to be governed from Moscow.'

Hardiman found his voice. 'But . . . they never would.'

'The cause of the poisoning will not be revealed.' Scolopendra had produced his silver dollar. 'If Britain will not capitulate, then further poisoned notes will be introduced and the death toll will continue to rise.'

James remembered the men from the police station, their flesh falling apart before his very eyes. He imagined millions more dying in Britain's hospitals. 'We . . . we won't have any choice.'

'So now we know why finding this cure is so important,' Jagua spat. 'You cannot sell your poison so well without it.'

'My pharmacological company is ready to produce the antidote in bulk, once I have radioed them the formula,' said La Velada. 'We don't know exactly when the British will surrender, but when they do, the cure must be ready.' She turned to Hardiman. 'Your facilities in the laboratory here are duplicated on board the yacht. You will prepare the antidote within two days.'

Hardiman was staring down at the table. 'And if I can't?'

'You know well that the poison can be passed undetectably through paper. Any paper can be used . . .' Scolopendra turned to James and Hugo. 'Even the pages of an old journal.'

James looked down at his clammy palm.

A small red blister sat in its centre.

'You've poisoned us?' he whispered.

Hugo looked incredulous. 'We're going to die within two days?'

'Father, no,' breathed Jagua. 'You wouldn't . . .'

'I do not baulk at killing children, if that is what you mean? For me, life is no precious miracle. It is merely a reflex of creation, a state of existence defined by chance and fragility.' He flipped the coin. 'This is why I set the odds myself. This is why I make myself strong.'

Tears rolled down Jagua's cheeks. 'This is why you are mad.'

'Once a poor orphan from a starving village, now I stand ready to reshape the global map.' Scolopendra laughed as he caught his coin. 'This is not madness. It is destiny.' He gestured to Ramón and El Puño to take James and Hugo away.

Still stunned, James followed his friend's meek example and did not resist.

'I hope, for the boys' sake, that you will no longer stall for time, Gerald.' La Velada walked round the table and placed her hands on Hardiman's shoulders. 'The clock is ticking . . .'

James didn't hear any more: Ramón pushed him into the hallway, and El Puño followed on with Hugo.

James forced words out of his dry mouth. 'Ramón. I . . . I'll tell Scolopendra you lied about falling asleep – that we beat you – unless you help us.'

'Help you?' Ramón sneered. 'I help you die, maybe?' He pushed James up against the wall, then held a switchblade to his face. 'Or maybe I better slice out your tongue . . . huh?' He mimed slashing at James's face, then pocketed the blade and pushed him on again. Hugo followed in silence, head bowed.

The door to their bedroom stood open. James and Hugo were shoved inside, then the door was closed and locked.

'How are you feeling?' James asked.

'Bloody petrified.' Hugo sat down on his bed. 'My stomach's

churning, but whether that's fear or the poison, I don't know.'

James paced the room, thinking desperately. It was one thing confronting an opponent you could see, but an invisible enemy, hiding inside you, attacking remorselessly . . .

Hours passed. Again and again, he looked down at his palm. The blister stared back like a tiny red eye. His stomach had started to cramp as well. *Hardiman will find a way to cure us*, James told himself. But relying on others meant accepting that he was helpless, and for James there was no worse feeling. The image of the walking corpse at the police station filled his head. The prospect of such a death, his body unravelling from within . . .

'How much poison was on those pages?' he muttered. 'I suppose we've had a lower dose than the officers got from those poisoned banknotes, but a higher dose than they gave Lana Barbey and her friends.'

'On their playing cards, most likely. Hideous bloody business.' Hugo was peering down his shirt at his chest. 'I've got no marks yet, as far as I can see, and I'm smaller than you. Why's that, d'you think?'

'I don't suppose height's got much to do with it. It must come down to natural resistance.' James went over to the window, looked out through the curtains. Outside, a guard with a machine gun walked slowly up and down; clearly Scolopendra didn't plan to be caught unawares by any more CIP agents – or risk James and Hugo making an escape. In the night beyond, the pulsing tune of the cicadas mingled with the noise of Scolopendra's men preparing for departure.

'What do you think those thugs are doing out there?' Hugo

wondered. 'Scolopendra's yacht is splendid to look at, but surely it can't hold much in the way of cargo.'

'Where did La Velada take us? To that giant log raft.' James nodded slowly. 'Plenty of room on board for transporting whatever they need. Towed by a tug, it could drag a whole flotilla of boats behind it.'

Hugo swallowed. 'So what happens to whatever's left behind?'

'On past evidence, they'll be getting ready to blow it to smithereens, or raze it to the ground.' James lay back on his bed. 'If only I'd just let the CIP diver take the money. If I had, perhaps this would all be over by now.'

'Perhaps.' Hugo sighed. 'Or he might have taken the box back to his team, counted up the money – and they would have wound up dead. Instead, we know that the rest of his team are still out there – perhaps they're talking to that copper you saved in Batabano right now, getting confirmation that Scolopendra's leading lady and hired thug were behind the blast.' He shrugged. 'At least while someone else is on our side, *something* might turn up—'

The French window behind him exploded inwards in a great crash and clatter of glass, and the guard came staggering backwards into the room. A huge furry *thing*, like a spider with too many legs, was wrapped around his face. James stared, horrified, and Hugo jumped behind his bed as the guard wrenched it off and the creature hared off into a dark corner. The next moment Jagua leaped in through the door frame. Before the man could react, she brought a big stone down on the side of his head, and he fell back and lay still.

'Good God,' Hugo called weakly from behind the bed. 'What *was* that monster?'

'A camel spider.' Jagua rubbed her bandaged wrist. 'One of Father's imported specimens. I found it in the grounds.'

Hugo rose warily to his feet. 'Weren't you locked up in your room like us? How did you get out?'

'I stole a fork from dinner and picked the lock with it.' Jagua pointed to the guard. 'Though this man saved me the bother of breaking into your room, yes? I do not think he likes arachnids.' James and Hugo looked askance at the skulking creature in the corner. 'Stories say that camel spiders feed on human flesh. This is not true – I carried her and she only bit me once. It is a good omen.'

'Seriously?' Hugo wondered.

'Luck is with us,' Jagua insisted. 'There are only a few guards on patrol – they all help to destroy evidence of the work before Father flees . . . And so before I came here, I spoke to Hardiman through the door to his room.'

James nodded. 'Well?'

'La Velada was right to say he stalls.' Jagua's dark eyes shone. 'He has *already made* some of this antidote since he was brought here, but pretends to her more work must be done. He prepared it in case he could get it to CIP so they could make more—'

'Where is this sample?' James felt a rush of adrenalin. 'Is there enough for two?'

'How is it taken – swallowed, injected?' Hugo vaulted the bed and grabbed hold of her sleeve. 'Jagua, where *is* it?'

'He told me the sample is in the lab. It is in a jar marked . . .' She closed her eyes, as if trying to remember what she'd been

250

told. 'The label says *Sodium Nitrite*. I do not know how the cure is given – a guard came to check on him, and I had to go.' She headed back towards the broken French window. 'We must hurry. Father's men will be clearing the lab too before they destroy it . . .'

'One way or another, we've got to get hold of that jar.' James picked up the guard's MP18 machine gun. It was an old weapon: there was no selector for single shot – it could only fire in fully automatic mode. 'This thing might persuade people we mean business.'

'Come, I know the way,' hissed Jagua, stepping through the ruined window. 'See, no one came to investigate the noise. The guards are too scattered.'

'But they'll be rattled. Expecting trouble.' James held the gun close. 'Let's be careful.'

The scene outside was eerily still. The moonlit palms and bushes stood like strange sentries. Even the cicadas' chirrup seemed muted; it was as if the night were holding its breath. James pinched his cheeks, trying to stay alert, peering about in the soft white light of the streetlamps. The thump of his heart was clearing his head; he felt stronger, but his palms were hot and itchy against the smooth metal of the machine gun.

'That will make things quicker,' said Jagua, pointing to one of the roadsters on the path leading from the patio.

James jumped behind the wheel. The key was still in the ignition and he hit the starter. The engine tore at the quiet, and James was sure they would be challenged, but no one appeared. He passed the MP18 to Hugo, who took it reluctantly.

'This way,' Jagua said, pointing.

In the dim light, surrounded by palms and the distant humps of outbuildings, James found it hard to get his bearings. As he drove, he glanced instinctively up at the sky to check the stars, forgetting the canopy of leaves that stretched overhead.

'We are almost there,' Jagua told him after several minutes. In the back, holding the gun, Hugo moved his head from side to side like a furtive crow.

As he rounded a thicket of tall, spiky trees, James saw the great X of the central laboratories. The lights were out; all was quiet and still. It wasn't too late . . .

He accelerated just as the doors opened. Two guards stepped out, saw the car coming towards them. They raised their MP18s and opened fire.

'Look out!' yelled James. Hugo and Jagua ducked down and he slumped in his seat as the windscreen shattered. As he drove into the storm of bullets, James felt terror shutting off his senses; it was as if an automaton had taken hold of his reactions. The roadster shook and sparked in the gunfire. He heard Jagua shouting at the guards – '*¡Soy yo! ¡No disparen! ¡No disparen, idiotas!*' In the dark, the guards didn't realize they were trying to kill their boss's only daughter.

James floored the accelerator pedal, dropped the gearshift into low and veered sideways, heading for the other side of the building. Lead bounced off metal and tore through leather. A tyre blew, and James fought to keep control. Wadding and dust burst from the upholstery about him.

Finally the roadster made it round the corner.

'Look out!' Jagua shouted.

Sitting up again, James remembered too late that the

building was shaped like an X; the protruding wing of the lab was right in front of him and he was on a collision course. He hit the brakes, turned the wheel, but with the flat tyre the steering had gone to hell.

And they were ready to join it.

The crash was inevitable. The lab wall caved in, and thick glass cracked like ice. James was thrown forward, felt the bite of the steering wheel on his ribs, gritted his teeth against the pain.

'James!' came Hugo's panicked cry. 'Are you all right?'

The roadster had stalled, and seemed in no hurry to start again. 'Never better,' James muttered.

'Why is no one coming after us?' Jagua wondered.

Suddenly the dreadful penny dropped. James realized that the guards had come out because they'd finished whatever they'd been doing inside. And if Scolopendra was looking to dispose of all the evidence . . .

'Quickly,' James hissed. 'Get out and run!'

Hugo and Jagua jumped clear without argument and sprinted for the cover of the nearest trees. James ran after them—

With a roar of thunder and a blaze of light, the lab blew apart. James was thrown to the ground beside his friends. Flames belched from the shattered building to set light to the canopy of leaves and branches above. Debris smoked through the sky like points of light tracing alien constellations, crashing down on the lawn and gardens. A blackened brick missed James's head by inches. Panting for breath, he watched the flames dance in the ruins where the lab had stood just seconds ago.

'The cure . . .' Jagua said softly.

'It's all right,' Hugo whispered hoarsely, 'Hardiman can make more.'

'But only in the lab on the yacht, as a prisoner.' James got up stiffly, looked down again at the blister on his hand. 'So either we give ourselves up and join him . . . or we get Hardiman away from here.'

'The CIP diver,' said Hugo, 'Franklin whoever he was . . . He could help us.'

'Agreed,' said James.

'If we can find him.' Jagua stooped to scoop up the machine gun from the ground – then froze.

Stepping forward through the smoke came El Puño, a chunky revolver in his gloved hand – and behind him, like a phantom in flowing black, was La Velada.

Her Derringer was aimed at James.

'I supposed as much.' Her voice was quiet, but still carried over the crackle of the flames. 'When the guards reported three intruders, my thoughts went straight to you.'

'I . . . I caught these two, La Velada.' Jagua cocked the machine gun and covered James and Hugo, emotion draining from her face. 'I told them, it will only make things worse if they struggle now.'

James wondered where the bluff was going. Would La Velada believe her?

'You know, the guards are jumpy tonight, my dear. Expecting trouble. You might have been killed, coming at them like that in the dark. And, then . . .' She shifted her arm, aimed the pistol at Jagua. 'I would have been rid of you.'

La Velada fired. James flinched and Jagua cried out as the

machine gun jumped from her grip. A stripe of red appeared on the back of Jagua's hand.

'I'd sooner you didn't join us at sea, my dear. Your father will be so much easier to manage.' The woman tutted softly. 'You've tried so hard to set him against me, gathering your evidence, building your case. And, of course, you're quite correct. I *am* using him.'

Jagua's eyes narrowed. 'You still work for the NKVD?'

'Under the deepest cover,' she agreed proudly. 'I will be handed a very senior administrative position in the new Soviet Socialist Republic of Great Britain. I fear that will leave me little time to indulge your father's dreams of a fresh start together.'

'He will kill you,' Jagua hissed.

'Once we have reached England, I will kill *him*. My superiors will not allow such a potent weapon of war to be wielded by someone so unstable . . . so easy to manipulate.' La Velada paused. 'He even wanted to spare your friend Maritsa's life, you know.'

Jagua shook as if she'd been hit again. 'What?'

'Misguided sentiment for the family that helped to raise you, I suppose.' The woman nodded. 'I assured him that was out of the question, of course.'

'That money he gave her . . .' Hugo looked at James. 'We thought it went up in flames to teach her a lesson—'

'When really it was destroying the evidence.' James glared back at La Velada. 'More poisoned banknotes?'

'I couldn't risk them being found and studied, so they had to burn up after only minimal contact with the skin.' She paused, considering, matter of fact. 'It could take Maritsa as long as a week to die – in the most terrible agony. I hope that's some small comfort for you.'

Jagua's legs seemed to give way; she fell to her knees. '*Puta.*'

James nodded to El Puño. 'And will you leave your gorilla behind to raze her village to the ground to cover all trace?'

'Two police officers in their prime dropping dead after handling Scolopendra's money would have attracted . . . unwelcome attention. Much could've been learned from the bodies . . . On the other hand, the slow demise of a scrawny child in a rural backwater, well – few will hear, and fewer still will care.' La Velada aimed her Derringer at Jagua for the coup de grâce. 'Goodbye, my dear.'

'No.' Heart in his mouth, James stepped in front of Jagua. 'You can't shoot through me, or Hugo. You need us alive. Your poison's too dangerous to use without a cure.'

Hugo stepped up beside him. 'And if we're dead, you'll have no power over Hardiman to make one.'

'Step aside,' La Velada insisted, 'or you'll be sorry.' When neither James nor Hugo moved, she turned to El Puño. 'Remove them.'

The huge man set off at a lumbering run. As he did so, he moved in front of La Velada, blocking her view.

Jagua lunged for the fallen machine gun, snatched it up and fired. The recoil knocked her backwards and the bullets sprayed high. El Puño threw himself to the ground. When James looked for La Velada, he saw nothing; she had vanished, wraithlike, back into the smoke.

James snatched the machine gun as Hugo helped Jagua to her feet. 'Run!' he snapped. 'Go!'

They charged away. El Puño was rising to his knees. James tried to fire another warning blast. Nothing happened. *Barrel's jammed? Out of bullets?* Either way, the gun was useless.

And the giant was bringing up his gun arm.

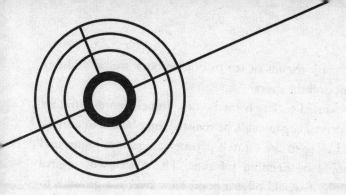

28
Five Minutes to Midnight

In desperation, James hurled the MP18 at El Puño. The big stone fist smashed it away, but by then James was already running off into the night. He heard the blast of the big man's revolver, made for the cover of the long grass. A kind of unreal, campfire light was brightening the night above, cinders falling like tiny comets as the canopy high above went on burning.

Where were Hugo and Jagua now? James wondered. Had he outrun them? Had they blundered into another patrol? If Jagua were captured and taken back to Scolopendra, could she ever convince him of the truth about La Velada? Or would he beat her again, adding to those terrible scars . . . ?

Moving as stealthily as haste would allow, James tried to clear his head but uncertainties kept crowding in on him. Had La Velada left to recruit more assassins like El Puño, who would search out Jagua and kill her without a qualm? Should he look for his friends or try to double back round and free Hardiman and the diver?

As he paused to catch his breath, James heard a distant rush of water. *The paper mill*, he realized; an obvious landmark that stood close to the estate's perimeter. Perhaps Jagua and Hugo would be heading for that. The tower was several storeys high; it would offer a good view over the grounds to assess the dangers. Plus he might find tools or equipment to use as weapons.

Mind made up, James ran towards the sound of water. Soon he was rewarded with a view of the mill's rustic silhouette against a dark sky pockmarked with gaping, cinder-fringed holes. No lights burned in the mill's windows. No shadows shifted at its base. The place seemed deserted.

Cautiously James approached the door and pushed it open. In the dim, unearthly light the great vats stood silent, their chemical reek acrid in his throat. Wire-mesh drums, vast machines as big as a motor bus, stood ready to snap into life.

A dim orange bulb eyed James steadily from the wall beside a staircase. There was a large red button beneath it, but he didn't dare turn on the lights and give away his location. Instead he started down a passage, searching slowly, methodically, looking for a tool store. A clock ticked off the seconds as James felt his way along. His hands brushed against a bulky package fixed to the wall, and a sickly sweet smell caught in his nostrils.

Peering more closely, James realized that the ticking was getting louder. A small white clock face had been attached by wires to a metal tube, and the tube inserted into a solid waxy block.

High explosive, thought James. *Enough TNT to bring the whole mill crashing down, and I'm close enough to kiss it.*

He backed quickly away. Of course, the mill would hold the most damning evidence of Scolopendra's plans, and all trace would need removing. How many more time bombs had been set here?

James knew he couldn't risk remaining. He turned back along the passage – and flinched as electric lights hummed into life, high above him. He could see the whole mill now – the steps and walkways, the giant vats linked by conveyers and complex systems of mesh.

A huge hunched figure stepped into the passage, barring the way out, staring with cold dead eyes.

El Puño.

James ran straight at the killer as if to shoulder-charge him, but at the last moment feinted left. He dived past El Puño, heard the whoosh of the great fist as it swung overhead, striking the wall like a wrecking ball.

Scrambling back up, James made for the exit. But El Puño was incredibly fast; his flesh-and-blood hand grabbed James by the arm and pulled him back. James was slammed into the side of a vat and saw that another timed explosive had been fixed there. The clock showed five minutes to midnight. Was that when the bomb was set to blow?

James squirmed free.

Desperate now, he started up the flight of stairs, passing two buttons on the wall – one green, one red. El Puño came lumbering after him and hit the green button. With a slow and sinister rumble, the drums began to rotate. In the vats, blades swivelled through the dregs of rank solutions.

First switch on the lights, then set the works going. James felt his heart sinking. *This area must've been cleared of personnel after the bombs were set – this is a summons to bring back reinforcements.*

He ran onto a walkway leading to a further flight of steps that headed upwards into the mill, and caught sight of a small dusty square on the upper landing – a window. If he could get out, perhaps he could scramble down the brickwork? The whole mill was now throbbing with the thunder of machinery – siphoning water from the bowels of the building, turning mechanical blades through liquid thick with rag and linen, firing up the dryers.

He turned and saw that El Puño was striding after him.

James reached the dusty window, but it wouldn't budge; it was locked. He beat on the glass with his fists, looking frantically for something that might smash it. But the landing was nothing more than a narrow walkway, bare whitewashed wall on one side, and a wooden safety rail on the other.

Now El Puño had closed the distance between them and was standing at the other end of the walkway. 'You not run.'

'What about the bombs?' James panted. 'How long before they go off?' El Puño stared blankly, and James tried again: 'How long till *boom*?'

'*Boom*,' El Puño agreed, his voice soft. 'You not run. Never again.'

As if to demonstrate his intent, he brought his stone fist down on the rail, smashing through it in a rain of splinters. Then he pointed to James's knees and nodded.

He's going to cripple me. So I'm no more trouble. Blood running cold, James turned, hoping against hope to find some last escape route. But there was nothing: a bare ceiling, a vertiginous view of the factory below—

And then El Puño lunged forward. His good hand caught James by the throat, slamming him back against the wall. 'Ha!' He grinned, eyes dwindling to black dots as he squeezed.

James gasped and retched, thrashing in the big man's grip. The world shrank to that ugly face as the fat fingers choked the life out of him. The heavy granite fist was drawn back high over his head, ready to give the killer blow.

Braced against the wall, James lifted both feet into El Puño's bulging gut. Then he pushed out hard with his legs, breaking the big man's grip at last. James gasped for breath as he slipped down to the floor. Meanwhile El Puño tried to steady himself against the safety rail – but he'd severed its support at the far end of the landing. With a crunching, splintering noise, the rail gave way.

For some moments El Puño balanced on the edge of the precipice. Then he toppled and plunged with a colossal splash into one of the great vats far below. Only then, as the automated knives on their rotating mesh set to work on this new matter, did one final scream escape El Puño. But it was silenced almost immediately: his head was severed from his body and the stew of chemicals turned crimson.

As nausea bubbled inside him, James looked away. When he glanced back, he saw something slosh out of the vat and drop with a crash to the concrete floor.

A cracked granite fist.

James closed his eyes. He had to get out of here . . . But suddenly the clank of the great machines began to slow. Fear ripped through him: was this something to do with the time bombs or—?

Then he saw Jagua on the steps, one hand on the red button, the other bloody and clutching her thin black jacket. She looked exhausted, sickened.

'Jagua!' Rubbing his throat, James hurried down to join her. 'Are you all right?'

'Better than El Puño.' She wiped the sweat off her face with her sleeve. 'Better than Maritsa. The back of my hand is only scratched . . .'

This was no time for sentiment; James was brusque. 'How'd you find me?'

'This place was lit up like a lighthouse, with no one around.' She shrugged. 'We thought maybe it was a signal—'

'Everyone will have seen it. We need to get out.' James took the last of the steps down to the factory floor. 'There are explosives set all over the place. I don't know how long we've got. Where's Hugo?'

'Hiding outside.'

'Let's find him.' As he ushered Jagua towards the exit, James saw the clock face protruding from the package on the wall: the minute hand was edging towards twelve.

He followed Jagua out. The racing water in the stream was churning like his stomach as he peered through the dark. James thought he heard a crash, a shout . . .

'Hugo?' Jagua called uncertainly.

There was no answer.

'Where did you leave him?'

'Underneath the mill supports.'

James ran round to check, squinting into the gloom,

stomach tight with fear. There was no sign of Hugo . . . but now he could hear more shouting, a crashing through the foliage, shouts in Spanish.

Guards, he thought. *On their way*.

'James!' Jagua had come up behind him, her eyes wide. 'They said the mill is about to go up.'

'How soon?'

'Seconds!'

In desperation, James turned to the stream beside them. 'We'll have to jump in. The current will pull us clear faster than we can run.'

Eyes fearful, Jagua nodded. She dropped her jacket, sprinted for the bank and launched herself into the black water. With a deep breath, James did the same. Cold gripped him as the current snatched him away. He glimpsed Jagua beside him, skinny limbs knifing through the foam. Then he dipped beneath the surface.

When the explosion came – when hell broke loose – James was still under. It was like viewing an open furnace through thick glass. The water seemed to clench around him like a fist, flinging him forward. Stone and timber rained down, and the perimeter fence buckled and tore. The pressure built inside his ears.

He shut his eyes, held his breath and finally surfaced. He saw that smoke was billowing from the shell of the mill. The stream was still pulling him along fast, a soup of rubble and debris, with no way to—

Something smashed into him. The stars above danced with flames for a moment; then night swallowed everything.

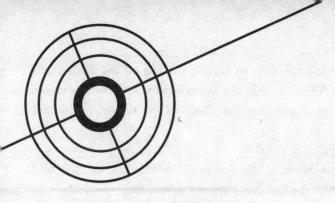

29
Desperate Flight

When James opened his eyes, it was still night. The air tasted of smoke. He was cold and wet, and his head throbbed. *Some debris from the mill must've hit me . . .*

He winced as he touched the back of his skull; it was bruised, but the new blisters on his palms stung too.

James tried to take in his surroundings. He was lying on a riverbank, his lower legs submerged in water. The current must have swept him into the reeds. But where was Jagua – and Hugo?

James got up unsteadily, shivered, felt the burn in his guts again. There was no time to rest; he knew he had to go back to Scolopendra's estate and get Hardiman out. And if Jagua and Hugo had been recaptured too . . . or worse . . .

One step at a time, he told himself, hands prickling, stomach clenched as he moved his weary limbs. *One step at a time.*

He stumbled on beneath the silver of the clouded

sky, following the river upstream, staving off the doubts and questions. After what felt like hours he saw sullen flames across the stream, made out the shadows of the mill's blasted ruins . . .

And voices.

The low boom of Scolopendra's words carried first and loudest; then the familiar purr of La Velada.

The pulse of adrenalin made James's senses sharp again. He dropped to his belly and crawled closer through the long grass like an alligator.

Now he could see them, lit by the flames: Scolopendra and La Velada, with Ramón hovering to the rear.

James couldn't understand the words, of course – the conversation was in Spanish – but it was clear that Scolopendra was angry and upset: Jagua's black jacket was clutched in one hand. La Velada was speaking more calmly. She put a hand on his shoulder, moved it slowly down his arm, then prised apart his fingers so that the jacket fell to the ground. Scolopendra stared down at it as the woman went on talking. James caught the name 'Franklin Ford'. After a few minutes Scolopendra turned decisively, and walked away from the mill, with Ramón behind him. La Velada looked briefly down at the discarded jacket. Then she turned and followed them.

Cautiously James knelt up. He could see chunks of masonry strewn across the millstream like stepping stones. To follow would be an easy matter. But before he could move, he heard a rustling in the grass behind him. He turned, fists raised, ready to—

'Jagua?' James felt relief cascade through him. 'You're all right?'

'Not very.' She was swaying on her feet, her wet braids plastered to her face. 'You heard them?'

'I don't speak Spanish,' he reminded her, 'without Hugo . . .'

'He is missing still.' Jagua sat down, and James knelt beside her as she went on. 'Father found my jacket near the ruins of the mill. His men were looking for me in the grounds – but La Velada has convinced him that I am dead. That it is *best* I am dead. That I hold him back. That this is . . . evolution, like in nature. Growing beyond the man he was . . . to become the man he shall be.'

'I'm sorry,' was the best James could think of to say.

'They think you and Hugo must be dead also.'

James felt an ember-glow of relief. 'So they haven't caught Hugo?'

'No. They found . . . the remains of El Puño. That and my jacket . . . They assume he went in there after us.'

'But then what about Hardiman? They have no hold over him now. No way to test the cure.'

Jagua looked troubled. 'Hardiman is already being held on the yacht.'

'What?' James took the news like a punch to the guts. 'We're too late.'

'La Velada says they must all act as if you are alive and held on board the tugboat. Hardiman will not know any different.' She paused. 'They will infect the CIP diver – Franklin Ford – with the poison in your place. But La Velada said he is' – she searched for the right word – 'too spirited. He will make trouble, and needs to be broken first. And Father said his men would enjoy that . . .' She shook her head, wiped her nose. 'I am sorry. My father . . . he gave no tears for me. Only anger at my disobedience. I should not care, but . . .'

James didn't reply. An awful tiredness was dragging at his senses. Each breath felt like the swing of a pendulum marking off time; each heartbeat another second closer to the end.

'I don't know what to do now,' he said quietly, 'except try to find Hugo.'

'I am sorry. I should be glad – I am free now, but you . . .' Jagua reached for his hand. 'Rest, James. I will look for Hugo.'

'La Velada said we only had two days.' James closed his eyes, fighting dizziness. 'What can I do?'

She helped him to lie down. '*Rest.*'

He heard her move away, too tired to open his eyes. The stream rushed on beside him, and he heard the calls of nocturnal animals. Exhaustion smothered all thoughts and fears except one.

How bad will I feel . . . when I wake . . . ?

James stirred to find that it was daybreak, stretches of pink and white warming the horizon. He looked down at his palms, at the blisters that festered there and now dotted his arms, got to his knees stiffly.

'You can still move,' he told himself. 'You can still think.'

'*James!*' That was Hugo's voice.

'And there's still hope.' James got to his feet and saw his friend hurrying towards him with Jagua.

'I found him.' She looked triumphant, her arm around Hugo's shoulders. 'Washed up further downstream.'

'Thank God you're alive, James.' Hugo looked pale, but his smile held its usual warmth. 'Dear Lord, that mill looks like I feel.'

'Seconded,' James said. 'What happened to you last night?'

'I was hiding inconspicuously amongst the mill's supporting timbers, then realized I was curled up beside a bomb. I jumped away and fell in the drink.' He showed James the red spots on his arms, and the warmth faded from his face. 'What are we going to do, James? Jagua told me that Hardiman's all at sea . . .'

'Come to the house.' Jagua's smile was strained. 'It is safe now. I will find you aspirin. It will not cure, but maybe it will make you more comfortable?'

James realized that Jagua was desperate to do something positive in a hopeless situation. 'Thank you,' he said. 'It may make it easier to plan our next step.'

'How much planning do you need to drop dead?' Hugo sighed. 'I'm sorry. Not so good at the brave face and stiff upper lip.'

'This isn't over yet.' James rested a hand on his friend's shoulder. 'For a start, we can try to get hold of the CIP. Tell them that Franklin Ford is alive – though he won't be for much longer unless they do something about Scolopendra.'

Hugo gestured around. 'The evidence here has been destroyed.'

'Suspicious in itself,' James pointed out.

'Father has faked evidence to make the boss of a rival timber company seem responsible,' said Jagua. 'I heard him discuss it with *her*. It will appear to be an attempt on his life.

This is why he "goes into hiding" – for his own safety, you see?'

'His own safety, and the murder of millions.' Hugo shook his head. 'I can't see hardened CIP agents attacking a giant log raft in the middle of the Atlantic on the say-so of three teenagers, can you?'

'No,' James agreed. 'But if someone *official* were to tell them . . . Someone from the British Secret Intelligence Service . . .'

Hugo's weary smile transformed his face. 'In particular, someone from the office of Agent Adam Elmhirst.'

Jagua looked baffled. 'Agent who?'

'Long story, from England to LA,' James said. 'Before we left, Elmhirst gave me a number I could telephone in an emergency. I don't think he imagined I'd use it so soon, but it's our only hope.'

'There is a telephone in the house,' Jagua told him.

'But if he's still at sea it will take time to reach him.' Hugo pondered. 'And even if he believes us, and convinces the CIP we're telling the truth . . . how long will it be before they take action?'

'Father did not leave so long ago,' Jagua pointed out. 'The tugboat and log raft can still be reached.'

'Reached how?'

'I have taken lessons in my father's seaplane – the one that brought you here, I think.'

James suddenly remembered. 'Of course. We saw notes on board, in your handwriting.'

'You would call them *crib sheets*, yes?'

'Yes.' James felt some of the old fire creeping back into

his frame. 'You told me seaplanes weren't so easy to handle . . .'

'I have flown it over the sea a little way before. With a co-pilot.'

'You can have two for this flight.'

Hugo groaned quietly. 'What are we going to do when we get there?'

'If we find the log raft and get down in one piece, we'll do the same as always . . .' James set off for the house. 'Improvise.'

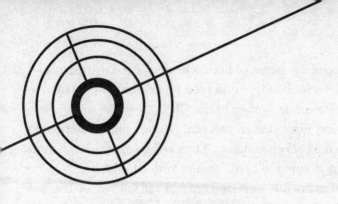

30
Air Burst

The seaplane turned in an uneven circle over the port of Scolopendra Industries. Sitting in the co-pilot's seat, blistered hands gripping the wheel, James felt his heart pounding: Jagua had not taken the flying boat up this high before, and with her injured wrist and hand, Hugo often had to help her with her own controls. The takeoff had been decidedly shaky, the seaplane skimming and splashing over the water like a demented duck. But now Jagua was growing in confidence.

Even so, James had seldom felt closer to death.

He'd put his call through to the number Adam Elmhirst had given him – thank God he'd remembered it correctly, and, thank God again, a secretary had picked up. A highly sceptical secretary: James told him the whole story, including every little detail he could remember, but the man seemed more concerned with how James had gotten hold of this number. James supposed Elmhirst's report was not yet filed,

but dropped the name of his old beak at Eton, Mr Merriot –
also known to the SIS – and pretty much begged the man to
contact Valentine Barbey at the CIP.

'The log raft's cleared harbour,' Hugo confirmed, peering
through the cockpit window. 'How will we find them? Tracks
left in the ocean don't tend to stay visible for long.'

'And I'm not sure how long our fuel will last.' Jagua checked
the cockpit's crowded instrument array. 'If the log raft is too
far from land, we won't have the range to find it.'

'I saw a map of the route in Scolopendra's apartment in
Havana,' James recalled. 'I *think* it followed the coast of the
mainland, but as to how far out it was . . .' He winced as his
stomach cramped painfully. 'We'll just have to gamble, get as
high as possible, look down over as wide an area as we can.'

Gamble is right, he thought dismally. *Place your bets. Heads or
tails. Live or die.*

They had been flying for four long hours with nothing to
report. James's arms ached. A light rain was spattering on the
windows, and turbulence was tossing the plane to and fro.
James knew that Jagua was nervous, on the verge of turning
round while they still had fuel enough to get back. The only
thing stopping her was the knowledge that if she did, James
and Hugo would be dead within two days.

James stared sullenly at his hands. Pus was gathering
behind the blisters; they itched and stung and scared the hell
out of him.

He jumped as Hugo suddenly cried out, 'Look to port. I
think I can see something . . . Might be nothing, or an oil
slick, or . . .'

'Let's follow it up, Jagua,' said James.

They headed into the squall; the wind rocked the plane, and water smeared their vision through the glass. A sense of mounting excitement filled the cockpit.

Finally James's stomach stirred at the sight of a dark mass, shaped like an enormous flattened rugby ball, rolling with the swell. Jagua had explained how the great log rafts were put together, painstakingly, over many weeks. A gigantic cradle, similar to the ribs of a ship, was half filled with logs of different sizes before the first of over 175 tons of chains fastened them together into one incredible mass – as long as two football pitches laid end to end, its width a quarter of that, and fully twenty-four feet deep.

The mass was towed from its cradle into the open water; no longer constrained, the logs shifted and flattened out to form a gargantuan artificial island. Additional cargo could then be secured to the top, ready for the tugboat to pull it all through the open sea using a sixteen-inch towing hawser.

Of course, James reminded Jagua, this particular log raft must be carrying millions of counterfeit notes for smuggling through Customs. He imagined them, sealed in layer upon layer of oilskins and hidden amid the logs beneath the surface. Presumably, when the vast raft docked, it would be dismantled and the timber distributed according to prebooked orders all across Britain – together with the money.

As the plane dipped lower, James spotted the tugboat – it looked like a child's toy – some way in front of the raft, smoke steaming from its funnel. Roped to the rear, bobbing like baby ducks swimming after their mother, were smaller craft and runabouts, while to one side, Scolopendra's sleek 200-foot motor yacht cut smartly through the grey-blue waters.

'Can you try to take us lower?' he asked.

Jagua nervously obliged.

James remembered La Velada's visit to the raft to check that all was ready for departure. Now he saw a dozen large wooden crates set at precise intervals on the top of the timber. Six or seven men were standing at the side of the raft, pushing another man into the water. 'What's going on down there?'

Jagua was looking too. 'Franklin Ford?' she murmured. 'La Velada said they must break his spirit, remember?'

'And Scolopendra said he'd let his men have some fun.' James nodded grimly. 'Yes, I remember.'

'An old punishment at sea: keel hauling. Being dragged under the boat from one side to the other.' Hugo looked disgusted. 'Ten minutes at sea, and they all think they're pirates.'

The men were looking up at the seaplane now. One of them pointed; James recognized Ramón at once. 'We've been spotted.'

'Only the henchmen travel tugboat-class,' Hugo noted. 'Scolopendra and La Velada will be aboard the yacht with Hardiman.'

'I'm sure they'll find out we're here soon enough,' said James.

The high-explosive shell came at them so fast there was barely time to react. A violent flare burst at the window and the seaplane shook violently. James was thrown to the floor. Glass panes cracked.

'Air burst!' Hugo held onto the back of James's seat as he and Jagua steered the plane unevenly upward. 'We just took a broadside of shrapnel.'

James looked down and saw that four of the crates had

been tipped over to reveal field guns and heavy mortars. Figures were scrambling over the logs to man them. 'Yes, they know we're here all right. Take us higher, Jagua!' he shouted – as there was another explosion below them. The seaplane lurched and groaned with the impact.

'Deliberate misses,' he decided. 'Of course, this is a Scolopendra Industries plane . . . They'll want to know just who's on board.'

'One of those misses was a hit.' Jagua tapped angrily at a dial. 'It must've holed the tank – we are losing fuel.'

Hugo barely kept his balance as the plane encountered fresh turbulence. 'They'll shoot us down!'

'Not if they know Jagua's on board.' Adrenalin was James's saviour once more: his body tingled with purpose. 'When Scolopendra learns that his daughter's alive, and that it's no thanks to La Velada—'

'He will not believe the truth,' said Jagua.

'Then we'll work out some lies that'll trip his trigger.' He turned to Hugo. 'Find something white.'

'My face?'

'A flag of truce.'

Hugo nodded and vanished into the cabin.

James looked at Jagua. 'It's *your* face we need to show. Wave, shout, anything – just make sure they see you down there. You've got to hold their attention, and give the performance of your life.'

'A diversion, you mean?' Jagua stared at him suspiciously. 'And what will you do?'

James took a deep breath . . .

★　★　★

Standing on the broad mahogany deck of the yacht, Scolopendra held his powerful Krauss binoculars to his eyes. The seaplane was one of his, and it was being buffeted not only by gunfire but by the growing summer squall.

Suddenly he saw that a white towel was flapping out of the co-pilot's window.

'Who the hell is that up there?' He picked up a loudhailer and bellowed across to Ramón on the log raft, 'Cease your fire!'

'Really, my love?' La Velada had stolen up behind him. 'I thought we agreed that the seaplane must be on a recon-naissance flight . . . It should be blown out of the skies.'

'If it is the CIP, why do they pursue me in my own air yacht?' Scolopendra shook his head. 'We let the plane land. We have firepower enough to destroy it on the water as easily as in the air.'

La Velada inclined her head, respectfully. 'As you say, my love.'

He put the loudhailer to his lips again. 'And get Ford out of the water,' he shouted. 'We may need to put him on show.'

The seaplane's engines throbbed as it came in to touch down on the water.

Hunched beneath the side window, James peered out through a set of Fujii Brothers 'Victor' 8x20 binoculars as Jagua traced a vast anticlockwise circle about the gargantuan raft and the tugboat that towed it.

James could see Franklin Ford more clearly now: he was lying on his back at the edge of the raft; he had clearly been towed through the water by a rope tied around his middle. His face was swollen, the left cheek marked with a deep diagonal slice. *Ramón, no doubt*, thought James darkly. The CIP agent had survived his interrogation; now he was ready for the poison.

Jagua shouted in Spanish as they circled round ahead of the tugboat: '*¡Tengo que hablar con mi padre!*' – 'I need to talk to my father!'

And let's hope he believes what you tell him this time. James crossed to the co-pilot's door, hidden from sight by the other side of the seaplane, and stood braced to exit. *Is the tug travelling too fast for me to hitch a ride?*

As it circled round, the seaplane would be invisible for several seconds to those on the log raft, obscured by the tugboat. From the tug itself the blindspot would be very brief – in order to emerge from the plane unseen, James had to time his jump perfectly, just as the seaplane circled round in front.

'Good luck, James,' Hugo called.

Taking a big breath, he jumped into the cold, choppy waters. With the enormous vessel bearing down on him and the raucous babble of engines in his ears, his mission seemed terrifying, impossible: *I have to get aboard that thing, and I have to stop it.* With the tugboat engine sabotaged, the flotilla – and the poisoned money – would be stranded, an easy target, its progress towards Britain halted. James tried to imagine himself saying to Scolopendra: *Give us Hardiman and that jar of sodium nitrite from the lab, and we'll be away. You can have your tugboat back . . . good luck outrunning the CIP.*

The tug's bow was already starting to thunder past, the truck tyres along its sides like black hollow eyes. The tail end

281

of the ropes trailed in the water, and James braced himself.

If my timing isn't right . . .

He bobbed close to the tug as it swept past, the wake sucking him in, drawing him down. He strained to reach the dangling ropes as they came towards him; the first couple brushed by, just out of reach, but he managed to grab the third – and cried out in pain as the thick wet twine was pulled through his blistered palms. Gritting his teeth, he clung on as he was towed alongside the boat. Slowly he pulled himself up until he reached the tyre, and held on for a moment, shivering. He felt exhausted and dizzy from the poison spreading through his body. He remembered scaling the sheer wall to Scolopendra's penthouse; it felt like it had happened in another life.

James heard the seaplane circling slowly round again, the box floats under each wing holding her steady in the water. Hugo gave James a worried thumbs-up from the cockpit as they passed. Then the seaplane was out of sight again, and the dark emptiness of the ocean was absolute.

Over the rumble of the tug and the drone of the seaplane came a further rasping tone. *Scolopendra's motor yacht . . .* James realized. *He's coming to face his daughter.*

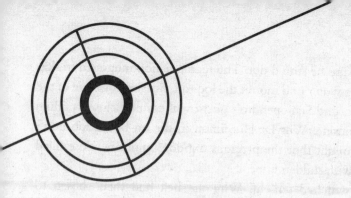

31
Starting Fires

Scolopendra's voice crackled through the loudhailer. 'Jagua!' Even over the din, his passion was plain enough in the single word, and in the rush of Spanish that followed.

Yes, your daughter's back from the dead. Teeth gritted, James began to climb over the tyre. *Let's hope that's a big enough distraction.*

He swung himself painfully onto the deck. There was no one in sight. A tugboat crew wouldn't be large, he thought – no more than four or five men.

Warily James peered through the windows of the mess room beside him. It was empty. The captain would be in the wheelhouse just above it. The rest of the crew must be watching the seaplane and awaiting further instructions.

A deep vibration and a hard scraping noise from the raft drew James's attention. *What was that . . . ?* He crept along the deck to the stern and found a short, stocky man there, shaking his head as he stared out. The seaplane had managed to skip over the water and mount the log raft, not far from one of the mortars, and Scolopendra's yacht was coming closer, pulling up alongside. Was Dr Hardiman in the on-board lab now? The thought that the precious antidote might be close filled James with sudden hope.

He watched tensely. Why the hell had they chosen to strand the seaplane like that? Then he noticed the leak from the holed fuel tank pooling over the logs below, and knew that the seaplane would never take off again in any case. The men on the log raft, Ramón included, had brought automatic weapons to bear on the intruder.

As if sensing James's presence behind him, the crewman turned suddenly. James jerked into action, instinctive, determined. He brought one fist up under the man's chin, knuckles finding bone. The blow left bare neck exposed; James chopped hard against the flesh and brought the man down, unconscious.

With a gasp as his stomach cramped worse than ever, James sank down beside the prone body, panting for breath. *One down* . . . Blood was weeping from the blisters on his hands; he wiped it away on his shirt, tried to clear his brain and stay alert. Somehow he had to stop the tug's engines. *Come on*, he told himself.

Slowly he raised his head above the deck rail.

With a chill, James saw that Scolopendra and La Velada had come out onto the deck of the yacht. The skipper had steered as close to the raft as he could, and a crewman had secured the yacht to a mooring post. Now Scolopendra casually vaulted over the side, a drop of at least fifteen feet.

He landed panther-like on the logs before rising to his full imposing height and calling: '*Jagua!*'

Scolopendra's voice boomed into the cockpit of the seaplane. Jagua felt sick.

'You can do this,' Hugo whispered to her. 'I'm right here.' He swallowed hard. 'I'm not much, I know, but I'll help you with what to say.'

'You *are* much, Hugo.' Jagua squeezed his hand, then opened the door of the seaplane.

The elements rushed in at her – gusts of warm wind and the peppering of rain. She felt like an actress, and here was her audience: twenty men with guns and mortars, the bitch she hated worse than anyone, and there on the logs below her . . .

'*Papito*,' she said.

'Jagua . . . ?' Her father stared as if not quite certain she was real; he started forward, arms raised as if to hold her, to help her down. 'My little goddess, I thought you were dead. To see you alive—'

'I cannot come out, *Papito*.' She pitched her voice higher, like the lost little girl she had once been, and pointed a finger at La Velada. 'She tried to kill me. I ran and she sent El Puño after me to finish the job. She wants me dead—'

'An absurd delusion,' La Velada broke in.

'She told me about Maritsa!' Jagua shouted. 'She laughed at how she persuaded you to do it. She has been tricking you all along, on Moscow's orders.'

'My love, do not listen to a jealous girl's—'

Scolopendra rounded on La Velada. 'How would she know of Maritsa?'

She shrugged her shoulders, serene as ever. 'One of the guards, perhaps, when she escaped our custody?'

'When La Velada shot at me, I ran.' Jagua found it easy to summon tears to her eyes. 'I ran straight into the CIP chief . . .'

'Valentine Barbey,' Hugo hissed behind her.

'This man, Barbey – he killed El Puño and captured me. He had already captured James and Hugo—'

La Velada leaned forward on the deck rail. 'You cannot believe this fairy story!'

'*Enough!*' Scolopendra rounded on her. 'You don't tell me what to believe.'

'She knows how close we are, *Papito*, despite everything . . . *because* of everything.' Jagua knew how to press all the right buttons. 'I have disobeyed you and I know I have shamed you, but always I love you, *Papito*, whatever you have done . . .'

'Jagua' – Scolopendra reached out a hand to her – 'if all this is true—'

'Barbey is sending the American ships at Guantanamo Bay after you.' Jagua took a deep breath and shouted into the wind: 'He found the corpse of Chester MacLean, *Papito*!'

'Tell him about the laundry truck,' Hugo whispered.

'The driver of a bogus laundry truck told him where the body was dumped.'

The words clearly hit home as Scolopendra turned to La Velada. 'No one knew of this but us.'

'You'd be surprised . . .' Hugo muttered.

(As the drama unfolded, no one, either in the seaplane or on the log raft, noticed that Franklin Ford had managed to untie the rope around his waist. Now he was slowly dragging himself on his front over the logs towards the nearest of Scolopendra's men . . .)

'The CIP know everything now, *Papito* . . .' Jagua looked down anxiously at her confounded father. 'Even the bullet in MacLean's head, it has been matched to your gun, the Colt Woodsman.'

'But . . . only someone who was there in that room could know this.' Scolopendra turned slowly to Ramón. 'You acted strangely when we came for MacLean. You said you were sleeping . . .'

'It's working, Jagua,' Hugo said. 'Keep piling on the paranoia. We have to give James all the time we can . . .'

'*Move!*' James muttered, willing away his nausea as he rose painfully from the deck. He had to reach the engine room – but how much longer could Jagua and Hugo keep all eyes on the raft? He couldn't understand the snatches of Spanish that reached his ears, but recognized the shock and anger in the words. Scolopendra had turned to Ramón, who was shaking his head, protesting, '¡No hice nada!'

Movement at the edge of his vision made James tear his gaze away.

A crewman with a revolver was creeping up behind him.

Desperately James launched himself forward and made a grab for the gun. The sores on his palms burst open again and he gasped in agony, but managed to force the muzzle of the

Colt 1908 away. Then he head-butted the crewman before he could fire, and floored him.

James swung back round – just in time to watch a lethal chain reaction unfold on the giant log raft.

It happened within a few seconds: Scolopendra marched up to the terrified Ramón and grabbed him by the throat. Ramón twisted free but fell against the nearest rocket launcher; under the impact, his finger squeezed the trigger of his machine gun. Scolopendra barked in anger and his men scattered as bullets bit into the timber and struck sparks from a thick length of chain. The petrol leaking from the seaplane caught light instantly, sending fierce blue flames streaking hungrily across the raft.

'Oh my God . . .' James breathed as the craft became an inferno. He glimpsed Jagua jumping out of the blazing cockpit, hand-in-hand with Hugo. Then thick diesel smog blew across from the burning plane, blinding him. He choked, rubbed at his eyes, staggered back from the rail.

Hugo? Jagua? He could no longer see them.

One of Scolopendra's thugs slipped on the logs as he tried to outrun the flames, landed on his back and skidded into a rocket launcher. The fire caught hold of him and he screamed, but the noise was soon lost to the rattle of automatic fire: in the chaos, Franklin Ford had snatched up a fallen machine gun and was spraying bullets in a wide arc. Scolopendra's panicking henchmen twitched and danced in a bloody rain.

More of a distraction than I could've hoped for . . . Trembling, James turned from the horrific display, picked up the crewman's gun and stumbled away. He opened the bulkhead door to the engine room, and swore at the sheer size of the air-starting, six-cylinder diesel engine: it was as big as a tank and looked just as hard to damage, all well-oiled metal pipes and pistons, flywheels and rivets.

Where's Boody when you need her? James looked at his stolen gun. Could he force one of the crew to put the engine out of commission?

Outside, men were shouting, their desperate voices instantly ripped away by the wind. James wondered what was happening and prayed that Hugo and Jagua could stay safe amid the carnage. Quickly he searched around for anything that might help him damage the engines and leave Scolopendra's cargo adrift. He stopped at the sight of what looked like a miniature short-nosed cannon, about the size of a collie dog – the boat's Lyle gun. James had seen the Sea Cadet Corps demonstrate the gun back at Eton: light the fuse and an explosive charge fired a ball attached to a length of rope. It was often used as a lifeline for people who'd fallen overboard. Perhaps if he removed the charge itself, he could—

A tall, weaselly-looking crewman with a long moustache came rushing into the engine room. James ducked behind the Lyle gun as the man turned off the engine. As machinery sputtered and shut down, he took a heavy camshaft and slid it along until it engaged into another set of lobes. Then the engine was restarted. As the floor seemed to shift beneath him, James realized that the heavy tugboat had been thrown into reverse.

That's going to bring her up against the log raft, he thought. *To pick up the panicking crew? Or to transfer the poisoned money before it all goes up in flames?*

James held his stolen revolver like a club and steeled

himself. If he could knock out the engineer, it would be one less crewman to worry about . . .

Crouched behind a wooden crate lashed to the log raft, Hugo and Jagua clung together. There was smoke everywhere, and the whine of bullets – and the screams from those they hit – seemed to come from all directions.

Jagua looked fearfully into Hugo's bloodshot eyes. 'We cannot stay here, Hugo.'

He coughed on smoke. 'If only we could get to your father's yacht, and Hardiman!'

'And La Velada,' Jagua reminded him. 'Still, I would sooner face her than all this, yes?'

'Yes. And this raft is towing other boats,' Hugo reminded her. 'If we could reach one of them . . .'

'We try,' said Jagua. 'Ready?'

Heads down, they scurried out of their cover into the heat of the battle. As Hugo peered around for the little motorboats, he almost tripped over something . . .

It was Ramón's body, or what was left of it. The face was blackened, the eyes charred jellies, the scarred lips drawn back to make a large black cross beneath the nose.

Hugo turned away and vomited. Jagua put an arm round him, tried to pull him away, but he shook his head. 'Wait. What . . . what did that?'

She pointed to their right. Hugo saw that flames from the seaplane had reached two of Scolopendra's mortars, perhaps fifteen feet away. Now unmanned, their wide muzzles pointed drunkenly up into the air. Without warning, one jerked violently and pumped out orange fire. The sizzling shriek of a shell whooshed through the smoke and confusion.

'Come on.' Jagua grabbed Hugo's hand and hauled him away. 'If that hits something—'

The explosion threw them flat on their faces. The screech of rending metal tore at Hugo's senses. He clutched his ears, rolling over and over as timbers moved beneath him on the swell of the sea. 'Jagua!' he yelled. 'Jagua, where are—?' But he broke off as he saw the tugboat lit crimson, spewing smoke into the grey-pink sky.

'James . . .' he whispered.

It was the engineer who was meant to see stars, but before James could bring the gun down on the man's skull, the day flashed incandescent through the doorway. The explosion hurled him against the wall, winding him. The engineer fell against a pounding piston and screamed as the workings crushed and mangled his arm. James tried to reach him, but was thrown back by a second explosion. Above him, the roof fell away as if kicked by a giant's boot. The engineer's shouts died as he was crushed beneath iron debris.

Shaking his dazed head, James realized that the engine was still running; the tug was still shifting backwards through the water – and now there was no one to stop it. He ran outside to find help, and quickly hit the deck as a three-inch shell tore past and nearly took his head off. Behind him, the bow of the tug bloomed with fire, its heat scorching his back. Looking up, he saw that the wheelhouse was on fire, its walls shattered.

Terrified, James scrambled up and ran astern. He needed to know what the hell had been happening.

Gerald Hardiman hung back in the doorway to the upper deck of the motor yacht, *Estrella de Jagua*. His guards had left – drafted to join the rest of Scolopendra's men in tackling the fiery, chaotic battlefield that the log raft had become. Only La Velada and her bodyguard remained on board now. They watched from the deck rail as Scolopendra prowled through the smoke and debris, directing survivors to shift the artillery and extinguish the flames before the counterfeit money hidden beneath the logs could be damaged.

'You are a fool, Scolopendra,' she hissed. 'Am I to stand here and watch my future burn?'

And what of my *future*, thought Hardiman. He looked down at the sealed glass bottle in his hand, the last remaining sample of his precious antidote. He knew it couldn't remain here, in La Velada's possession.

He looked out at the smaller boats, lashed to the log raft, towed along in its smoking wake. If he could only reach one of them! But to take such decisive action . . . to take his life in his own hands like that . . .

It wouldn't be much of a life, thought Hardiman, *if you knew just where you'd land up.*

Before his courage could fail him, Hardiman dashed out from hiding, ran across the deck and clumsily vaulted the rail. He heard La Velada shout –

Then the ocean broke around him, and its rush and roar was in his ears, and Hardiman swam. Swam for his life.

James stared over at the blazing log raft, at the bodies and the carnage, praying that he'd glimpse Hugo and Jagua through the smoke. Someone was escaping in a motorboat, making for Scolopendra's motor yacht. Or perhaps they were heading for the man James could see thrashing and shouting in the water . . . ?

Distracted as he was, James suddenly realized that the tug was still reversing steadily closer to the raft.

'Hugo, Jagua, wherever you are,' he yelled, 'brace yourselves. She's going to ram!'

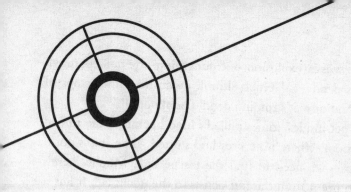

32
What Will Break

It was too late for warnings. Steel crunched into timber as the tug came up against the logs. James was sent sprawling. The stern of the tug dipped sharply downwards as the hull crumpled with a nerve-jarring, metallic shriek. A crewman fell overboard with a cry that was quickly lost in the roar of another shell exploding. This time a chunk of the raft was blown apart, and charred white confetti was whipped about in the wind.

James saw scraps of paper marked with ornate writing whirl about him. Ice filled his body. *The poisoned banknotes*, he realized, *concealed in the logs, until now . . .*

Smoke blew across his vision and he fell back, choking. He suddenly saw that a figure was crawling over the tugboat's rail. A *small* figure, his face black with soot.

'Hugo?' James scrambled over, helped his friend down to the tipping deck. 'Are you all right? Where's Jagua—?'

'There was an explosion, and guns firing — we got separated. Ramón's dead . . .' Hugo shrank away from the scraps of paper. 'And now it's raining deadly banknotes!'

'Let's get inside.' James pulled Hugo back into the ruined engine room, where little fires had started. 'The ship's got a Lyle gun — we need to find the rescue line. Maybe there's a way to fire it from the raft across to the yacht . . . It has a fair range. Then we can find Jagua and make our way across to Hardiman and the antidote.'

The roar of another explosion set the whole tug shaking; it felt ready to split apart.

'Who are you trying to fool, James?' Hugo looked terror-stricken. 'We'll never make it out of this!'

'We have to! Keep looking . . .' Somehow, though his gut was cramping and hands bleeding, James managed to steer the little cannon out onto the deck without letting it skitter down the slope. The yacht seemed to be well clear of the raft now. 'Quickly, Hugo!'

'Here!' Hugo emerged, clutching the length of waterproof rope. 'At least there's no shortage of fire about to light the fuse— Whoa!' As the tug rocked again, he stumbled over something on the listing deck. 'What the hell . . . ?'

'Loose hatch cover. Leads down to the hold.' Through the hatch James saw that the floor, twenty feet below, was slick with seawater, pooling in through the damaged hull. He scanned the space for anything of use: old wooden planks, a roll of tow-chains, the massive freshwater tank the crew used for drinking and washing, and some fishing net shifting in the seawater.

James turned back to the Lyle gun and fixed the

waterproof line into the barrel. 'At least you didn't fall down there, Hugo. A lucky escape.'

'*No.*' The deep voice sent a chill through James. '*No* escape.'

Scolopendra strode out of the smoke. His clothes were charred, his dark barrel chest gleaming with sweat. In one gauntleted hand he held a smoking length of timber like a club; in the other, a tattered sack of oilskins.

'You did this, Bond.' The brooding eyes were fixed on James. 'Years of planning . . . all the deaths, so many sacrifices . . . and all I have to show for it . . . *this.*' He dumped the oilskins on the deck, and James saw the wads of banknotes stuffed inside. 'La Velada has gone, she took the yacht . . .'

James felt his stomach clench. 'And Hardiman?'

'I don't care about them. Any of them.' Scolopendra's glare was murderous. 'I just want Jagua. Now.'

'I don't know where she is.' James got carefully to his feet. 'I saw her jump out of the plane—'

'*You turned her against me.*' Scolopendra came towards him, raising his makeshift club.

Suddenly Hugo ran and shoulder-charged the big man's legs, hoping perhaps to push him over. But Scolopendra simply turned and swatted him with the back of his hand, knocking him senseless.

James tried to rush Scolopendra, but the sinking tugboat lurched under his feet and he stumbled. Scolopendra brought the club swinging down. James barely rolled aside in time; the weapon struck splinters from the deck as he scrambled back up. Bellowing with rage, Scolopendra swung again. This time James took the blow to his stomach and was slammed against the bulkhead, winded.

Scolopendra charged forward again. James tried to throw a punch but the big man caught his fist in his palm and squeezed. The pain burned up James's arm and it was all he could do not to whimper.

'You can't fight natural laws, James.' Scolopendra's smile was as wild as his eyes. 'Superior force will always win.' Releasing his grip, he rammed the end of the club into James's chest.

Pinned against the bulkhead, James felt as if his ribcage was going to split. He kicked Scolopendra in the kneecap, forced him back a pace, got hold of the club and managed to twist it free. But a second later he dropped it as Scolopendra punched him in the stomach. James bounced off the bulkhead and twisted as he fell, landing on his back, dazed and gasping for breath beside the Lyle gun. The tug pitched again, sinking lower still as it took on even more water.

'Down we go . . .' Scolopendra loomed over James, his long hair coiling about his head like black snakes. 'Everything else has gone to hell, Bond, all the evidence lost. Now you go with it.'

'You'll . . . go too.' *Keep him talking*, James thought desperately. 'Heads . . . you lost.'

'I'm still rich. I still have my poison and a boat out of here. I'll find a way.' Scolopendra pulled off his gauntlet, reached into his pocket for the silver dollar. 'Your country's won breathing space. Nothing more.' He flipped the coin, caught it, laughed. Then he placed one foot on James's aching chest. 'Time to die, Bond.'

'*No, Papito.*'

James craned his head round, looked past the Lyle gun.

Jagua had come aboard. Her braids had burned away on one side, her dress was torn and she was shivering. She knelt down beside Hugo, who was just beginning to stir.

'Jagua?' Scolopendra turned to face his daughter.

'Leave James alone' – her hand hovered over the oilskins – 'or I will touch your poison. Take it into my body.'

'You would not do this.' He shook his head fiercely. 'Not to yourself, and not to me.'

'It's what you did to Maritsa, no?'

James lay very still, summoning his strength. His arms and hands were burning, his stomach cramping, but he knew that Jagua was buying him time, that he had to use it . . . To do what?

'My little goddess, my only daughter, listen to me.' Scolopendra's words were like a punishment. 'La Velada, she has gone. Now you and I can go too. I – I can start again. *We* can start again, together.'

'Do this again?' Jagua pulled at her dress, exposing the scars of her beatings. 'Wherever we went, Father, I'd always be running.'

'No. Because you know now – you know what happens when you try to think your own thoughts, decide things for yourself. Look at you . . .' Scolopendra held out his arms to her. 'I'm saving you from that, Jagua.'

'Saving . . . ?' Her eyes were cold, her face set. She looked at James and Hugo, then back at her father as, with a low moan of metal somewhere below, the tug shifted again, almost levelling out. Jagua stood up. 'I love my *papito*.' She stepped into his embrace, and as he lowered his head to hers, she whispered in his ear: 'But my *papito* was killed – by Scolopendra.'

James suddenly glimpsed the knife concealed in her other hand. With a cry, she forced it deep into her father's back and his body went rigid. 'Go, James! Take Hugo – there's still a runabout left—'

'*¡Perra, te mataré!*' With a bellow of pain, Scolopendra hurled Jagua to the deck. He reached drunkenly behind him for the hilt of the knife but couldn't reach it. Instead, he grabbed what was left of Jagua's braided hair and hauled her onto her knees, then slapped her face with the back of his hand.

'No!' James shouted as Jagua dropped like a dead weight. He got to his knees and gasped as a piece of burning banknote brushed against his arm, blew onto his chest. He stared at it for a moment, watched flame and paper curl.

Then he grabbed it, pressed it to the fuse on the Lyle gun. The cannon's barrel was pointing past him, but if he'd gambled right . . .

'When will you learn, Jagua?' Shaking with rage and pain, Scolopendra picked up his club, lifted it above his head, ready to bring it down on his daughter's skull. 'It is a law of nature – superior force always wins. The weak *must* break.'

James snarled, 'You before her.'

There was a crack like thunder as the Lyle gun fired. If Scolopendra liked natural laws, he could try Newton's third: *For every action there is an equal and opposite reaction.* The recoil was powerful enough to send the little cannon jerking backwards a good six feet. It smashed into the backs of Scolopendra's legs and knocked them from under him. He fell on his side across the hatchway to the hold, realized the danger, and scrabbled for something to hold onto.

His fingers closed on the oilskin sack, and he dragged it down with him. 'No—'

A wet thud echoed up from the hold.

'Jagua . . .' Hugo crawled forward to help her, held her bloody hand in his. 'Are you all right?'

She nodded, eyes shut, lips tightly clenched. Unbreakable.

James staggered over to the open hatchway, looked down. Scolopendra was lying face up, sprawled over thick chains in a pile of paper money. Dark water foamed around his huge body, first lapping at limbs, then closing on the torso – until finally the proud features were taken by the blackness.

Jagua lay on her side, shivering. 'He saw it coming, didn't he?' she whispered. 'He told me I'd stab him in the back the moment he looked away . . .'

'You had to do it,' James muttered. '*We* had to.'

Hugo placed a hand on Jagua's scarred shoulder, then joined James looking down into the gloom. 'Is it over now? Is Scolopendra—?'

The tugboat gave a rending screech and tipped sideways. James was thrown onto his face, Hugo tripped over him and fell through the hatch. There was a clatter of timber, followed by splashes.

'Hugo!' James stared down into the hold, afraid of what he might see. 'Are you all right?'

'The accommodation's distinctly third class,' came the weak reply.

'Jagua . . . ?' James turned to her for help, but she made no reply: clearly in shock, curled up on her side.

Heart pounding, James ignored the pain from sickness and injuries and swung himself down into the dark hatchway.

The tug lurched again just as he landed in the water – which was already up to his knees – and overbalanced, almost falling onto Scolopendra's corpse. 'Hugo?' His voice echoed around the hold. 'Where are you?'

'Here.' James could now see that his friend had knocked over some lengths of timber. He had a cut on his forehead and was crouching on the wood in the water, tugging at his foot. 'Tangled up in this damned net . . .'

'Let me see.' James splashed over and saw that the tough netting, undulating in the rising water, must have snagged on something. 'It's all right, Hugo. Soon have you out.'

The freezing water was flooding in faster. Hugo looked up at James, terrified, as the water rose up around his waist.

James took a deep breath and dipped under the water, groping about in the darkness; the net had got caught in the timber and wound tight about Hugo's ankle. James pulled at it, his raw hands burning. Resurfacing, he spat out water.

'The net won't give, will it?' Hugo shouted.

'I'll find something to cut it with.' James looked around, frantic now. The hold was filling up fast, and poisoned notes swilled about them. He could see no way to climb back to the deck above.

'James!' The water was up to Hugo's neck.

'Help!' James screamed up through the hatchway. 'Jagua? Please, I need you! For God's sake . . .' He snatched another breath, splashed down into the water, pulled and heaved at the tangle of thick twine. There was no way it would break. He surfaced again, panting, desperate.

Hugo was spluttering, desperately trying to keep his nose above water. He clasped James's hand tightly. 'Get out.'

'No!'

'Go on!' Hugo shouted. 'You're always playing the damned hero, James. Give someone else a go.' He strained for air, choked on seawater as he snatched a last breath. 'Tell my—'

The water closed over Hugo's head. His hand was still gripping James's.

Slowly the grip weakened.

'No!' James bellowed. The water was pouring in even faster now. He was about to duck under again when he glimpsed something bobbing towards him like some dark predatory beast, and started.

It was Scolopendra's body . . .

With a knife in the back.

Hope surging, James grappled with the corpse, found the knife-hilt, and pulled with all his might. The blade came free, and he shoved the body away through the water. Desperate now, he scrabbled at the netting, sawing with the blade, hands stinging, lungs burning, pain bringing one last burst of strength.

Finally the twine snapped free.

Elated, James hooked an elbow round Hugo's neck and dragged him to the surface. The hold was flooded almost to the hatch now. Looking up, he saw a figure standing over him.

It was Jagua, bruised and burned and fierce. 'I am sorry.' She reached out with her good hand. 'Come on.'

James forced Hugo's dead weight through the hatch and Jagua dragged him out onto the listing deck. With the last of his strength, James pulled himself up after him.

'He's not breathing!' Jagua cried.

'Come on, Hugo.' James felt for a pulse in his friend's neck. There was none. He applied chest compressions: one, two, three, four . . . 'Help me, Jagua.'

She held Hugo's nose, placed her mouth over his and breathed air into his lungs.

When she stopped and moved away, James tried again with the chest compressions.

'Everything is sinking – the log raft too.' Jagua pressed her lips to Hugo's, breathed and looked up at James. 'The tug will be dragged down in minutes—'

'Keep going.' James's hands pummelled down on Hugo's chest. 'One more time.'

Jagua forced her breath between Hugo's lips – and finally his body twitched. His face twisted away from hers in a spray of water and he choked, gasping for breath.

'Was that a kiss?' he gasped, staring at her. 'I ruined it, didn't I? Oh God, I ruined it.'

'Not God.' James looked at Jagua as she held Hugo tight. '*Goddess*.'

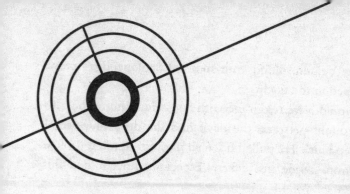

Epilogue
Liberty

Oil slicks and charred lengths of timber were the only markers of that watery grave. Together with Jagua, Hugo and Hardiman, James watched them disappear from sight as Franklin Ford steered the motorboat away.

If the CIP man hadn't been there to take them aboard with Hardiman, James had no doubt that they would have drowned. The tug had sunk within fifteen minutes of Hugo's resuscitation; they'd barely made it off in time.

'Hope the rescue makes up for trying to kill you back there on the beach, kid,' Ford called over the buzz of the engine. 'Nothing personal – just thought you and Jagua were Scolopendra's people. After what happened to Sarila, I figured you'd kill me if I didn't kill you first.'

James nodded vaguely, looked out over the horizon. *Scolopendra's people* . . . Most of them were dead now, like the man himself.

But La Velada, along with some of Scolopendra's crew, had escaped in the yacht.

'She would have taken me with her.' Hardiman shook his head. 'Caught between the devil and the deep blue sea, I chose deep blue.' He pulled a sealed glass jar marked SODIUM NITRITE from inside his jacket. 'Especially since I had this with me.'

James smiled in relief. 'You really can cure us, then?'

Hardiman nodded. 'This compound alleviates the development of symptoms. It's not instant, but we'll begin the moment we get back on land. The damage can be undone.'

Can it? James thought of all he had seen, all he'd been through since arriving in Cuba. *Can any of that be undone?*

'With all those burning banknotes flying around,' Hardiman went on, 'I think I'd better administer a complete course of treatment to us all.'

'And you must treat Maritsa also, in Sabana de Robles,' said Jagua. 'She does not deserve to die.'

'She had a milder dose, she'll show a slower decline. I could learn a lot more about the way this poison works on the human body . . . and ensure that a fully effective antidote is available in every country in the world.'

Ford grunted. 'Taking no chances?'

'None. Not after all this, eh?' Hardiman said. 'No more gambling.'

'I am glad. Because this is all I have left of my father now.' Jagua looked down at the silver dollar in her hand. 'One coin that changed everything. Perhaps it will change me too.'

'You can change yourself, if you choose to.' James looked down at his blistered, bloody hands. 'You're free now.'

'Free . . .' Jagua smiled, then tossed the silver coin to James. 'A dollar is worth a dollar. But free is worth everything.'

The little boat was running on fumes by the time they reached the Isla de Pinos. Night had fallen. They stopped off at Scolopendra's estate to eat, rest and begin the first course of treatment. James's hands throbbed and his stomach groaned, and he felt little better for his first injection; Hugo was the same.

'Bound to take time to get you well again.' Ford wasted no time contacting his office; he learned that a call had been put through from the London office of Britain's SIS, but while logged, it hadn't been acted upon. 'We're kind of thin on resources, out here. Some wheels take time to turn, and your story wasn't the easiest to sell.'

'I suppose we can't always wait around for someone to slay our dragons,' James said. 'Sometimes we have to play St George ourselves.'

'Well, if there's anything left of these particular dragons, the US navy is sending boats out to find it,' Ford said. 'Any evidence could prove useful . . .'

Just, please, don't find a trace of that poisoned money, James thought. *Let it be lost for good.*

The five survivors ate a simple meal of leftovers from the previous night, before Hardiman helped Ford search the house for any evidence La Velada might have left behind. James doubted they'd find anything. He sat on the porch with Hugo and Jagua, looking out over the gardens in the glow of street-lamps and moonlight.

'I hope we can call in at Playa Caimito on our way back to the harbour,' he said suddenly. 'I left Queensmarsh hidden in the Indian's sidecar.'

'That poor motorcycle courier.' Jagua sighed. 'Sidecar in Caimito, motorcycle battered and abandoned in Batabano . . .'

'With those earrings I gave him, he can buy at least three more,' said James. 'Still, perhaps we should try to trace him and apologize.'

'Stick to an anonymous tip-off once you've collected your things,' said Hugo. 'Best keep a low profile till we leave the country.'

'I just realized . . .' James declared. 'Aunt Charmian's arriving tomorrow.'

'To make sure you've been getting lots of rest after all you went through in LA.' Hugo went cross-eyed. 'Still, I'm glad I shall get to meet her at last.'

James nodded. 'I'm sure Mr Hardiman will enjoy seeing her too.'

'I wonder if he will stay on here in Cuba,' mused Jagua.

'If he does,' said James, 'I hope you'll keep an eye on him.'

'Of course.'

'And then you must write to me,' said Hugo quickly, 'and let me know how the old fellow's getting on.'

James raised his eyebrows. 'Very caring of you, Hugo.'

'Of course, I'd like to know how *you* are too, Jagua,' Hugo went on quickly. 'You could send postcards as well as letters. Every other day will do. And perhaps . . . perhaps you might include a small portrait of yourself?'

Jagua smiled. 'I will be busy, hmm?'

'Well, you'll need something to occupy your mind once I'm back in dear old Blighty,' Hugo said solemnly. 'I can't believe that in three weeks we'll be going back to school for ordinary things like lessons and tests and sport and' – he smiled self-consciously at Jagua – 'pining for you, of course.'

She shook her head, fiddling idly with the stubs of her burned braids. 'You should be glad to go. Home is . . . important.'

'Speaking of which, Jagua,' said James, 'I suppose all this is yours now. Will you stay here?'

'I think Mr Ford will make many investigations into my father.' Jagua grimaced. 'But once he is gone, and I am alone, yes, I think I shall stay.'

'There aren't too many bad memories?'

'I will make better ones,' Jagua said. 'I . . . am going to come to the mainland with you tonight.'

'Can't bear to say goodbye, eh?' asked Hugo hopefully.

'I am coming because Maritsa was wrong to say, *Life is what we do while we wait to die*. Life must mean something, must be *worth* something. Today we made a difference. I want to make more differences. And so I will go to Sabana de Robles. Not because I wish to live in the past as it was, but because I want to make life better as it could be.' She smiled sadly. 'We cannot live in the past, James, for the past is full of old beginnings. We must follow them to the ends. Yes?'

James nodded. *No matter how steep and unsafe the paths*, he thought, *or how unhappy those endings prove*. 'I suppose you could let the villagers run their own factory, for a start?'

'Or invite the whole lot to live with you here in the grounds.' Hugo shyly reached out a hand to Jagua. 'How's that for a difference, eh?'

'Maybe too much . . .' Jagua took hold of his fingers and closed her eyes. 'Or maybe anything is possible.'

James walked quietly away and looked up at the moon. He felt cold, put his hands in his pockets – and pulled out Scolopendra's silver dollar.

He flipped it: *heads*. Liberty's imperious face stared out across the back of his blistered hand, as if choosing not to meet his questioning gaze.

Win or lose, life had to mean something. But what?

Alone beneath the great bowl of stars falling over the Caribbean, James Bond absently tossed the coin again. Even if he could catch every last light in the sky, he thought, it would never be enough.

Acknowledgements

Special thanks to Sophie Wilson for editorial guidance, along with Ruth Knowles, Mainga Bhima, Josephine Lane, Corinne Turner and all at Ian Fleming Publications Ltd.

Thanks to Phoebe Taylor for Spanish assistance.

Support was provided by Jill Cole, Philippa Milnes-Smith, Harriet Venn, Elizabeth Briggs, Jo Cotterill, Beth Bottery, Emma Lamont, Mike Tucker, Paul Simpson, Alan Barnes, Tony Bradman, Anthony Horowitz – with added backbone brought, of course, by the novels of Ian Fleming.